Praise for Off Menu

"Written as a series of charming and hilarious diary entries, this novel is a fantastic blend of Helen Fielding's *Bridget Jones's Diary*, Nora Ephron's *Heartburn*, and the humor of Molly Harper, Janet Evanovich, and Emily Henry. Perfect for foodies who love a bit of fun, hijinks, and romance."
— *Library Journal*, starred review

"A delicious romp! The cooking is as irresistible as the love story. An exhilarating peek behind the doors of culinary school, filled with passion, purpose, and puff pastry."
— Olivia Potts, author of *A Half Baked Idea*

"[This] was such an entertaining book, and it was a pleasure to read a foodie fictional piece where the dishes, places, and culinary terms are actually accurate! A delicious way to daringly dine and swoon from the comfort of your cozy chair."
— Anna Olson, pastry chef & cookbook author

"What a wonderful and delicious debut novel! This read like a breath of fresh air, and I absolutely loved how reminiscent it was of *Bridget Jones's Diary*. So much heart and so much good food!"
— Jamie Varon, author of *Main Character Energy*

"*Off Menu* is a must-read for anyone who knows someone who cooks. Hilariously accurate, it brings Canadiana to the stage when we need it most."
— y, pastry chef and judge on eat Canadian Baking Show

Off Menu

Off Menu

a novel

Amy Rosen

Copyright © Amy Rosen, 2025

Published by ECW Press
665 Gerrard Street East
Toronto, Ontario, Canada M4M 1Y2
416-694-3348 / info@ecwpress.com

All rights reserved. No part of this publication may be reproduced, stored in a retrieval system, or transmitted in any form by any process — electronic, mechanical, photocopying, recording, or otherwise — without the prior written permission of the copyright owners and ECW Press. The scanning, uploading, and distribution of this book via the internet or via any other means without the permission of the publisher is illegal and punishable by law. This book may not be used for text and data mining, AI training, and similar technologies. Please purchase only authorized electronic editions, and do not participate in or encourage electronic piracy of copyrighted materials. Your support of the author's rights is appreciated.

Editor for the Press: Kenna Barnes
Copy editor: Jen Knoch
Cover designer: Jessica Albert
Cover & interior artwork illustrator: Kenna Barnes

This is a work of fiction. Names, characters, places, and incidents either are the product of the author's imagination or are used fictitiously, and any resemblance to actual persons, living or dead, business establishments, events, or locales is entirely coincidental.

LIBRARY AND ARCHIVES CANADA CATALOGUING IN PUBLICATION

Title: Off menu : a novel / Amy Rosen.

Names: Rosen, Amy, 1969- author

Identifiers: Canadiana (print) 20250140616 | Canadiana (ebook) 20250140632

ISBN 978-1-77041-786-1 (softcover)
ISBN 978-1-77852-400-4 (ePub)
ISBN 978-1-77852-401-1 (PDF)

Subjects: LCGFT: Novels.

Classification: LCC PS8635.O6487 O34 2025 | DDC C813/.6—dc23

This book is funded in part by the Government of Canada. *Ce livre est financé en partie par le gouvernement du Canada.* We acknowledge the support of the Canada Council for the Arts. *Nous remercions le Conseil des arts du Canada de son soutien.* We would like to acknowledge the funding support of the Ontario Arts Council (OAC) and the Government of Ontario for their support. We also acknowledge the support of the Government of Ontario through the Ontario Book Publishing Tax Credit, and through Ontario Creates.

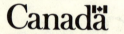

PRINTED AND BOUND IN CANADA   PRINTING: MARQUIS   5 4 3 2 1

Purchase the print edition and receive the ebook free. For details, go to ecwpress.com/ebook.

For my BFF, Natasha.
Sometimes you're born with sisters,
and sometimes you meet them along the way.

June

JUNE 12
9:45 a.m.

This story begins with me, Ruthie Cohen, slogging away in an open concept office that's a shade of green not found in nature. The building itself: grey, sloped, glass. The architectural equivalent of a slap in the face, while the people working within can best be described as Smurfs, mindlessly following Papa's orders. I should talk. I'm just another blue dude in a toque.

But not by this evening. By this evening, I will be free, galivanting with Trish and Lilly, celebrating that I finally (FINALLY) got the courage to quit my job. ("Courage" — also known as privilege, also known as an inheritance from Bubbe Bobby Grace passing away last month.)

Truthfully, I can't believe I'm journalling. I feel so Bridget Jones circa 1996. But even I know that some things, some life events, require structure. Enter: this notebook.

Since I haven't kept a diary before, or a journal, or even sent myself a voice memo for that matter, we'll have to backtrack a bit. Actually ... quite a bit.

For the past year I've been working at TelecorpMedia on contract for an app, which they say will be "*the* authoritative guide to the movies from A to Z, with insight, analysis, plus all of the insider Hollywood dirt!" The thing is, we're all in Toronto, none of us knows anyone in Hollywood, and I'm fairly certain that Greg over there, the one with his finger up his nose, only watches movies of the pornographic variety.

This week, for my assigned film blurb entries, I'm cataloguing the letter "S."

> *Say Anything*: This poignant comedy contains an iconic scene in which anti-hero Lloyd stands outside brainy beauty Diane's house holding a boom box blasting Peter Gabriel's "In Your Eyes" with a look of quiet desperation. The best of the 1980s romantic teen comedy genre. Dir: Cameron Crowe. Cast: John Cusack, Ione Skye, John Mahoney, Lili Taylor. 1989. 100 min.

I'm basically doing data entry, but FYI, I'm the best one at it. Which is probably why Keith has offered me a full-time job with benefits. (Benefits! In this day and age!?) He called me into his cubicle yesterday to discuss "long-term employment" for "an increased wage" and a "free Green Bean coffee loyalty card." I told him I'd sleep on it and let him know tomorrow, which unfortunately is today.

Despite being my manager, Keith began flirting with me a couple of months ago, soon after he broke up with his long-term girlfriend. I had noticed him carefully sizing me up, and I guess I was doing the same to him, even though I hadn't really thought of him that way before. But when you realize you've just hit the one-year mark at what was supposed to be a temporary job, you start re-evaluating just about everything. I liked that Keith was 34, not exactly old, though he seemed quite a bit older than my youthful 27 since he wears bifocals, not to mention a vintage corduroy jacket with elbow patches — in June. After a well-placed joke here and a few surprise desk latte drop-offs there, he correctly deduced that any girl who loves being regaled with a good projectile vomit story probably wasn't the sort of girl who would report him to HR should he ask her out for artisanal soft serve.

I said yes to a date because, straight up, I was bored. But I was also sad. I didn't realize it at the time, but I was still majorly pining away for Dean.

Sigh, Dean. *Sigh*, Dean and me in Thailand. Honestly, how could that trip Trish and I took to Thailand have been only six months ago when it seems like it's been a lifetime since I saw Dean for the very first time?

I was wearing my favourite red bikini, sitting in the water just where the ocean meets the sand, cooling my tanned tush while Trish read under a nearby tree. She had set herself up in roughly the same spot where we had noticed two new guys to the island eyeing us the night before. The fact that they hadn't come over was odd, because Koh Tao island is a very friendly place, and Trish and I are especially approachable because she has a crazy laugh, the best red bob, and we wear nothing but bikinis all day long. These two were a bit standoffish, which obviously intrigued us to no end.

After our typical breakfast of grainy toast with natural peanut butter and the best mango ever, we made our way to the beach, where Trish dove into her book (a voracious reader, this was her third book in a week, *Lessons in Chemistry*) and I dove into the water. I watched her skim her book for a minute before she yawned and lay down for a nap, resting her tented paperback over her slender nose.

There was a heatwave happening in Thailand, so we spent most of our days wading or sitting or standing in the water. But just standing in water started feeling weird, so Trish and I began a bit of a handstand competition, which meant I could never practise too much. (What can I tell you? Life could not have been simpler on Koh Tao.)

When I emerged from a particularly successful sideways split with full body rotation and looked towards the beach to see if Trish had caught it, one of the new guys, the taller one, was standing in the water right in front of me.

"Is that all you've got?" he asked, without introduction. He proceeded to dolphin jump into the water before re-emerging in a truly spectacular handstand. He included a neat scissor kick motion that

I would have to attempt later. But more importantly, *Well, well, well. What do we have here?*

Apparently, Trish was also impressed. She had risen from her book nap and was laughing and applauding from the beach. He bowed, then took two water strides closer to me, looked me in the eyes, and pulled a large clump of turtle-green seaweed from my chest.

That's how I met Dean.

And now a bit about him: Dean earned his medical degree from Pritzker in Chicago. He's single. His last name is Stein. (I can't help but think of Bubbe Bobby Grace's all-time favourite piece of advice: "It's just as easy to marry a rich man as it is a poor man, and if you can snag a Jewish doctor, your children will never go without summer camp.") Dean has spent three years in internal medicine and is now about to enter a subspecialty in infectious diseases after a trip to Ghana changed his plans.

Ian Sanchez, the guy he was with, has been Dean's best friend since childhood. Ian is a graphic novelist and also happens to be a talented beach juggler. But for the purposes of this journal, or diary, or whatever it is, let's concentrate on Dean.

On Koh Tao you learn a lot about the people you hang out with, because all you really do is sit and talk and eat and drink, with mini bouts of physical activity — one day we climbed a nearby mountain and another time we went snorkelling — and longer bouts of swimming and napping. What would normally take three weeks to learn about a new friend back home takes roughly three minutes on vacation.

Since Dean and Ian are a few years older than us, together we were like the grand elders of Koh Tao — everyone else seemed to be 21. Newly 30, Dean is showing a bit of age; he has laugh lines around his brilliant blue eyes (a good sign!), can't see without his contacts, and is a bit soft around the middle, though his sandy mop knocks about five years off his looks. Ian, meanwhile, has straight dark hair that looks exactly how you would draw a man's hair with a brown crayon if you were in grade one.

Turns out, Dean and I both have a love of:
- Fresh mango
- Hot weather
- Banana shakes
- My bikinis
- Travel — though we travel for different reasons. I mostly go for the food and beaches while Dean goes to heal the sick. (Six of one, half a dozen of another, as Bubbe Bobby Grace would say.)

Trish and I had found our perfect island vacation boyfriends in Ian Sanchez and Dean Stein. Beach time, hike time, reading time, rest time, movie time, and nighttime, when the EDM starts pumping, and everyone hits the beach and starts drinking and dancing. We also ate most of our meals together, and our different likes and dislikes had somehow morphed into the perfect Thai smorgasbord for four: Trish and Dean liked the nut tofu (a waste of space involving bland firm tofu stir-fried with tri-coloured bell peppers, tomato, onion, and a scant handful of cashews), while Ian and I were crazy for the tamarind shrimp (a sumptuous melding of tiger shrimp, ginger, garlic, chili, and green onion tossed in a tangy tamarind sauce and topped with crispy fried shallots). Dean and I enjoyed the spicy eggplant (the heaps of fresh Thai basil totally made it), while Trish and Ian usually went for the curry beef. (I'm not a fan.) We all shared in the perfectly balanced salty, sweet, spicy, and sour green mango salad and deep-fried honey bananas for dessert when we were stoned.

It was only three weeks together, but I grew incredibly attached to Dean. It's a little bit amazing how he instinctively knew what I needed when I needed it, like when he absentmindedly swung me in the hammock while I read, or when he would push the green mango salad towards me without necessarily knowing that I wanted more (even though it is obviously my favourite).

We talked for hours on the beach and he never bored me. And at night, when we drank, or especially when we danced, he looked at me in a way that no one else has before. It was like he was looking *into* me instead of *at* me. But my absolute, all-time, #1 favourite was when he would lie beside me on a sarong on the beach, and he would hold my hand and then just say, "Oy."

It made my heart do backflips!

Things with Dean felt real and felt great. But Dean and Ian left to continue travelling through Vietnam and Cambodia. And even though he promised to keep in touch . . . I still haven't heard from him. Then again, I haven't reached out to him, either. I just don't know what I feel. Could we have worked in real life, or was Koh Tao just a vacation fling?

So, here I am at TelecorpMedia, no Dean, no Dean replacements, in a job I pretty much hate: it's obvious why I agreed to go out with Manager Keith. We even fooled around a bit on our third date, but after that I ended it as gracefully as I could. (Read: not gracefully at all. Turns out guys don't like being broken up with in bed while still holding a Kleenex of wet stuff.) But I knew it was unfair to lead him on; he would be better off without me. "I'm doing you a favour," I said.

5:15 p.m.

I did it. I quit (sort of). I crawled past Keith's desk and slipped my letter of resignation under his green cubicle wall. Probably not the most professional way to quit, but I've never been accused of being professional. Besides, I couldn't bear to disappoint him in person yet again by turning down his job offer. That said, apparently, I'm not nearly as stealthy as I thought since Keith headed me off at the automatic-locking, glass-encased elevator banks, waving the resignation letter.

"What are you doing?" he asked, looking equal parts bemused and bored, staring at me on hands and knees. I stood up, brushing off my pants while trying to act like it's perfectly normal to be caught crawling out of a midtown office tower.

"Wow. You really don't want to work here anymore," said Keith.

"No," I said, flicking a stuck-on paper clip from my palm and embracing my growing confidence. "I really don't." Mic drop.

5:50 p.m.

I'm still not 100% sure about journalling but people who seem to have their shit together do it, so here I am getting my shit together. Trish and Lilly were on their way home, walking down College Street, when I called to tell them to come over for some snacks and bigtime news.

"How big?" asked Lilly, as if she wouldn't be coming over anyway for free feta dip.

"In-person big," I told her.

"Good big news, or sit down, it's bad news, big news?"

Do people really talk like this? And on that note, do they actually transcribe it into their journals?

"Champagne news big," I said.

"Champagne-drinking-away-your-sorrows big or . . ." Trish mercifully grabbed the phone from Lilly.

"What can we bring?" she asked, knowing that snacks are going to become a full-on dinner. Like always.

"Just get your asses over here — maybe bring more hooch if you've got it." I hung up. Click.

Trish and Lilly are my best friends. They live together, I live alone, and we're all happier that way. We met at McGill and bonded instantly. We had all ended up in Mr. Draker's film theory class called Icon, Index, and Symbol — I think the point of the class being how they all relate to the central themes in film. All I know is that I wrote a 40-page dissertation on the spiral imagery in Hitchcock's *Vertigo*, and, in a surprise plot twist, got an A.

11:45 p.m.

Trish and Lilly helped me take all the empty wine bottles (yikes) out to the recycling before walking home. I can't help but wonder if all of those celebratory bottles for quitting my job became the fuel that gave me the courage to make such a major life decision (leading to two more celebratory bottles) . . .

"Here you go, bella, a bottle of red and a bottle of white," Trish said as she arrived, handing over a couple of dependable Argentinean labels. "Now, what's this big news?"

"Manager Keith offered me a full-time job," I started. Manager Keith was their nickname for Keith. I love that my friends always come up with the least imaginative nicknames yet think they're a total riot. For instance, sometimes they call me Ruthie C.

"Great," said Lilly, trying to sound upbeat, not realizing that her expressive brown eyes were betraying her.

I looked at Trish. Then I looked to Lilly. Then I looked down at the table for a good 30 seconds. I rubbed my palms together. I placed them in my lap. I decide against that — I never quite understood what people were meant to do with their hands during bouts of quiet contemplation — I placed them back on the table...

"Oh, for Jesus's sake!" screamed Trish.

"I turned him down," I said with a smirk, loving nothing better than milking a juicy story.

"Great!" said Lilly, now looking honestly happy.

"And I quit my job," I casually revealed while unscrewing the red.

"Holy shit!" they shrieked in unison.

I poured the wine and then we all cheered and toasted to me.

"Not to immediately burst your bubble," said Trish, while immediately bursting my bubble. "But... what are you going to do for money?"

The big revelations to share didn't end there. I had another surprise for my girls, a little bit of life-altering info I'd been sitting on for a few days. In what can only be called perfect timing, I suddenly had the wherewithal to make a major life change, thanks to a generous inheritance from Bubbe Bobby Grace.

My Bubbe Bobby Grace died just over a month ago, and while it shouldn't really shock a grandchild when her 89-year-old grandmother passes away, it was a real blow to me because not only was Bubbe Bobby Grace one of my favourite people in the entire world, but she was also no ordinary granny, either. It's still pretty hard to talk about her because it's all so new, but I will talk about her because I've heard a big part of journalling is writing down your feelings to help with the healing process. Worth a shot. So, here are ...

Ruthie's Feelings
- I loved Bubbe and miss her a lot.
- She was a great cook and a mediocre baker.
- Everything reminds me of Bubbe, from the Sweet'n Low packets she kept in my kitchen junk drawer for when she visited, to the fuchsia sun visor she bought me with the hopes I'd take up golfing.
- Bubbe was hilarious, even when she wasn't trying to be. I miss both laughing with her and at her. And I *really* miss her laugh.
- Maybe I should take up golf.
- I'm going to use the inheritance in a way that will make Bubbe proud and will make me proud of myself.
- I'm going to lead a bigger, bolder life. Just like Bubbe Bobby Grace did.

Bubbe's husband, my Zaidy Murray, had died when my dad was just 12 years old, so Bubbe had to raise her five children on her own, and somehow figured out early on that real estate would be her ticket to financial freedom. She was right for the most part, spending the better part of 40 years working as a real estate agent, often keeping the best gems for herself and buying up whole blocks of downtown Toronto in the '80s, suffering through the real estate slump of the early '90s, and rebounding with the market, ultimately making a very good living.

After seeing all her children through university, she happily retired to Miami on her 61st birthday.

From the time I was eight years old, my parents would fly me to visit her for a week in late February while they took their annual sojourns to various Club Meds. They claimed the resorts were "adults only," but I later learned that this was not the case at all. But I didn't care. I loved my special week each year with Bubbe Bobby Grace, going for early bird specials with her and her friends, shopping in malls so big and air conditioned that she'd have a blanket waiting for me in her Cadillac so that I could warm up on the drive home to her gated community.

"Ruthie," she'd say, as we drove the 20 minutes back to the manicured palms and overly chlorinated swimming pool of her condo, a time she often used to dispense important life lessons. "I want you to remember three things. If you learn nothing else from me, please remember this." At this point I'd usually turn towards her, adjust the blanket, and listen carefully.

"Never buy green bananas. They will never ripen properly and will ultimately disappoint you. And while we're talking, never wear banana yellow. Sorry, doll, it's just no good on you." I'd nod in agreement, suddenly embarrassed by my cheery yellow bike shorts yet thankful for the honest advice. Then we'd drive for a little while in silence while she mulled over a final lesson: "Give money to street people, even if it's just a nickel. And make eye contact, too. They're just like you and me, only they haven't been so lucky."

The thing is, our chats almost always started with these life lessons, so, fearful of forgetting any of the very important "three things," I'd always rush into the bathroom as soon as we got back to the condo to write them all down in my little notepad. I later learned she thought I had a weak bladder. When Bubbe died, I numbered all her life lessons I'd saved in my spiral-bound pads and added them up. There are exactly 7,853, and I swear at least half of them are totally useful.

Bubbe loved taking her daily swim, an hour after playing canasta and two hours before dinner. That usually meant a 3 p.m. swim in the Atlantic Ocean each day. I used to marvel at this fit, leathery woman as she pulled on her swimming cap, so colourful and floral that her head looked like a giant frosted cupcake. She'd leave me on the beach, on a big pink towel under a blue umbrella, to watch her purse and eat a Snickers bar while she did her 45-minute swim. "Don't talk to strangers," she'd instruct as she pulled on her swimming goggles and kicked off her wedge sandals. "But if you do, be sure to offer them a stick of gum. And don't forget — Lipton onion soup mix is the secret ingredient to a flavourful brisket." Boom — three more without even trying.

From what the police told us, a Jet Ski hit Bubbe as she was swimming back to the beach, even though I have no idea how he hadn't spotted her elaborate swimming cap. A bunch of people ran into the water after witnessing the accident and helped carry her ashore while others called 911. But it was too late to save her. Apparently, as the life faded out of her on the powdery white sand, her last words were, "Go to Charlie's Seafood Restaurant on 15th Street. They really give you a nice piece of fish." And then she gasped, and then she died.

After that, it all came down to money and possessions. Bubbe was the matriarch of our family; the eldest of four (though her younger brother, my great uncle Stan, had died while fighting in the Korean War . . . of gonorrhea), she was the mother of five, and the doting grandmother to 11. After they divvied up her real estate holdings and stock portfolio, I inherited $62,873.42 from Bubbe Bobby Grace, and as of last week, that inheritance was suddenly sitting in a brand new "Inheritance" savings account.

There were some stipulations as to how the money should be used, but as was Bubbe's way, they were actually really good suggestions: "There are three ways I'd like you all to try to use this inheritance," started Auntie May, the executor, as we all gathered in the lawyer's office to hear the reading of Bubbe's will. Auntie May was reading the will in a spot-on imitation of Bubbe Bobby Grace, which, I'll be honest, I was having mixed feelings about. "Use it for education — why not learn a new trade? I'm not saying you should become a metallurgist or anything, but carpentry, locksmithing — you'll never be without a job if you've got one of those under your belt." True, true, we all nodded. "Or use it for travel — maybe you'll learn some things about yourself along the way. For instance, remember that time I went to northern Norway and went dogsledding? How else would I have known I hate dogsledding?" *Hmmm*, I thought. *I do love to travel.* I definitely got that from Bubbe. "Finally, you could use it to open up a small business," Bubbe Bobby Grace a.k.a. Auntie May continued.

"Learn to be self-sufficient; there's nothing better than being your own boss."

I contemplated Bubbe's final pieces of advice while I set out some marinated olives and focaccia on the coffee table.

"You know you were never meant to be what, in essence, has turned out to be a glorified temp, right?" Lilly gently asked. A third-year medical resident, Lilly knows she's fulfilled her obligation as a useful member of society so never wants to seem judgmental when her friends aren't necessarily living up to that level. She's always so careful about that, which I really appreciate.

"Go on," I said. We were sitting down on my poofy red couch, and I popped a spicy olive into my mouth. (I marinated them last night — they're a killer match with the Malbec.)

"So, let's think about it. What do you know how to do? What do you like to do? What would you be happy doing every day for the rest of your life?"

"I think the latest catchphrase for it is 'following your bliss,'" added Trish, as she tore off a piece of focaccia and swiped it through the fruity olive oil. I watched her close her eyes briefly, letting the flavours take over.

"Ruthie, you already know what to do," said Lilly. "You're the only girl I know who can take an empty refrigerator and turn it into something decadent. Where others would have been happy with these plump deli olives, you took them home and marinated them with olive oil and rosemary from your garden..."

"You're forgetting the fresh chilies, slivered garlic, and orange zest," I thoughtfully reminded her.

"Right. While most people invite their friends over for dinner *never*, you invite your friends over for dinner *always*. Your bliss is food."

I popped a pitted olive in my mouth and chewed slowly, considering what Lilly had said. Glancing around my apartment, I started to notice things. The stack of cookbooks on my TV stand. The food magazine clippings tacked to the fridge. The massive peg board I had Dad install to manage my ever-growing collection of spices.

She was right. I said it out loud to make it true: "My bliss *is* food."
And there it was, the delicious epiphany.

I leapt to my feet, nearly knocking over a wine bottle in my excitement.

"I've got it! I know what I'm going to do!" I announced to my girls.

The lightning bolt moment had arrived, with some helpful prodding from Trish and Lilly. I need to dive in and learn to master the art of food using the inheritance in a way Bubbe Bobby Grace would have definitely approved of. I'll cook my way to both financial freedom *and* happiness. It sounds *so* doable! My savings from work would cover rent and day-to-day living for about a year (if I'm frugal), and by my calculations (made under the influence of too much celebratory prosecco), that would be plenty of time to reinvent myself and become a rousing success in the culinary world! It's such a great plan!

As for the rest of that night, I won't bore you with the details. All I will say is that three petite women ended up drinking more wine and pink prosecco than is considered reasonable. We also polished off a pot of my go-to pasta — linguine in garlic oil swirled around marinated artichoke hearts, Niçoise olives, red pepper flakes, and oven roasted tomatoes, topped with some chèvre, parsley and a mittful of toasted crushed walnuts. Then we got on my laptop and before I knew it, I had paid the tuition for the next session of l'École de la Cuisine Française, along with all the necessary accoutrements. I was going to train at a traditional French cooking school. It would seem, if I listened to what Trish and Lilly were saying, my bliss was being followed. I was going to become a chef.

JUNE 19

Went to Mom and Dad's condo for brunch today. They seemed to have mixed feelings on the phone about me suddenly quitting my stable job and going back to school for something they consider more of a hobby than a career, so we decided to talk things through in person amidst their museum-white walls and sky-high windows to allay any fears they had about me being reckless with my inheritance and life choices. Being risk-averse professionals — Mom's a tax lawyer and Dad's a high school math teacher — they weren't fully understanding the whole "following my bliss" thing.

When I had called to tell them my big news, all Mom said was, "Speak to your father." I think they were both more surprised than disappointed, but one of the benefits of being an only child is there are no other offspring to measure up to. So I pretty much always end up on top.

I love my parents and I've always felt loved in return. I've also been privileged in that they supported me all the way through university. Right after the graduation ceremony, however, Mom said, "That's it, Ruthie, the bank of Mom and Dad is closed." *And fair enough*, I thought, but at least she could have waited until after we'd cut into the ice cream cake.

Today they put out the usual spread at the condo: Montreal bagels and little bowls of egg salad, tuna, cream cheese, and some nice lox. I was relieved to see the lox. Bagels and lox meant they'd decided they were happy for my happiness. If they weren't, it would have just been egg and tuna salad. And just in case the lox didn't prove it, they surprised me with a little back-to-school gift: an IKEA cake carrier. "It was my idea," said Dad. "Wouldn't want any of your tasty creations to go to waste, kiddo!" Dad was totally on board, but Mom still had misgivings. "Cooking is a thing you have to do to live," she said. "It's not something you bet your savings on." This struck me as odd since she loves food and has always encouraged me in the kitchen. (Then again, Mom also made me start a retirement account when I was eight.) But their reactions were par for the course: Dad is my biggest fan and loves everything I do, while Mom is my second-biggest fan but also my greatest critic. Just last week she called to tell me the lemon pasta recipe I gave her didn't work, which struck me as odd because all you do is toast angel hair in some butter, then cook it down in chicken stock and stir in a bunch of fresh lemon juice and Parmesan. I literally make it all the time. It's delicious. "Well," she said, "I didn't have angel hair, so I used linguine, and I didn't have lemons, so I used tomato sauce. I also threw in some leftover salmon and peas to bulk up the dish. Sorry, honey, not your best work."

JUNE 25
3 a.m.
Just got in from one of my worst dates ever. It's too bad because it had such potential.

The girls suggested I have a Summer of Love before diving into school in August, try to get Dean out of my system once and for all, so I swiped right, and after some reasonably entertaining online flirting, Dave the Man and I decided to meet in person. (Nickname c/o Trish and Lilly, of course, because he had showed off his hairy chest in one of his profile pics.)

I liked that he took charge and got us $20 tickets for *Boxhead*, a one-man show at a rep theatre on Ossington. It's the kind of theatre that doesn't have a real name, let alone a bathroom. And this is how cool you have to be to go there: you actually have to know someone to get tickets and be confident enough to know that you won't have to pee during the entire play. And then you have to know enough to head down a back alley at 10 p.m. on a Wednesday night and sit with 49 other people in a square, dark room with black risers and try not to cough because the space is so small and silent that you wouldn't want to disturb the rest of the audience watching the naked man onstage with a cardboard box on his head.

Normally, the thoughtful consideration, the weighing of pros and cons that must have gone into organizing such a risqué first date would have impressed the pants off me, just like Boxhead's. But as things turned out, even with its undeniable moxie factor, it ended up being super boring.

"What did you think?" Dave nervously asked, following the show. In other words, four hours later. In other words, worst piece of shit I've ever seen. Poor Dave. He was visibly shaken and knew this was probably it for us (and Dave the Man was right about that). If the play went badly for me, it went doubly so for him. He had a sudden coughing fit around hour three ("First coughing fit of my life," he later claimed), and by the end of the show he had to pee so badly that he bolted during the climax, missing the part where Boxhead pulled on some white tube socks and started playing "Blue Moon" on an electric ukulele.

So, I decided to be nice. "He had really lovely testicles," I said.

I don't think I'll hear from Dave the Man again.

Inheritance: (to be used only for school-related costs and materials) $62,873.42

Expenses: tuition $12,000, uniforms $125, knives $340, small wares such as Y-peeler $55, books $400, black safety shoes $100, subscription to Cook's Illustrated $27.

Balance remaining: $49,826.42.

July

JULY 5

Saw a viral news story about a bunch of teenagers in Houston who decorated an Independence Day slab cake with fireworks instead of sparklers. That's right. They set off fireworks inside. Kids these days! It went as well as one would expect. Some of them suffered cuts and burns and there was red, white, and blue buttercream frosting absolutely everywhere in the formerly white kitchen. It actually looked delicious. But how would you even clean that? I would just move.

JULY 8

I ate the most incredible mango today. The only problem is, now whenever I slurp back a great mango, I also get a pang in my heart because it reminds me of Thailand. And Dean. I called Trish to commiserate.

"Remember the freshly baked bread and homemade peanut butter? Will you make me homemade peanut butter?" she asked. The bread was always warm and the peanut butter extra smooth and salty. I told her I would.

During the oppressive late afternoon heat of Koh Tao, we'd watch movies in the main hut — usually some god-awful Avengers movie or decades-old comedies like *Turner & Hooch*. Our shady-time breaks included snacks of coconut shakes and skewered cubes of juicy mango, oftentimes eaten while playing cards with each other or Connect Four with little Chet, the five-year-old son of Charlie, the owner of our huts. Chet usually beat me eight out of ten games at Connect Four. (Actually, he beat me every single time. Why would I lie about that?)

"Remember that day we took a walk to the other side of the island, where the beach was rocky, and we saw six wild horses charging along the shore?" sighed Trish. Of course I remembered. As breathtaking a sight as you could ever imagine. But then we found a human skull and we shrieked and ran around in circles for a minute and then charged like wild horses all the way back to the safe side of the island.

"I don't think anything will ever be as good as that Thailand trip," said Trish, snapping me out of my reverie.

"We peaked too soon," I agreed while polishing off my mango.

JULY 10

Recent Swiping Sample
- Dan: Cute smile. Loves dogs. Holding a giant fish in his main pic. Wants a woman who takes care of her body. Swipe left.
- Tom: Very blond. Very thin. Enjoys chess and coding. Is looking for someone who enjoys playing D&D and eating "chicky nugs." Swipe left.
- Chris: Handsome! Loves to travel, likes funny people, long walks, and fine wines. Swipe right. No match. Humiliating.
- Ryan: I like his glasses. Warm smile. A journalist. He's holding a puppy. Swipe right. No match. I hate this.

But I did match with Mitch.

- Mitch: Tall. Into sports. Big finance bro. Not my usual but I liked his bio. We went for drinks. Things that worked: He's tall. Things that didn't work: Literally everything else.

JULY 13

Trish and I took the streetcar to the Beaches to escape a particularly steamy day in the city and couldn't believe how packed it was. I always assumed the majority of Toronto's downtowners escaped to cottages when the city emptied on summer weekends, yet here they all were, walking the boardwalk, blasting music, making out under sun umbrellas, and wading in the water with kids in colourful floatation devices.

We were sprawled out on the sand on beach towels, sipping wild cherry White Claws, eating Cheetos, and feeling summertime relaxed.

"Doesn't this remind you of Thailand?" asked Trish. The oppressive heat was definitely making for some Koh Tao flashbacks these past few weeks.

"A bit," I said. "Though Lake Ontario is a sad substitute for the aquamarine Gulf of Thailand. And those guys in the Speedos are definitely no Ian and Dean."

"Oh!" said Trish, bolting upright from her languid lean. "Speaking of which . . . Ian texted last night."

WHAT.

"Out of the blue. He said he wondered how I was doing and asked if I wanted to come visit him in Chicago."

"Let me ask you something, lady. Why have I been lying here listening to you drone on about your job, and why have you been listening to me drone on about my bad dates, when we could have been talking about this huge Ian news this entire time? So, what did you say?!"

"Well, I thought about it for a minute and realized that most of the fun we had involved the four of us hanging out together and I decided I wanted to remember that magic for what it was, a perfect three weeks in Thailand to be preserved for the ages."

Okay, this was odd, even for Trish. She'd rather preserve old memories in her mind than create new ones in real life? While I admire her ability to make snap decisions, sometimes her haste, be it ditching Ian or telling me I looked like Dwight Schrute that time I got a haircut that leaned into my cowlick, can be a little insensitive. "Please tell me that's not what you told him." I said.

"I said it was really great hearing from him, but that it's been over six months and time marches on." Then Trish took a big old gulp of her drink and relaxed back onto her towel as if it was just a day at the beach.

"So that's that?"

"He texted back a sad face emoji," she said. "And then that was that."

I've got to admit I was baffled. Then I considered what my reaction would be if Dean surprised me with an out-of-the-blue text and I decided there would be no sad face emojis involved. It would be a steady stream of red hearts, sparkles, fire, thumbs up, smiling face with heart-eyes, and face with tears of joy emojis.

JULY 15

I feel like I've wasted most of the summer lying on blankets and towels with Trish, listening to podcasts (loving *SmartLess*), reading, scrolling, swiping, and eating pizza. Maybe I shouldn't call it wasting; for the most part it's been pretty great.

Today I switched things up and played tennis with Lilly, who finally had a day off. As we took to the fenced-off hard courts at Trinity Bellwoods Park, she told me that she and Craig are having problems, but I'm not too concerned as this happens now and again and they always work it out.

"Maybe I'm to blame because I've laid the groundwork for an imbalance in labour over the years," she started. "I'm the one booking all of the dinner reservations, buying all of the theatre tickets, and planning all of the trips. I don't think he even has Uber on his phone. And why am I ironing his dress shirts? We don't even live together!" she continued while effortlessly serving. She really is a great multitasker. Also known as Type A.

"So, what does Craig contribute?" I asked.

"He's supposed to upload the grocery delivery for his mom each week," she said. "But he usually takes too long and does it wrong, so I end up doing that, too."

I volley the tennis ball back. "Lill, have you asked him to maybe take some things off of your plate?"

"My residency is clearly demanding," she said. "I had hoped he'd figure it out on his own."

"Have you met Craig?" I joked. She served again, and I was forced to leap to my left so the speeding ball didn't hit me in the boob. Not the time for jokes, Ruthie. Got it. But why is she so angry? We're talking theatre tickets here, not arson.

"I shouldn't have to ask," said Lilly. "He's a grown man. And we were finally going to start looking for a house together." Then Lilly took a ferocious swing with such a spin on the ball that when I tried to return it, the ball popped clear over the fence and landed on the grass. A nearby cockapoo grabbed it and ran away.

"I also think he's cheating," she said.

Damn it, Craig.

"Think or know?"

"I'm pretty sure."

She said all of the telltale signs of a cheat were there: the scent of another's perfume, sundry excuses for missing dates, and he was acting distant, too. I'll admit, it doesn't sound good. But this is Craig we're talking about. Our sweet, funny Craig. I grab another ball from my tennis skirt (feeling very Zendaya in *Challengers*) and serve an easy lob right to her.

"How can I help?" I asked, following one of our best volleys of the day. "Want me and Trish to disguise ourselves and spy on him?"

"Now's not the time for your Nancy Drew shenanigans," she said.

I told her everything would be okay, because they are Lilly and Craig — Lilaig — the best couple I know. *Get your shit together, Craig!*

Oh, and FYI, Trish and I will definitely be doing some Nancy Drew shenanigans.

JULY 23

I swiped right on Steve, and it was a match. I think I like him. He's a photographer who just had an art show opening at one of those shoebox-sized galleries on Queen Street West. He specializes in food shots, mostly fuzzy on one part of the plum and then sharp focus on another, and mostly for a small but national magazine called *Fooding*. He's not exactly creative but his work is technically sound, so he's found a niche that serves him well, and his client base is growing. But more importantly, he says he loves to cook. Here we go, Summer of Love Part Two!

JULY 26

Was just thinking ... when writing in a journal are you speaking to your present self or future self? Or someone else altogether? I'll have to ask Lilly. Either way, another great date with Steve. A couple of days ago we hit it off over iced coffees at Sugar Beach, and today we took a walk down College Street, ending at the Big Scoop. I ordered a single scoop of peanut butter and chocolate in a cup, which is by far my favourite. Steve chose a double scoop of tiger stripe with sprinkles in a waffle cone, and I was incredibly turned off. We sat in the sunshine on the neon-painted Muskoka chairs assembled in a jumble on the sidewalk, eating and watching as children used their powerful little tongues to dislodge fresh vanilla scoops onto the hot pavement. There was crying, there was laughter, there were new couples and old marrieds. Everyone loves ice cream. And everyone loves love. *Maybe that could be me and Steve one day*, I thought, as he leapt to the aid of a little blond girl whose strawberry milkshake was teetering.

Inheritance Update: *Balance unchanged at $49,826.42. Used work savings for park snacks and drinks. So responsible!*

August

AUGUST 2

Trish and I went on our first stakeout to spy on Craig. (I'm starting to think we may have a little too much time on our hands.) Yesterday, she casually asked Lilly what Craig was up to, and Lilly said he had a chiropractor appointment at 11, was meeting a friend for lunch, and taking his car in for an oil change after that. In other words, poor, naïve Lilly. That's more than Craig usually does in an entire week!

Trish and I biked over to the chiropractor's at 10:40 a.m. — Trish goes to the same one and had actually recommended Dr. Bessie to Craig, so she was able to saunter in under the auspices of "being in the area" and "booking her next appointment," while I hid around the corner outside, nervously giggling in anticipation of Craig showing up. When he did, a whole 15 minutes early, I texted, "THE EAGLE HAS LANDED! CHARLIE FOXTROT!" but it was too late. Craig had already entered the clinic.

A few minutes later, Trish burst out of the building, yelling, "CHARLIE FOXTROT?!"

"I'm sorry, I choked!" I was doubled over, laugh-gasping for air.
"What happened?"

"Well," she said. "I said, 'Small world.' And he said, 'I see you here all the time.' Then I asked what he was doing after his appointment, and he said, 'Going for lunch.' Then I asked where and with whom, and he said with Bruce, to Ramen on Bloor."

(We know Bruce and we know Craig loves Ramen on Bloor. His story checked out.) "Then he asked why I was asking so many questions, and why was Ruthie staring at us through the front window? And then I saw your face pressed up against the glass and I shouted, 'BYE!' before running out the door!"

"I blew our cover! It couldn't be helped! I had to see what was happening!"

We'll do better next time, Lilly.

AUGUST 7

Steve and I broke up. Nice guy, not so funny, but he gets a punchline. And when he said he loved to cook, he meant HelloFresh boxes. My biggest peeve about him had to be those fingers of his. That man and his fingers! I'd be watching TV and all of a sudden there were his daddy-long-legs digits making their way down my panties. I'd be washing my face and all of a sudden, his little twigs were crawling down my backside and up my centre. He mistook my writhing and occasional wrestling moves for orgasmic pleasure. Boy, was he wrong. We're in our twenties, not 15. You finger until you've had sex. Once you're having sex it's bye-bye fingerbangs, hello penis and tongue. Am I wrong? I don't think I'm wrong. Warm a gal up, is all I'm saying. And even with all of that probing and jabbing he never did find my clit. Obviously, we were just getting to know each other's bodies, so I tried to make it work. I liked his sandy bedhead, inquisitive brown eyes, and awe-shucks charm — until I didn't.

Like Bubbe Bobby Grace used to say, "You can't kid a kidder. And you, dollface, are a grade-A kidder."

AUGUST 11

Craig and Lilly are doing better but not great, I'm getting anxious for school to start — and am *this close* to giving up on the Summer of Love. I have a callus forming on my thumb from swiping left. So, the girls decided we all needed a night out amongst other people, or rather, people other than us.

"Let's be part of a larger society," suggested Trish. So, we went for icy shrimp cocktails and martinis at the rooftop bar at the Kiefer Hotel — they've also got really yummy smash burgers topped with caramelized onions and aged cheddar.

We reclined on couches tossed with Moroccan-themed pillows while sipping gin martinis under the city stars (read: three visible stars that are probably satellites). All in all, it was shaping up to be a pretty good pity party.

"This isn't a pity party," said Lilly. "We're here for practice. You've gotten so caught up with swiping left or right that you've forgotten how to meet guys in real life."

"So, here's a challenge," added Trish. "Make eye contact with at least three guys tonight."

"Not eye contact," I moaned. "My nemesis."

"Just do it," said Trish. "Guys are chicken-shit. But all they need is a sign that it's okay to come over, and that's where eye contact comes in handy."

After my second strong martini I gave it a shot. I cast my gaze upon a cute guy with green eyes wearing a white V-neck T-shirt at the bar, and he stared back. Soon after, his girlfriend returned from the bathroom, and he swivelled away and patted her ass.

For my second attempt, I made eye contact with a tall guy with a little afro wearing a pale blue button-down and he threw me the warmest smile. But then he leaned in closer to the guy next to him, putting his hand on what I assume is his boyfriend's inner thigh.

Even though I was 0 for 2 so far, I had to hand it to my girls, simple eye contact is truly effective. Later in the evening we met "Curly Jimmy" after I had eyed him over, and we had a blast. We all left the Kiefer around 2 a.m. and headed to a booze can Curly Jimmy knew about just down the street. I ended up dancing with him in the bar, then going downstairs and making out with him in the washroom, until the girls banged on the stall door and said it was time to go home. I told Curly Jimmy it was nice meeting him and wished him luck with his pet hotel startup as I tucked my undies into my purse and left the loo.

"Who needs Tinder when you've got eyeballs?" said Trish as we stumbled home.

AUGUST 12

Was so hungover today that when I walked out into the midday sunshine, I felt like I was staring directly into a solar eclipse. The outside world just felt weird. Went back to bed and slept for another four hours before ordering an obscene amount of Chinese food.

AUGUST 14

Have officially given up on the Summer of Love — it pretty much turned out to be the Summer of Bad Sex. Or, Bummer of Love. (Haha, good one.) Besides, school is starting in a week, so I've decided to get excited about that instead. Also, I *am* excited! It's time to buckle down and concentrate on my new life. I've deleted all the dating apps. And I probably won't even make eye contact anymore. It's time to forget about men and focus on l'École de la Cuisine Française. Oui, Chef!

AUGUST 17

All comfy on the couch, I can hear the summer siren song of the ice cream truck outside my window, and the laugher of kids running to catch it.

I think I'm finally getting the hang of this diary thing: it's basically therapy for the price of a notebook and a Bic pen. So here I am jotting down life events and inner thoughts like it's the Dead Sea Scrolls. For instance, the fact that on a sultry end-of-August night, instead of being sad that I'm stuck inside thumbing through a school syllabus, I have a giant grin on my face. This is actually happening!

Mom and Dad just called to wish me good luck on my first day tomorrow: "We've always thought of you as our little chef," Mom said, "and now it may actually come true."

"More importantly," Dad chimed in, "when do we get to eat the leftovers?" (The girls secretly call Dad "Trashcan Eddy.")

AUGUST 18
Lunch Break

Welp, my new life got off to an interesting start. I was whistling my way down Dundas, arms full of newly purchased cookbooks — everything from Auguste Escoffier's *The Escoffier Cookbook* to Anne Willan's *La France Gastronomique* to M.F.K. Fisher's *The Physiology of Taste*. (I left Julia Child's tome *Mastering the Art of French Cooking* at home because I'm a burgeoning chef, not a professional weightlifter.)

I had just missed the Dundas streetcar but left myself plenty of breathing room to get to my first class on time; I heard these chef instructors were real sticklers for punctuality. They probably figure if you can't get yourself to class on time, there wasn't much hope that your rib roast would emerge from the oven nicely crusted and properly pink.

So, with plenty of time to catch the next streetcar, I plopped myself down on the metal bench in the bus shelter next to a silver-haired lady who was piercing a juice box of V8 with a pointy straw.

"V8, huh?" I said. "I haven't had one of those in years."

"That's wonderful, sweetheart," she said, taking a savoury first sip.

I continued eyeing her healthy beverage while deep in thought — my cardiac health suddenly at the top of my mind. Last night, I read we'd be making béchamel and Mornay sauces, poulet poché sauce suprême and hollandaise. There would be rich potages of crème de moules au safran, bisque d'étrilles and homard, soupe à l'oignon gratinée, and then a whole lot of les oeufs: oeufs durs mimosa, oeufs mollets à la Florentine, oeufs cocotte à la crème, and oeufs frits au bacon. Oof!

Leçon 16 would feature compound butters and nothing but. Followed by la leçon on braising (lamb stew, braised crown roast of pork nivernaise, beef à la mode), which begets frying and sautéeing (beignets de gambas, sole meunière), which begets a whole section on "au gratin." Even the salads are full of lardons and heavy cream. And the desserts! Apple Charlotte with custard, crème brûlée, crème caramel, and sabayon. Just thinking about it again, I feel my chest constricting — owing to both the pressure of making these complicated dishes and their excessive fat content. This was going to take some getting used to, that's for sure.

Which was why I suddenly needed a V8.

Kippy's Korner was right across from the streetcar stop. So close. I had time to grab a juice, right? The streetcar wasn't coming. Bubbe Bobby Grace would want me to go for it.

Since I didn't know when I'd be eating next, I grabbed the large two litre plastic bottle. Not only would it quench my craving and curb my appetite, but I figured I'd make some instant friends when I showed up with enough juice for the class: "Ruthie! So thoughtful," they would all say in amazement. "She's a leader *and* a team player," the chef instructors would be forced to conclude.

No sooner did I leave Kippy's Korner than the streetcar pulled up at our stop and the doors slid open.

"This is your lucky day," said the old lady who had inspired my juice mission, as she climbed onto the streetcar ahead of me.

The morning rush hour was already underway. I was left teetering near the front, my arms full of chef's equipment, a leaden bookbag, my white chef's cap, and my latest addition, the jug of V8. It was all more

37

awkward than it was heavy, but still, I desperately wanted a swig of my juice, as the chef's cap I was holding in my mouth was absorbing any residual saliva I may have had.

I did the calculations in my head and figured I could coordinate getting the sip I needed. And so, following the next streetcar stop, I launched into action.

I unclenched my teeth and the chef's cap dropped squarely onto the chef's kit. (Score!) I slid my bag off of my shoulder as I moved out of lunge position and wedged it between my legs. (All on track!) I wavered momentarily, but so far it felt good. (It was almost juice time!) I gave the bottle a haphazard shake, opened my mouth so wide that my jaw clicked, and then I grasped the lid between my rear molars and started turning the bottle counter-clockwise with my hand. (So close!) The lid popped off, and I suddenly realized I hadn't factored in what to do with the lid. Ah ha! I spotted the breast pocket on my new chef's jacket, and I dropped it in there. (Vegetable juice plan a-go!)

But just as I was about to go in for that first swig, I noticed a commotion in the aisle ahead of me. A toddler had broken free of her stroller and was on her feet, her mother screaming; some teens started talking even louder at each other and people were looking up from their phones — it was chaotic. The toddler was holding one of her pink polka-dotted shoes in her tiny hand like a trophy . . .

As the tiny shoe sailed through the air of the crowded streetcar seemingly in slow motion, all I could muster was an "Ah, nuts," shortly before the wee shoe made contact, hitting me squarely on the mouth.

My bookbag dropped, my tool kit crashed, and my brand-new chef's cap slumped to the filthy floor, followed by the tiny pink polka-dotted shoe. Followed by me. Followed by the jug of V8.

Glug, glug, glug. I was on my back and fellow passengers were trying to help me up, but I was splashing around in a pond of tomato juice. The streetcar driver slammed on the brakes, making things even worse.

I was now officially the girl who showed up at l'École de la Cuisine Française on her very first day of class, drenched in vitamin-enriched tomato juice. This stain will forever be my scarlet letter, and it is how my classmates will remember me, always.

"Maybe this is a lucky *and* unlucky day," offered the old lady as she waved goodbye and exited the streetcar. Our elders . . . so wise.

When I arrived soaked in juice a few hours ago, instead of feeling sorry for me and my messy predicament, my instructor, Chef Antoine, used me as an example in front of the entire class.

"Don't be like this one," he said of me, not yet knowing my name. About 20 of my new classmates stared at me from their seats, some chuckling, others offering up sympathetic smiles.

"Do not be late and then come into my lecture room with sloshy shoes and expect me to fix what mess you have made."

"But Chef, I . . ." I started, hot with embarrassment.

"And don't make excuses and don't waste my time. If you have a problem, you must find zee solution!" But then, as he noticed my bottom lip fluttering, his voice softened and he handed me a kitchen towel and told me that Monique, the school secretary, would help me find a replacement chef's outfit for the day.

"And zee OxiClean should help remove zee stain du tomates."

8 p.m.

I just spilled mint tea all over my journal and the couch. What is even happening with me and liquids today?! Public humiliation aside, I'm happy to report I survived my first day of school.

During this morning's demonstration class, Chef Antoine explained that each day would start with learning recipes and techniques we'd later attempt to duplicate during pratique classes in the afternoons. He seems to enjoy teaching through storytelling, which I obviously love. He told us his family would go through 20 pounds of butter a week, so we shouldn't be afraid of butter. Someone put up their hand and asked how many people were in his family, and he said four plus an uncle. Then someone else asked if they were all still alive, and he said everyone but the uncle. Growing up in rural France, the chef's recollections of the summertime markets in Cannes filled me with both wonder and hunger. So vivid are his stories that in my mind, even though we're firmly in Toronto, Chef Antoine was leading us through the throngs of French marketgoers who are strolling about with baguettes tucked under their arms like so many Sunday papers... "Bonjour, Pierre!" "Bonjour, Amélie!" The locals happily waved to one another before pressing on. Chef explained some of the fresh products they'd use in their prized regional dishes, which we'd soon be cooking too: the smooth Niçoise olives and the lovely fruity oil; bouquets of zucchini flowers, born to become fritters; fresh almonds; more cheeses than there are days in the year; eggs with yolks the colour of the Côte d'Azur sun; and, of course, the butteriest of butters. He said there is a seasonality and simplicity at work, which is why French recipes don't change: "A classic is always timely."

To think, I went from Bubbe's chicken schmaltz to Mom's low-cal Pam spray, and now this man with a frying pan for a face and a banana for a nose is suddenly telling me it's all about the butter.

And let's just say butter in a pan wasn't the only thing sizzling in my class today. I made eye contact with a guy named Jeff...

Dear Diary, I loved the first day of my new life!

AUGUST 19

I never realized a beautiful glance from across the room could make my ears go hot. Chef Antoine tasked us today with choosing kitchen partners for the semester, and with that we suddenly had the makings of a meet-cute as Jeff made his way over to me.

"Hey," said Jeff.

"Hi," I said.

"I'm Jeff. I think we should pair up."

"Hi," I said again, suddenly rendered mute by the fact that this tall, cool drink of water was actually speaking to me. (Refreshing!) I hope he didn't notice my ears had gone bright red.

"You were the one covered in tomato juice, right?" he asked.

"Well, V8, actually, but yes. I'm Ruthie," I said.

"Well, Ruthie, would you like to be station partners with me?"

I snapped out of it and also laid down the law: "Sure. As long as you can cook well and follow orders, I see us getting along just fine."

What a smile on this guy!

AUGUST 22

Third day in a row that Jeff has saved me a seat in class. He leaves his backpack on the chair beside him until he sees me walk in, then he waves me over and puts it on the floor. I brought him a coffee today, with cream, no sugar. "Just how I like it," he said.

I know.

Not in, like, a creepy way. We went to Timmies together on our break the other day.

AUGUST 24

My iPhone contacts now officially include Jeff!

"We should probably exchange numbers in case one of us is running late or gets doused in V8 on the streetcar," said Jeff.

"Good thinking. I'm assuming you already have an extra chef's coat on hand for me for just such occasions?" I'm playing it cool, but my insides are doing backflips. Jeff wants my phone number! I give him my digits and he immediately texts me.

Jeff: "Hi Ruthie. This is Jeff from class."

Me: "Hi Jeff. Can you see me waving at you?"

Jeff: "Yes. Can you please pass me the chinois?"

Me: "With pleasure. Here you go." And then we start laughing because we're standing right next to each other, just two new pals being silly. This is the best thing ever.

AUGUST 27

Each day I learn a little more about Jeff, so have decided it's time to give him a proper introduction in the annals of this journal.

Jeff Wilson is youngish (my age), gorgeous, and willing. A star of track, former lead singer in a band, it's as if the world was created solely for his pleasure. Born with gifts, he takes without malice and gives when it strikes him. You cannot fault a man born with gifts. I certainly don't. Jeff may be my partner in Basic Cuisine and Pastry, and we may just share a stainless-steel workstation and a six-element gas burner for now, but my hope is that soon we'll be sharing a lot more. (Simmer down, Ruthie!)

> **Things I Like About Jeff**
> - He's super easygoing. The definition of water off a duck's back in human form.
> - He's 6'2" and has a swimmer's body. (Lithe, inverted triangle, smooth.)
> - He's funny and he gets my humour. After spending all summer having guys on dates explain my own jokes to me, this is a welcome change.
> - He's a talented chef. Definitely standing out in class as a top student. You can tell it's innate. I'm a bit jealous.
> - He's kind. Hasn't said anything mean-spirited about anyone or anything yet and believe me there have been ample opportunities.

Is he too good to be true?

AUGUST 29

Sometimes I catch a glimpse of myself in my oversized chef's whites at school and think I look like a background character in *The Menu*. What must Jeff think? How am I supposed to act sexy in this?

Inheritance Update:

Expenses: bleach $2.99, Tide to Go stick $3.49, OxiClean MaxForce $4.99, dry cleaning $12.50, new uniform $65.

Balance remaining: $49,737.45

September

SEPTEMBER 2

During a study break in class today I casually mentioned that I was starving to death, at which point Jeff pulled a Snickers out of his bookbag and handed it to me.

"Hey, I didn't know you love Snickers, too," I said, while grabbing the candy bar before he could change his mind.

"I don't. I got it for you," he said as he retrieved his own snack of Reese's peanut butter cups from his bookbag.

Not to give this too much importance, but I think a guy who notices his new friend's favourite chocolate bar and thinks to have it on hand during study breaks is just about the most thoughtful person in the world. And the fact that Reese's, Jeff's favourite chocolate bar, just happens to be my second favourite, *has* to be more than a coincidence. As Bubbe Bobby Grace used to say, "A coincidence is just like a bagel with lox and cream cheese: it was always meant to be."

SEPTEMBER 5

While school is super demanding there's always time for a little chitchat. Jeff and I talk about everything under the sun, except for one meaty topic that somehow hasn't come up yet: whether he's single. And he hasn't asked me either.

"Red flag," said Trish while I was at the girls' for pizza last night.

"Not necessarily," said Lilly. "School is a professional setting, and you're culinary partners. He may just think it's inappropriate."

"So, if you weren't with Craig, you wouldn't be scoping out the other medical residents?" I asked. Trish threw me a nod in agreement.

"Actually, lots of residents date each other," Lilly answered. "Because they understand the job priorities and extreme time limitations placed on relationships. You're around these people for 16 hours a day so you see them more than anyone else in your life. It's one of the reasons Craig and I are having problems. My training is number one, and he's suddenly number two. Nobody likes being number two."

"Yes, thank you, we've all watched ten seasons of *Grey's Anatomy*. Can we please get back to Jeff?"

The girls rolled their eyes at me.

"Okay, you little brat," said Trish. "Go."

"Well," I started, "as previously discussed, Jeff is handsome and hilarious, and he brings me Snickers bars and he's got an amazing skill set in the kitchen." They both nod. "He understands I'm having some issues with my knife skills, and he's been helping me with that. And he's having some problems with his timing, and I'm helping him with that."

"So, kitchen partners helping each other," said Trish.

"Right," agreed Lilly.

"That's it?" I whined.

"We all see what we want to see," offered Lilly. "You see a potential boyfriend because he seems to have a lot of the attributes you enjoy in a partner. But has he done or said anything that makes you think this is more than a friendship?"

"He did compliment my pen this morning."

"Has he mentioned other women's names without referencing their relationship to him? Does he ever text or make calls out of earshot?" asked Trish.

Hmmm. I did see him texting earlier today and smiling a lot. But tons of men smile at texts they send their grandmas, right?

"You know what could solve all of this wondering and worrying?" offered Trish.

Of course I knew. We all knew. All I had to do was ask Jeff if he had a girlfriend.

I guess I was just afraid of the answer.

SEPTEMBER 7

Ugh. I hate being so intuitive.

Jeff casually mentioned that Kate was picking him up from school today so he couldn't stay to study.

"Who's Kate?" I asked.

"My girlfriend."

My stomach dropped to the rubber tile floor and my heart followed soon after.

SEPTEMBER 8

Still reeling, but Jeff is throwing a party this weekend and the whole class is invited. He said I could bring Trish and Lilly, too. He also said I may like one of his roommates. I wanted to tell him to suck an egg.

SEPTEMBER 9

Still processing the fact that Jeff has a girlfriend. Too embarrassed to tell the girls.

SEPTEMBER 10

At the rambling second-floor Annex apartment Jeff shares with his two roommates, our class bonded over copious amounts of beer, dancing to retro '90s hits, and eating cold pizza at 2 a.m. I liked Jeff's roommates, Sid and Ken, who he knows from his band days with the Wet Paint, who had a couple of minor hits and one major hit a few summers ago ("I'll Take the Moon, You Take the Sun"). Jeff was using part of the streaming royalties from that Billboard success to pay his tuition. Jeff had liked the vagabond lifestyle of the band, and, like the rest of his bandmates, he had also enjoyed sleeping with many devoted fans on the road — less than 500 but more than eight, he told me. The difference between Jeff sleeping with the fans and his bandmates sleeping with the fans is that, while the other guys kicked the girls out of bed as soon as they rolled over the next morning, Jeff at least cooked them fluffy omelets filled with sautéed mushrooms and Gruyère before showing them the door. Sid and Ken still play small gigs but, like Jeff and me, are mostly trying to figure out what to do with the rest of their lives.

"Wow, who's that?" asked Trish, pointing to the blond supermodel across the room. (Lilly was on call at the hospital so couldn't come.)

I was pretty sure I knew who it was, but I was hoping it wasn't who I thought it was. But then Jeff came up to us and said he wanted us to meet Katie, and lo and behold I met the first person in my life who didn't have any discernible pores.

"Oh, hey Ruthie," she said as she bent over to hug me. "I've heard such great things about you!"

What a bitch. But believe it or not, meeting stunning Katie wasn't the worst part of my night.

If you would have told me 24 hours ago that it was possible to embarrass myself even worse than that time I got my period in a canoe, and worse than that time I mistakenly slapped Miss Crawford's ass instead of Lilly's, and worse than that time I barfed in the bridesmaids line, and worse . . . you get the picture. Yet it happened again, last night, at Jeff's party. It's probably my fault for having a big bowl of split pea soup for dinner.

Trish and I were in a huddle talking to stunning Katie — Trish because she loves meeting new people, and me because I was gathering intel — when Jeff and his roomies started getting out their guitars and basses and someone in the crowd had a bongo, and someone else had a harmonica, and they set up a mic and amp, and what an enjoyable time we were having, with such a talented gaggle of musicians. I especially loved seeing Jeff shine in the spotlight.

After a while, they started playing popular sing-along tunes so everyone could participate, crowd-pleasers like "Mr. Brightside" and "Wonderwall." At one point I popped up to sing "Hey Jude" with Katie and Trish, and as I did, I somehow fumbled the mic. And as I leaned over to pick it up, Trish's mic was hovering right above my tush just as I let out a fart. It wasn't a huge fart, but it WAS amplified by ten. (I want to go on record in this journal as saying I rarely fart but unfortunately split peas are extremely high in fibre.)

My fart silenced the room. I tried to brush it off by saying, "And on that note . . ." but only Trish and Jeff laughed since everyone else was too mortified for me.

SEPTEMBER 11

First text I got this morning was from Jeff: "Hi Fartface!"

SEPTEMBER 13

When Jeff and I were walking home from school today (I was tired and he was carrying my bookbag for me, *swoon!*), we saw not one, not two, not three, not four, but FIVE near collisions. Drivers in this city have totally lost their minds. Meanwhile, pedestrians and cyclists aren't exactly paying attention, either. And don't get me started on the e-bike couriers.

"Did that guy just cross an intersection against traffic without looking, pull a U-turn, jump the curb into the middle of the sidewalk, and then just park there?" asked Jeff.

"He absolutely did," I said. "That's got to be at least 28 different traffic violations. Should I go over there and make a citizen's arrest?"

"Go for it," said Jeff.

"Will you back me up?" I asked.

"Maybe. What would something like that entail?"

"Probably some light tackling and punching. Do you have any zip cuffs on you? Or perhaps rope or duct tape for his wrists?"

Jeff rummaged through his pockets and came up empty-handed.

"By the way, I'm glad I finally got to meet Katie the other night," I said. "You seem like a good match."

"How so?" Jeff asked. Hmm. I wasn't really expecting any follow-up questions. I was just trying to be nice while lying.

"Well for one thing, she's gorgeous. And for another, she probably doesn't fart in the middle of a party."

"I enjoyed your giant fart," he said. "And I especially liked your reaction to it. Not everyone can stay cool when faced with such a massive humiliation." I gave him a friendly punch on the shoulder. I love that he likes me, farts and all.

SEPTEMBER 14

Trish and I met up at Café Roma. She had just ended her latest in a growing string of month-long relationships — I can't even remember this one's name, let's call him Bob — so we had to discuss that, and I was also hoping to slip in some Katie discussion, along with a soupçon of Jeff.

As we shared a classic Caesar and ate pan-seared gnocchi in fresh tomato sauce, I casually mentioned, "Hey, some asshole is miming in the corner..." and hadn't even finished half the sentence before Trish was already clear across the terrazzo floor, having astutely deduced what

I had thought to be a poor attempt at a dead art form as an excellent attempt at the universal sign for choking. A couple of scary moments, three strong Heimlich thrusts, and a half-chewed meatball later, the busy restaurant erupted in cheers, and we were the proud owners of a free slice of caramelized lemon tart. (Trish had learned the Heimlich years ago as part of her training to become a lifeguard and swim instructor. She had said: "Really, how many people are going to choke on a chicken bone while swimming laps?" But look at her now...)

Anyway, let's skip over the boring Bob part and get straight to the Jeff discussion.

"Ruthie, you're thriving in culinary school, and I'd hate to see you screw it all up over some guy — even if he is the yummiest thing in your class," was Trish's gist. She and I share similar tastes in men. When she met Jeff at the party she couldn't believe how "our type" he was.

And talk about chemistry. Whether Jeff is checking on a veal stock reduction or doing a little jig as he's whipping egg whites (he's sooo funny!), when our bodies are close together it feels like we hum. Sometimes when I'm bent over my saucepan reducing heavy cream, he'll lean in so close that I can feel his warm, minty breath on the back of my neck. Major shivers! And one time, when I was folding puff pastry, I even felt a buzz. But then Jeff reached into his pocket and pulled out his phone set to vibrate. Gorgeous Kate, poreless, sweetly bland Kate, his beloved girlfriend of over two years, was on the other end.

"Hey, Katie," he answered in a hushed voice while pivoting away from me. "Yeah, sorry. Probably late again. Okay. Bye, babe."

Yeah, so what if Kate is a stunning fashion influencer who has 152,000 followers on Instagram and he calls her babe? And so what if Kate's sweet and tall and blue-eyed and blond and everybody loves her more than they love me? Blah, blah, blah! Trish says I should start acting my age and less like a giddy schoolgirl but *whatever*, Trish. I even bought a new Fenty lip gloss and underwear (just some black cotton bikini-cut Jockeys to replace my old ones with the saggy waistbands). You know. Just in case.

"Here's the thing, Ruthie," said Trish as she polished off her meal-ending cappuccino. There was always a *thing* with Trish. "Even though we love Jeff" — there's that "we" again — "until he leaves Kate or Kate leaves him, he's off-limits. Honestly, from what I could tell, they're a pretty solid couple, and Kate seemed really cool. Remember when she found you a piece of plain cheese pizza because you were complaining about the pepperoni?"

"I wasn't complaining," I corrected Trish. "I was voicing an opinion."

"And think about what Lilly is going through right now, worrying and wondering about Craig," said Trish. "Do you want to be the type of person who causes that sort of angst?"

"Of course not," I sniff. "But don't you think you should be the sort of person who supports her friend when she tells you she feels a connection with her classmate, and she senses the feeling is mutual?"

"Is this about the Snickers bar again?" asked Trish. Of course it was! But doesn't that type of kindness mean something? And his gentle teasing? Or am I losing my mind?

"Well, what about that time you stole Roger from Alison?" I countered.

"Yeah, what about it? That sucked," said Trish. "I sucked. And I felt so bad that I couldn't enjoy the relationship, which lasted, by the way, all of two weeks if you remember."

Great: now I feel like an ass and a bitch. "You know, I think Kate may be an anti-Semite."

"No, she's not. And you can't use that excuse every time things aren't going your way, Ruthie."

"But yesterday she brought me a bagel. A bagel!"

Then Trish started giving me the "Do you want to make a joke out of this, or do you want to be serious?" look and obviously I want to make a joke out of it — my go-to for eluding hard truths.

"That's what's known as a kind gesture," she said. "Everyone knows you love bagels. You don't shut up about how you could eat bagels every day for the rest of your life and then still eat some more after that. Come to think of it, I overheard you doing your bagel shtick at Jeff's party the other night, which is probably why Kate figured it would be thoughtful to bring you a bagel. Which, by the way, it was."

"You mean a bagel with *caraway* seeds, even though everybody knows how much I hate caraway seeds?" I said. (Trish has also seen my caraway seed bit).

Still, I know when I'm beat. "So, you're saying this Jeff thing is really a no-go?" I'm putting on a brave face, but I'm crushed — even though I'm not ready to give up on Jeff just yet. I finish the last bite of Trish's gifted lemon tart as a way of proving my displeasure.

"Besides," she said. "I think that 80 decibel party fart firmly placed you in the friend zone with Jeff."

"And whose fault was *that?*" I said, putting my mug down with a touch too much force.

SEPTEMBER 15

Trish told Lilly I was hoping to make Jeff more than just a culinary partner (such a tattletale!) and Lilly called to tell me that Jeff is off-limits. I hate it when my girls are mad at me!

"I'm not mad," said Lilly. "I'm disappointed."

Disappointed is even worse than mad!

SEPTEMBER 19

Katie sent Jeff to school with a container of her triple chocolate brownies for me, because I had gone on and on about how delicious they were at the party — truly fudgy through and through. How am I supposed to steal this girl's boyfriend when she's so gorgeous and thoughtful? Why does she keep sending me food? Moreover, how can I compete with these incredible brownies?!

SEPTEMBER 21

Trish and I had planned to tail Craig again tonight: suspicions are at an all-time high. But I had a hazelnut dacquoise emergency at school so had to stay behind. Trish said she'd still pop into Craig's gym — he had mentioned he'd be playing squash for an hour starting at 5:15 p.m.
    Trish rode over, and guess what? He wasn't there! And Trish said she checked, and the squash courts were all booked for the next two hours. Arrgh. I don't want our suspicions to be true. *Damn it, Craig!* Thankfully Lilly was headed to a fancy pharmaceutical dinner at the Bytown, so at least for tonight, she'll be none the wiser.

SEPTEMBER 22

Lilly and Craig broke up. Lilly caught him red-handed with some redheaded bitch and that's all I'll say because the last thing I want to do right now is gossip about poor Lill. (Also slightly annoyed that Trish and I failed as private detectives.) Lilly saw him canoodling with said redhead at the bar at the Bytown. Instead of making a scene, she picked up her phone, hit his number, and watched as Craig reached for his phone, looked at who was calling, and then placed it back on the bar unanswered. Lilly ran to the washroom and vomited.

SEPTEMBER 23

I've been making a super easy lemon meringue pie for years, prepared with lowbrow ingredients such as packaged tea biscuits and sweetened condensed milk (along with a ton of fresh lemon juice — that's the key), and my pie is great and probably best illustrates the main difference between my food and the stuff we're taught at school. My pie can be made in under an hour with no sweat, and people love it. And this is how you make tarte au citron meringuée at l'École de la Cuisine Française:

The first step is to make the sweet dough, a.k.a. a pâte sucrée. All you do is sift icing sugar, then add butter and mix. Add the yolks, one at a time, which will probably split the mixture, but not to worry, "the flour will bring it back together again," sniffed Chef Bertrand, the pastry teacher who was subbing for Chef Antoine today. You add lemon zest and a bit of milk, then combine, flatten, and form the dough into a disk. Wrap in plastic and pop it in the fridge.

Then it's time for the crème d'amande. That's right, there's almond cream in this lemon meringue pie. Weird, right? It's a mix of icing sugar and softened butter, combined with a ground almond and flour mixture, combined with beaten egg. Mix it all together along with the seeds from a vanilla bean, plus a shot of Grand Marnier. Mix well and refrigerate. (One thing I've learned when practising these French desserts at home is that you must clear the entire contents of the fridge to make room for the various components of one little tarte.)

For the lemon curd, I just juice and zest a couple of lemons and bloom the gelatin in cold water. Add half the sugar, beat in the eggs, add the rest of the sugar, and a bit of the hot juice to the mixture to temper the eggs.

Uh oh. What hot juice? Was the lemon juice supposed to be hot? Chef Bertrand never told us that in class this morning! Or maybe I wasn't listening! And now everything is mixed together and is supposed to thicken as I whisk but it isn't getting thick.

"Jeff, help me!" I yelped. I hate to admit it, but he's way better at pastry than me. Why must everything be so precise and have so many rules? So much to remember! Too many numbers and fractions! I hate it!

"It's okay, Ruthie," he said in his most calming voice. "What have you done so far?"

"Everything is in the bowl. And I don't think it's all supposed to be in one bowl."

"Where's your bloomed gelatin?"

"In the bowl."

"Where's your sugar?"

"In the bowl."

"And the lemon juice?"

"Oh that," I said. "It's warming on the stove."

"Well, that's lucky," said Jeff.

"I lied. It's in the bowl!"

We brought Chef Bertrand into our lemon curd conference, and he sniffed, "Start again." And so, I did, with rattled nerves, but Jeff helped me out and by the time I was adding my cubes of sweet butter to finish the slightly cooled lemon curd, my confidence was vaguely restored.

Just in time to start the Italian meringue: a slightly more involved meringue than the straightforward French meringue, it involves the added task of whipping together egg whites with sugar *and* water. However, when doing this properly, the sugar and water must first be cooked to the "soft ball" stage (120 degrees), and it appears there's no cheating it. Turns out egg whites are psychic or something because they know when you're trying to deceive them.

And so, my meringue separated.

And then it failed.

Again.

And again.

On the fourth try it seemed to hold.

But then it flopped.

"Jeff!"

"It's really not your day today, is it, Ruthie?" he said with a sympathetic smile.

"I quit," I whined.

"Come on. I'll help."

And that's exactly what he did, holding the candy thermometer in my fifth pot of sugar and water until it reached the proper soft ball stage, which he then drizzled into my last batch of whipped egg whites.

"Sweet success." He smiled as I waved my freshly whipped, stiff, and glossy meringue from the top of my whisk to the tip of my nose.

But we weren't out of the woods yet. It was time to revisit the dough: I rolled out my now chilled pâte sucrée with quarter rotations four times.

How thick? I sent Jeff over to ask Chef. He came back with the answer, "There should be three fingers of excess dough around the pie pan."

"Which three fingers? And pointed which way?" I asked.

"I don't think it really matters," said Jeff.

Uh oh. He was losing patience with me. That's what tarte au citron meringuée does to people: it turns them against each other!

After baking the dough and piping in the almond cream and then baking it again, at the four-hour mark we were finally in the home stretch: time for "assembly." You just take the almond-cream-baked tart shell and pour chilled lemon curd on top. Spatula it around to smooth, then put the medium star tip on the pastry bag and pipe on the meringue in continuous rosettes, starting at the edge and working into the centre. Then get out the blowtorch and finish that puppy off.

Finally. I was done. And it looked good. Restaurant quality, even.

"See, Ruthie," said Jeff as he casually finished torching his perfect tarte, "I knew you could do it."

"Yeah, I did do it," I said, as I carried it over to the presentation table like a proud peacock. Suddenly, I noticed the sides quivering, and the middle — if such a thing is even possible — sort of gurgling. And then the whole thing started shifting and the crust started crumbling and by the time I set it down on the table it had completely collapsed. Or imploded. Or whatever the hell you call a yellow gelatinous mess of broken dreams.

"Fail!" said Chef Bertrand with a little too much enthusiasm.

SEPTEMBER 24
9 a.m.

"Road trip!" squealed the voice on the other end of the line. It was Trish. And it was too early for a squealing phone call.

"Hello?" I answered back, pulling the phone away from my ear to check the time and date.

"Get a weekender bag together, Ruthie C., because you, me, and Lilly are going to Montreal. Today! In like, a half-hour," she said.

"Hello?" I asked again, rubbing my eyes open.

"Lilly's down about the big breakup, you're pining after Jeff and up to your ears in butter, I'm ... well, I'm just bored, and I think we're all in need of a little adventure," she explained. "So ... road trip!"

"I'm not pining," I corrected her. "I'm plotting."

In any case, Trish said she's taken care of everything. She found a cheap deal on a good hotel, her car is gassed up, and most importantly, she's got road snacks.

"Including Pringles?" I inquired.

"Obviously."

She also knew I was free for the weekend because all of my plans happened to be with her and Lilly (Saturday: brunch, then coffee, then naps, then a walk in the park, then dinner, and then drinks. Sunday: same itinerary but with a start time of two hours later.) Basically, I had no out ... and yet. "I don't know ..." I said.

"Come on," said Trish.

"But what if Jeff calls and wants to hang out?" I asked.

"He won't call," said Trish.

"Don't be mean," I said.

"Sorry," she said.

"I have to study," I said.

"We'll have you back by 3 p.m. on Sunday, promise," she said.

"I'm so tired," I said.

"You can sleep in the car."

Then Lilly got on the phone. "I'm sad, this is my one weekend off for two months, and I need to have fun," she said, sniffling

"Are you crying, Lilly?"

"Yes."

Sigh. I guess we're all going to Montreal.

"Pick me up in 45 minutes."

Noon

We've stopped at one of the Tim Hortons along the 401, somewhere between Kingston and Montreal. I just peed, Trish is filling the tank, and Lilly is getting the coffees and Timbits. (I told her to get mostly chocolate glazed and honey dip.) I'm going to join them in a minute but first wanted to pop in to say that while the girls thought I was sleeping in the back I've secretly been texting with Jeff for the past half hour! We've mostly been sending each other funny Reels (I'm surprised the girls haven't heard me chuckling), but the point is, Jeff ~~misses me~~ cares about me!

Lilly just came over and complimented me on keeping up with the journal. What a sucker.

Lilly can never read this journal.

1:00 p.m.

The girls switched places, Lilly is driving now, and Trish thought I had been quiet for too long, caught a glimpse of me texting and smirking, and practically dove over the front seat and tried to grab my iPhone.

"We are not going to be obsessing over Jeff this weekend," she said. "The next 48 hours are about the three of us being together and having fun. No texting, no swiping."

"What about DMing?" I asked hopefully.

"*Especially* no DMing."

I may not agree with her tactics but totally agree with the message. This trip is about cheering up Lilly.

But first I had to send one last important text to Jeff: "We just passed the Thousand Islands. This is where Thousand Island salad dressing was invented."

Then I handed my phone to Trish, and she has claimed it for the rest of the weekend.

4ish p.m.

Okay, I'll give Trish her dues where they are owed, the hotel is pretty sweet. It was a long drive — hours of snoozing, snacking, and belting out anthems or consoling Lilly when our playlist betrayed us (Lewis Capaldi is not your friend during a breakup). But the weather is great, the girls are unpacking (who unpacks for one night?), and I have claimed one of the two queen-sized beds in the junior suite for myself.

"Aaaahhh," I said while flopping around in our adorable boutique hotel room. "This is the life."

"Ew, ew, ew, don't lie on the bedspread," said Trish.

"I need to loosen up. Let's go out and get day drunk," suggested Lilly, who, between working long hours at the hospital and dealing with the big Craig breakup, definitely needed to blow off some steam. It's so unlike Lill to be the one suggesting debauchery. I like this side of her. And I'm glad I came.

"Better put on our game faces," I said. We freshened up in the little gilded bathroom — a pop of eyeliner, a swoosh of lip gloss — then they proved their phones were also zipped away in their purses. Nothing would be going on the 'Gram tonight.

The unspoken is understood — we are in Montreal to mourn the death of Lilly and Craig's relationship. And to do that properly we must return to where it all began.

7:00 p.m.

When I think of People's Pub, two words come to mind: beer and barf. Exactly in that order, and always those exact same words. And there are reasons for that: $9.99 pitchers of Belle Gueule and $2.99 spaghetti. Both went hand over fist during several years of being regulars here while we were at McGill. This is where we came to eat when we were out of groceries while studying for exams. This is where we would get too drunk on pitchers of beer that we drank through straws like giant Big Gulps. This is where we would end up in the washroom, having long, meaningful conversations with complete strangers as we waited for a stall to open up. People's Pub is where we pretended to enjoy watching hockey games, and where we met half of our friends during first year. But most importantly, it's where Lilly met Craig.

"Is your father a thief?" was the first thing out of Craig's mouth when he finally got up the nerve to walk over to our table. He was talking to Lilly.

Here we go, I thought while rolling my eyes at Trish.

"No, he's a doctor," answered Lilly. "Why would you think he's a thief? What have you heard?" (Oh, Lilly.)

"Well then, who stole the ... stars ... from ... um, I'll be right back," stammered Craig.

He returned to his table and bent down into huddle formation with the five friends who had been staring at our table, just as we started staring at theirs. They broke their huddle, fist-bumped each other, and Craig readjusted his Mets baseball cap as he started walking back towards us, looking a little more confident this time.

"So you say your father isn't a thief, huh?" asked Craig of Lilly upon his return.

I genuinely thought this sort of pickup line was only done in bad rom-coms. Happy to be proven wrong.

"Nope. He's an ear, nose, and throat specialist," she said.

"Well then, who stole the stars from the midnight sky and put them in your eyes?"

"Huh?" asked Lilly, not getting the pickup line, the pun, or even the fact that Craig liked her.

"He's complimenting you," said Trish helpfully. "He's saying your eyes sparkle."

"More like, um, twinkle," said Craig, now blushing.

"Have a seat," I said, and Craig pulled up a creaky wooden chair from a neighbouring table.

His friends applauded. He didn't look back at them, too busy gazing at Lilly, and bought another round for our table.

Lilly and Craig ended up going out for seven years, which is quite a long time for such a young couple, especially since the relationship got its start with such an awful pickup line. But there's no getting past chemistry, and they had that from the beginning.

"Feel my heart," Lilly said after her first official date with Craig. They had gone to see a movie and he had just kissed her goodnight at the door. Her cheeks were flushed and her eyes alight. I remember her reaching for my hand and putting it over her chest. It was beating like crazy. "I think I love him," she said.

They definitely had their ups and downs over the years but for the most part they were the sweetest couple you've ever seen — their hands always knitted together wherever they roamed. But once we had all left our utopian existence at university and moved back to Toronto, they hit some rough patches now and then. But nothing like this.

"I need a batch of your Toblerone chunk cookies big-time," said Lilly, weeping into her pitcher of beer between sips from her disintegrating paper straw. Poor Lilly. But she was right. She did need my cookies.

"We all need pedicures," I declared, as we were down to the dregs of our respective pitchers at the People's Pub. "We all need drunken pedicures right now."

So, that's where we are now. I'm jotting down some quick notes so that the girls don't talk to me during the pedi. I'm too buzzed and frankly I just need a few minutes of alone time. Man, this journal comes in handy on several fronts. That said, we were lucky to get into Spa Mermaid for side-by-side pedicures on a busy Saturday. There had been a last-minute bridal party cancellation (the wedding was suddenly called off but that's all we could get out of them), so one group's misfortune turned out to be our Red Hot Rio nails.

"I've decided that I never want to date again," said Lilly, perched atop her pedicure throne. "I'm going to concentrate on myself: learn how to be a better me."

"Dumb-b-b id-d-dea," I said from my vibrating massage chair, set to high.

"Ruthie!" said Trish. "Don't listen to her, Lill. She's just trying to shut you up. She must be the only girl in existence who likes to go for group pedicures while also insisting that nobody speak during the appointment hour..."

Midnight

For our final meal we decided on a blow-out dinner at the rustic and chic le Boeuf et le Cochon, where Quebecois chef Luc Roy brings fancy French peasant food to the Montreal masses by making it both comforting and extremely decadent. Like foie gras poutine with squeaky curds from his own dairy farm and seared duck breast with foraged chanterelles, all set amidst a simple room of rough-hewn beams and exposed brick.

After much deliberation, here's what we ended up ordering:

- seafood tower featuring crab legs, oysters, clams, shrimp, mussels, snails, and conch — much of it culled from the nearby St. Lawrence River (The furry conch shell was a tad challenging.)
- foie gras poutine (The consensus was "disturbingly delicious.")
- two-pound lobster stuffed with fall vegetables and doused in Béarnaise (Lilly's favourite: "Can you make this for me on my birthday?" she asked between mouthfuls. I'll have to remember. It'll be a nice surprise.)
- hanger steak with a sidecar of mushroom Bordelaise (Trish's favourite. She's super into protein these days.)
- lamb shank with green lentils ("Unappealing colour combo" was the verdict.)
- pouding chômeur (Warm, mapley heaven! New favourite dessert alert!)

"Hello, assholes," said the chef wearing his trademark blood-stained apron and smiling as he made the rounds to our table before dessert. We started coming here when he first opened and now visit every time we're in town. He loves us.

"Bonjour, Chef Roy," we all said in unison

"Did I fuck you ladies up good?"

"Yes, Chef!" I shouted, patting my full belly. "I feel the old gallbladder working overtime."

So delicious, so much fun. Such an amazing night. Best of all, Lilly is looking lighter and happier even if the wine and lobster are doing most of the heavy lifting.

SEPTEMBER 25

3 p.m.

I dumped my bag as soon as I walked through the door, grabbed some water, and have planted myself on the couch. I intend not to move for the next ten hours. God, I love this couch. What a great weekend.

3:04 p.m.

FUUUUUUUUCK THERE ARE 14 MESSAGES FROM JEFF ON INSTAGRAM. WHAT A WASTE OF A WEEKEND!

SEPTEMBER 26

Jeff seemed to be drunk in the messages (he's a bit of a drinker — cause for concern?) and was basically saying "hey" in various, wonderful ways ("Hi partner," "What up?," "Bonjour?," "Yo homeslice," "Having fun?," "Are you alive?"), which is a big deal to me but apparently not to Lilly or Trish. I don't care what they say. This is huge. He was thinking of me. ~~He cares about me.~~ He loves me!!

As exciting as it is, I've got to remain calm, act normal, and put this potentially blossoming relationship on the backburner for now, because today I was back in class and Chef was playing show and tell with a live crustacean and a ten-inch knife.

"To kill zee lobster, normally we don't just put him in zee boiling water," said Chef Antoine as he flipped a lively lobster onto its back and then rubbed its head as one would an adorable kitten. "First we take zee time to say hello." Then Chef abruptly stabbed the crustacean in the back with the point of his razor-sharp knife, its shell making a particular crunching sound. There were a few audible gasps from the class. "Sometimes they bite you," he explained, "then you take more pleasure in killing them." He was trying to be funny, but I'm afraid the jokes weren't exactly landing this morning, especially with some of my more sensitive classmates. But either he didn't notice or didn't care, and then, as is his way, Chef Antoine ended this lesson on lobster butchery on a serious note because even though he likes to joke around as much as the next guy, he is deadly serious when it comes to food: "I'm being serious now," he intoned as he dropped the lobsters into a pot of simmering water. "Zee animal must not suffer. We do it this way because zee lobster is not stressed, and it dies instantly. Also," he added with a sly smile, "it makes for zee more tender, sweeter meat."

I like Chef Antoine a lot. I think he's a wonderful person full of amazing insights and a glass half-full kind of attitude. And I'm naturally drawn to that. Even when the shit hits the fan during practique sessions, as it invariably does, he only yells when it's totally necessary, and only throws things (any overripe fruit is a favourite) when he truly needs to make a point. As in, don't throw hot oil into a pot of water. For if you do, not only will you get splattered with searing fat, but you'll also get beaned with one of the ripe tomatoes Chef regularly keeps at the ready, just so that you'll remember never to do that again. I honestly don't know how he gets away with it in this day and age.

The fact of the matter is Chef Antoine has to be on his toes because lives are at stake. When you think about it, there are just so many ways to mortally injure oneself (and others) at l'École de la Cuisine Française that I'm surprised nobody has ever died here. There are all the knives (obviously), but there are also propane torches and pots of boiling oil, and there's molten cheese and slippery floors and meat cleavers and gas elements and smoke and fire and ... well, there are just so many things that could possibly go wrong, and so many people who haven't a clue as to what they're doing. It's a recipe for disaster (haha). And sure, we all burn and cut ourselves now and then, but like I say, Chef runs a tight kitchen and apparently nobody has been killed on his watch, though he did tell us a story about that one guy who sliced off his pinky with his boning knife while butchering a lamb saddle.

A little later, as Chef Antoine smashed the emptied lobster shells into a pot (you do not waste a thing in French cuisine), the basis of what was to become a rich, coral-coloured bisque, Chef said with a furrowed brow, "Remember, he tried to kill you." And then, moments later, he switched gears yet again from madcap chef to philosopher: "Most people love to eat zee lobster, but they don't want to kill zee lobster. But somebody has to kill zee lobster!"

Jeff gave me the eyes and mouthed the words "Somebody has to kill zee lobster," and I chuckled then threw him a shush sign.

SEPTEMBER 28

Today at school I burnt my arm while taking a sheet pan out of the oven. And it turned out to be one of the greatest moments of my entire life! Jeff launched into action and put my arm under cold water before applying ointment to my screaming welt. Then, as he held my hand while wrapping my arm in gauze, I looked up at him and our eyes met — and held.

"Good as new," he finally said, holding my hand for a little longer than necessary.

Thank you, Chef McDreamy.

SEPTEMBER 30
5 p.m.
Our class is getting chummier. We're more confident, too. Today we were on leçon 15, and Chef Antoine has taken to pop-quizzing us more often. "How do you know eggs are fresh?" asked the chef. The class threw out a handful of old wives' tales and he put them to the test to put them to rest. In other words, he was making another point. "Float the egg in water," offered Christopher. (But was the egg supposed to sink or swim?) "Spin it on the counter," said Cynthia. (Should it spin fast or slowly?) Michelle suggested it must be spun counter-clockwise to really work. Chef let us have our fun for a little while and even threw a hardboiled egg into the mix as a prank. In the end, Jeff was the one who finally submitted the correct answer: "Check the best before date on the egg carton." Gosh he's smart. Swoon.

Bottom line: there really aren't too many tricks to this cooking game. The most obvious answer is usually the correct one.

"When you have a problem, don't wait for zee solution," Chef said as we gathered up our books and started shuffling off to lunch. "You must find it." And then, "Ruthie, stay here for a minute."

Uh oh. I didn't think I'd done anything wrong, but isn't that always the way? Take any sort of classroom scenario, be it grade ten math, or even a continuing education course in calligraphy at the local recreation centre, and if the teacher asks you to stay behind, a chill runs up the spine.

"Am I in trouble?" I asked when I joined him at his station.

"Non."

"Do you need help with something?"

"Non."

"Nice weather we've been having, huh?"

"May I speak now?"

"Yes, Chef."

"As you know, the Emerging Chefs Silver Platter Competition is happening in Vancouver next month. There will be student chefs from across Canada competing and l'École de la Cuisine Française is sending our best to compete, and of course to win."

Oh. My. God. I had gone momentarily deaf by the excitement of it all because I think I knew what was coming. I hoped I knew what was coming. In fact, it would be pretty embarrassing if I didn't know what was coming because I was already jumping up and down while clapping my hands. And then, ". . . I'm sure Jeff told you this morning that I have asked him to represent our school in zee competition and he said yes. But there eez an extra surprise. I also asked Jeff to choose a partner for the competition and he made a very good decision. He chose you. I think with your instincts and Jeff's skills — and *his* willingness to follow instructions — you should, in fact, do very well as a team."

A team!

"Thank you, Chef! Thank you!" I hugged him and he stiffened. I quickly released.

Jeff and I are going to the Emerging Chefs Silver Platter in Vancouver! And together, we will kill zee lobsters!

5:35 p.m.

"You're going to Vancouver with Jeff?" asked Lilly, mouth pretty much agape.

"What can I tell you?" I said after delivering the good news — along with a still-warm pithivier. "You and Trish plot against me, and Chef Antoine laughs."

I was kidding around because Trish and Lilly are concerned that my feelings for Jeff are misplaced even though I've been compiling a dossier detailing examples of our burgeoning romance in this very journal.

1. He left me 14 DMs when we were in Montreal.
2. He caringly tends to my wounds.
3. We spend every minute together at school.
4. He usually walks me home.
5. Once home, we text each other a lot.
6. He chose me to be his partner at a major culinary competition clear across the country.

But most of all it's the butterflies. And nobody knows that special feeling except for you.

Obviously, this situation isn't ideal. Not by a longshot. Gorgeous Katie is still on the scene.

And while I do like her, and Jeff probably loves her, over the past few weeks I've noticed he's been spending more and more time with me, and less and less time with her. Could it be that they've broken up? I know we're spending so much time together mostly because of school, but sometimes it's not. For instance, why is he texting me at all hours instead of her? Why does he smile so widely when I walk in the room. (And why do I feel a little empty when he leaves?) Why do we stand so close together when we're cooking in class, but so far apart when we're not?

Trish's and Lilly's hearts are in the right place, I get that. They're afraid I'm going to blow it at school again because of some guy. The problem with having old friends is they know everything about you, including your dating history, and specifically that time you let your film theory grade slip to a C-minus because you missed a midterm when Gary Shum dumped you after you told him you were falling in love with him.

"I'm excelling at school," I assured Trish and Lilly. "Chef Antoine says my pithivier is uncommonly good."

"Your pithivier *is* uncommonly good," said Trish while gorging on the frangipane-filled flaky pastry.

"We can taste that you're excelling," Lilly added. "And you also seem happier than you've been in ages, and it's so nice to see, Ruthie C. We just don't want you to lose your focus."

While I'm enjoying l'École de la Cuisine Française, the girls are absolutely loving it. It's like I went from leading a sepia-toned life to starring in a technicolor food dream. I feel like Remy in *Ratatouille*! I have to say I'm a lot more interesting now — they get a kick out of my Chef Antoine stories and are actually keen on learning about the history and cooking methods of these classic French recipes. But more importantly, I stop by their place with savoury dishes and cream-filled Parisian desserts almost every night.

Of course, once Jeff and I hit Vancouver, I may be pursuing two passions.

Inheritance Update:

Possible new boyfriend expenses: this obviously falls under "following my bliss" — *new mattress $2,050 (My first real bed. It even has a pillow top. Heaven!), gold hoop earrings $325 (I've always wanted a pair — trust me, Bubbe would approve), three-pack of black Jockey bikinis $35.*

Awesome weekend in Montreal: $523 all-in, am considering it a culinary "research trip" and totally, TOTALLY worth it.

Balance remaining: $46,804.45.

October

OCTOBER 3

I've watched *Top Chef, Iron Chef, MasterChef,* and *Chopped,* and let me tell you, they all make culinary competitions look like a cakewalk in Candy Land compared to what I've been through these past few days. I'm so busy I haven't had a second to speak to Trish or Lilly, and my mom keeps leaving passive-aggressive messages like, "I know you're busy, honey, so don't bother calling back. We just want to make sure you're not dead in a ditch."

The good news is I'm not dead in a ditch. Plus, all this practising outside of class is clearly making me and Jeff better chefs. The bad news is, it's really hard work! And I'm also freaking out a bit because a month isn't nearly enough time to prepare for a culinary competition, even though Chef has explained, and the rules clearly state, that student competitors may only be informed of their participation in the Emerging Chefs Silver Platter event exactly one month prior to the competition date. But I'm sorry, that's dumb. There's so much to do and I still know so little. I'm just a cooking school student, damn it!

While Jeff is awesome in every way, I find it hard watching him basically ignore my well-plotted timing during our practice sessions, relying on haphazard course corrections. When he sees me getting flustered, he gently says, "It's all good," or "Somebody has to kill zee lobster," which for some reason still cracks me up.

I may be stressed, but we're still having fun. Just last night I was experiencing some technical difficulties with my compound butter — marchand de vin to be exact, which we thought would be the perfect topping for the grilled ribeye in our Individual Plated Entrée entry. Anyway, compound butters are usually one of the easiest things we make, but I couldn't get the lemon zest, parsley, shallot, and red wine to incorporate into the softened butter in a smooth and cohesive fashion. It was the strangest thing. Following my third attempt, I walked away to get a baguette and spotted Jeff snickering while sneaking some ice water into the mix. Major prankster alert! Well, two can play at that game. I grabbed the day-old baguette and whacked him over the head with it. The loaf got a bit dented, but it didn't break so I hit him again and again with increasing velocity. It was hilarious. (Maybe you had to be there?) But honestly, what was I thinking? Jeff is double my size and twice as strong, so he effortlessly wrested the baguette away from me and started chasing me around the room with the semi-intact loaf. I was screaming and laughing — until we heard some familiar footsteps coming down the hallway.

Without a word I ran and grabbed a large stainless-steel bowl, Jeff started scooping up the bread from the floor, and just as Chef Antoine entered the kitchen, we regained our composure, me holding an oversized bowl of crumbled baguette, and Jeff a pound of butter and a litre of milk.

Chef was checking in on our progress.

"What will you do with this bowl of bread?" he asked while breadcrumbs audibly crunched underfoot.

"We were thinking something rustic," said Jeff, looking over at me expectantly, trying to hold in a chuckle.

"Like what?" asked Chef, looking none-too-happy.

Jeff was staring at me, Chef was staring at me, and I was staring at the bread bowl and thinking *hard*. And then, "Chef, for one of our desserts on the final platter, we were thinking of a new take on bread pudding. Small, dainty, and decidedly French, of course."

"Yeah," added Jeff, giving me a look that said "high-five." "Small diamonds of warm bread pudding, maybe topped off with a crème légère or salted caramel." (Nice one, Jeff!)

"Well," said Chef, "I suppose it's French by way of Acadia, and it does sound good. You will try it and I will tell you if it's a nice idea for zee competition. The judges may think it is too basic but maybe they will not." Then Chef made his way to the door, stopped short, turned around, and half-opened his mouth. But he didn't say a thing. And with that, he left, his authoritative clogs clomping back down the hallway.

"Do you think he heard us?" asked Jeff.

"A hundred percent," I said.

OCTOBER 4

I just got the worst haircut of my life. I tried a new spot that Claire from class recommended and now I look like Javier Bardem in *No Country for Old Men*. Never go back to Cheveux, future me! Back into a topknot it goes.

OCTOBER 5

Went for a coffee walk with Lilly today. She said she's doing okay with the Craig breakup and Trish confirmed she's doing as well as can be expected, but I'm not convinced. I wanted some alone time with Lill just to walk and talk — I find people open up more when they're not sitting and staring. (A rare example of when no eye contact is actually better for communication.) I suggested we get coffees and treats from Café Forno then stroll through Trinity-Bellwoods Park as the leaves are starting to change — tinges of orange and yellow but no crimson reds just yet. Warm lattes, Italian cookies, fall coats, a nature-imbued walk . . . I figure it's almost better than chicken soup for Lilly.

"Okay, lady, start talking," I said.

"I'm good," said Lilly. "Work is challenging. I've started kickboxing, and I've joined another book club."

What does she think this is? A job interview? I take a bite of my pistachio sandwich cookie and a sip of my latte. A perfect pairing, just like Lilly and Craig used to be.

"Lilly, can we talk about Craig for a minute?" I asked. "He's been a big part of your life for the past seven years. Don't you miss him?" (I mean, *I* miss Craig. I hate him right now, but I still miss him.) "Are you sure keeping so busy isn't just delaying the inevitable?"

"What's the inevitable?" she asked after taking a tiny nibble of her chocolate-dipped biscotti.

"Thinking about the breakup, being sad about the breakup, dealing with the breakup?"

Lilly stopped walking and met my eyes: "I'm specifically trying not to think about him so that I don't fall apart. Do you want me to fall apart?"

"No Lilly, of course not! That's not what I'm saying. I just want you to know that it's okay to be sad and it's okay to fall apart. You know that, right?"

"I know," she sighed. "If it makes you feel any better, I don't really have an appetite right now. Do you want my biscotti?"

"It doesn't make me feel better but of course I want your biscotti," I said as I snatched it. "Do whatever you need to do, Lill, and go at your own pace. I just want you to know that if you ever need me, I'm right here, and always will be."

"You're a good friend, Ruthie C."

"I know."

OCTOBER 8

It started with a bashed-up baguette and the promise of dessert.

Test One
"Okay, what have you got?" Jeff asked.

"What have *I* got? You're the genius who said we could make a competition worthy dessert out of a floor baguette," I said.

"I'm the big ideas guy. You're the flavour guru." (He's not wrong.)

We decided on a maple bread pudding, inspired by Chef Luc Roy in Montreal.

After a bit of fiddling with measurements and deciding on doneness, about an hour and ten minutes later it was ready and smelling like heaven but too sweet, too loose, and too close to a classic pouding chômeur.

Test Two
We decreased the milk, added another egg, and removed the maple syrup. But we still needed a core flavour. Hmm, core ...

"What about apple?" I suggested.

Test Three
We added some sauteed Golden Delicious, and it was good but still missing something. "Maybe a little crunch?" pondered Jeff. "Walnuts?"

"Yes," I said with a high five. "But pecans."

We were jiving like peanut butter and jam.

Fifty-seven minutes later we had another golden-brown bread pudding on our hands. It was moist but still had texture, and the flavour was definitely there. Yet it still wasn't competition-worthy.

Test Four
"I have an idea. Can you get me a small saucepan and a whisk, please?"

Jeff fetched the pan while I collected butter, sugar, cream, and Calvados, then whisked together a spiked butter sauce over the heat. I poured most of it over the still-warm bread pudding, so it absorbed the luscious sauce like rain on Kentucky bluegrass.

"I can't wait for Vancouver," Jeff said abruptly.

"This *is* some mighty fine bread pudding," I agreed triumphantly.

"No, not because of the bread pudding," he said.

"The competition?"

"Not because of the competition," he said, taking a step even closer. "Ruthie..."

"Well! Here you two are! I was starting to worry!" Kate suddenly said from the kitchen threshold.

"Oh, hi Kate!" I shouted, as Jeff and I each took a giant step back from each other.

"Shit, Katie, I totally lost track of time," said Jeff. "Sorry, babe."

"That smells amazing, you two."

"Want to try it?" I said, cheeks hot from embarrassment (and a possible near-miss sexual encounter?)

"We're actually on our way to dinner. Don't want to leave my parents hanging at the restaurant. I brought you a blazer, Jeff. Let's hustle."

"Shit, Ruthie, sorry. Are you okay to clean up?" he asked.

"Go, you two! Go! Enjoy the tableside Caesar!" I said as I shooed them out of the kitchen like an Italian grandmother.

I think I've got everything under control. Maybe...

On the way home from practising for the competition, I popped by Trish and Lilly's to check on Lill and also wanted them to taste the bread pudding Jeff and I had been working on. I still can't believe what a happy accident that idea was. And it's so good! "Good lord, what is this?" asked Trish, eyes rolling and fork waving in pleasure.

"I think Jeff and I almost kissed tonight," I blurted out, and then immediately regretted it. The girls stopped eating, looked at each other and did the *bad* type of eye roll.

"Well that's... a development," Trish said carefully.

"Poor Katie," said Lilly, poking at her pudding with her spoon. After a moment of silence, they returned to eating the bread pudding and Trish simply said, "I hope you know what you're doing."

OCTOBER 11

The whole class went for drinks after school to celebrate Claire's birthday. We drank too much beer and ate too many wings 'n rings and sang karaoke and some of us embarrassed ourselves while others showed off hidden talents. Do you ever notice how the person who suggests a karaoke bar usually "just happens" to be an amazing singer? More importantly, Jeff and I were sitting beside each other in a booth most of the night, and our thighs kept touching and I'm not even sure it was by accident. It made my nethers tingle. (Also, I'm adding it as #7 in the romance dossier.)

OCTOBER 13

My favourite photo of Bubbe Bobby Grace sits in a small sterling silver frame on the walnut sideboard in the dining room at Mom and Dad's condo. In it, she's about 70 years old, living her best life in Florida in a floral muumuu and feather-topped slides, large gold hoops and her short, thick bleached hair pulled back in a bright orange headscarf. A literal picture of extroverted elegance. She's been gone for six months, and some days I still can't believe it. I'll wake up in the morning and think of a funny story I want to tell her, will pick up my phone to FaceTime, and then I'll remember. Other times, when I'm walking down the hall to my apartment and smell chicken soup cooking, I think, *Maybe Bubbe's surprising me.* Of course, she isn't. Besides, she stopped cooking over a decade ago.

When I visited Mom and Dad today, I was staring at the muumuu photo while they were telling me about a little road trip they took to Niagara Falls this week. "We just felt like being spontaneous," said Dad. "We'd never taken the *Maid of the Mist* cruise at the Falls and wanted to do it before they shut down for the season."

"It was beautiful, but shockingly wet, and we were freezing," said Mom.

"Bubbe always wanted us to see it, and we never got around to it. So, on Tuesday I turned to Mom and said 'It's an hour away. We'll have some fun and I'll buy you a steak.'" Then Dad turned to me and said, "Like your Bubbe Bobby Grace always said, 'Slip the complimentary buns into your purse and a nice steak dinner turns into a great steak sandwich the next day.'"

"I didn't even want a steak," said Mom. "But I was happy to visit. And it *was* a great day," she added as she threw Dad the sweetest smile. "I had the branzino and a beet salad, and your father had a New York striploin with a baked potato and creamed spinach. And I stole the buns in honour of Bubbe."

Dad wiped away a tear.

OCTOBER 15

The fall colours are at their absolute peak this week; it looks as if the city is on fire. One of the reasons I love living in Toronto is the changing seasons. I can't imagine living in California or Florida where you're not freezing through the snow, then waking up to spring, then living it up during a short, shvitzy summer. But nothing beats fall. Or maybe it's more like nothing beats fall with Jeff. When we were walking home through the park after practice today, he told me to stay where I was, then ran off in all directions for a couple of minutes, staying within eyeshot. When he returned, he presented me with a beautiful little "bouquet" of multicoloured maple leaves. In other words . . .

> **Romance Dossier Update**
> 1. He left me 14 DMs when we were in Montreal.
> 2. He caringly tends to my wounds.
> 3. We spend every minute together at school.
> 4. He usually walks me home.
> 5. Once home, we text each other a lot.
> 6. He chose me to be his partner at a major culinary competition clear across the country.
> 7. Our thighs touched at Claire's karaoke party.
> 8. Bouquet of dead leaves.

And as always, those unrelenting butterflies.

OCTOBER 17

Trish texted to ask what I was bringing over for dinner tonight. I texted bouillabaisse, a fresh baguette, and Paris–Brest for dessert. She texted back an eggplant emoji.

OCTOBER 19

Now, I've already mentioned that Jeff is a perfectionist in the kitchen, which is odd as it doesn't exactly mesh with the rest of his personality (or what I perceive to be his personality), yet here we are. Where I'm a little more freewheeling, he's totally by the book, and in a way, I can't help but think our different cooking styles are part of what make us such a great team. Because we *are* a great team.

But the other day I found him sliding a new pair of small, offset fine tip tweezers into his chef's coat, and I totally lost it. Kitchen tweezers! Jeff had gone cheffy supernova on me.

"Well then you tell me how to grab and place microgreens with precision and confidence?" he chuckled back, his dirty secret revealed. Even though he was laughing with me, I could tell he wasn't joking. When it comes to French cuisine, Chef Antoine prefers perfection, so bully for Chef Antoine and Jeff and their pocket tweezers.

OCTOBER 20

I am officially exhausted. I fell asleep at lunch today. I was eating an egg salad sandwich on the couch in the student lounge and the next thing I knew Claire was gently removing it from my mouth. "Sorry," she whispered. "I didn't want you to choke." After I finished, I went to the vending machine and bought a Snickers and a Coke and was good to go for the rest of the day. Just under two weeks until the competition in Vancouver!

OCTOBER 24

"We live to eat," said Chef Antoine of his countrymen as he started caramelizing half a dozen onions in lots of butter for this morning's demonstration of French onion soup. "When someone has a wedding in France, zee first thing they talk about is not zee ceremony or that zee bride looked beautiful in her wedding dress. They say, 'We ate well. I've saved the menu.'" What's more, he said they have a tradition where the bride's and groom's parents prepare onion soup for the new couple that they all hand-deliver to the newlyweds' honeymoon suite. It's a lovely ritual that continues throughout the marriage. "And so, for zee anniversaire," Chef Antoine continued as he stirred the pot, "people bring onion soup to your house every year. It's tradition. It's a great tradition." He sliced a baguette and laid perfect pieces on the bottom of each ceramic soup bowl. He tasted his rich beef stock and added it to the pot in which he had been caramelizing the onions. He poured a couple of ladles of the hot soup over each baguette slice, and the bread floated to the top and became a raft for a mound of grated Gruyère. He put Michelle in charge of telling him when the cheese had properly gratinéed under the broiler, and then he started explaining the next soup we'd be making this afternoon, a classic consommé, which he warned will take at least two and a half hours of simmering once the egg white filter (or "the raft") had formed. He also said if we let the consommé boil, we were doomed. "It will all be sheeet."

Speaking of doomed, Michelle failed Chef Antoine's impromptu test: the first bowls of onion soup scorched to cinders. He didn't yell at her and didn't throw a tomato, but he did make her stay to clean up after his demo. Humiliating? Sort of. But we all knew the exact same thing likely would have happened had he called upon any one of us, so we just considered ourselves lucky. Chef was making another one of his none-too-subtle points. He wants us to be mindful of the fact that every step and every second counts when preparing fine French food, and instincts play a part too, even with a seemingly simple dish like onion soup. "Always be tasting," he said. "Always be thinking."

Chef Antoine kept his eyes on the next batch of soup bowls he'd put under the broiler himself. He wanted to show us what a perfect gratinée looks like. He always does this — pretends that he trusts us with his classic dishes but then fires off one of his own in the end. His perfect example of poached pears or scrambled eggs Portugaise or prawn fritters. The Way It Should Be Done.

He let the onion soup bowls go for a solid two minutes under the broiler, longer than I would have been comfortable with, really. And of course, they were perfect — a deeply satisfying tawny brown, just on the edge of danger. It's the danger that makes them extra delicious.

Just as he was about to take a first steaming spoonful of his Perfect Onion Soup, Chef paused and said, "Can you imagine knowing that friends are going to bring you bowls of this soup without fail, on zee same day every year? It's just fantastique," he said, as he closed his eyes and slowly took in the first soulful spoonful like a fond memory. "I like it better than my birthday. And it eez why I will never leave my wife."

OCTOBER 26

I can't believe it: my culinary journey has inspired non-cook Trish to start cooking! She wouldn't shut up about how much she loved the potatoes dauphinoise I brought over the other night and asked me to make them again. I said I was too busy but that I could empower her to make them herself. So, I sent her the recipe, walked her through a few key steps on the phone, and she made them. And they were delicious! The best part was I'd never seen her look so proud (or eat so many potatoes).

"See?" I told her. "This is one of the benefits of learning how to cook. It gives you the ability to make anything you want, whenever you want."

"Well now that I know how to make these potatoes, I don't need to learn how to make anything else," she said, completely missing the point.

OCTOBER 27

During lunch break I was sitting on the couch in the student's lounge when Jeff came by, plopped down between me and Claire, and told me he liked my pink sweater: "It looks super soft."

"Touch it," I said. And he did, surprising both me and Claire by reaching his arm around my shoulders and squeezing me in while rubbing my upper arm for a few magical seconds. Claire shot us both a quizzical look, then continued eating her banana.

"Bubbe Bobby Grace got this for me at a clearance sale in Miami a couple of years ago," I said, diffusing the situation like a pro. "She would want you to know it's 100% cashmere and that you have excellent taste."

"Don't I know it," he said, smiling at me for just a beat too long.

OCTOBER 28

Timing is everything in the kitchen, even more so when practising for a competition. Not having your timing properly mapped out will result in food going to the table cold when it should be hot, or, god forbid, *raw* when it should be cooked, or sloppy when it should be neat and beautiful. Basically, bad versus great. And I think people wrongly assume that competitions like the Emerging Chefs Silver Platter boil down to the exciting final few moments, the rush to the plate, the sprint to the garnish. But they're dead wrong about that. Culinary success really has more to do with the first moments in the kitchen — sourcing the best ingredients, getting the mise en place ready, retrieving all of the necessary pots and utensils, and then going over your game plan again and again and again. Oy vey, look at how serious and studious I've become! But I need to be. In just a few short days Jeff and I will be flying to Vancouver for the competition, and I haven't been this nervous since that time I tried luging. Chef Antoine was watching us all day as we did a run-through of our dishes, and he said that everything looked and tasted very good. He suggested I concentrate on the savoury courses and that Jeff concentrate on the sweet ones. He likes how well we work together, and even finished off the day with an uncharacteristic pep talk.

"You have worked very hard this past month and I think zee work has paid off," he said. "You will go to Vancouver, and I am quite sure your chances of success are strong. You are ready and I am proud of you both."

"Wow, Chef, thanks," said Jeff.

All I could do was nod, seeing as I was too busy holding back the giant lump in my throat.

As Chef made his way to the door, Jeff gave me a celebratory high five that turned into a brief finger clench, just as Chef turned around.

"And none of zee funny business," he added, giving us both a sideways glance.

OCTOBER 31
3 p.m.

We're on a midday flight from Toronto to Vancouver. Jeff and I are in the same row, but we messed up so aren't actually sitting next to each other. Instead, he got the window seat, and I got the aisle. When I asked the guy in the middle seat if he'd like to swap so he could be more comfortable and I could sit with my friend, he said no. He said he always books the middle seat. That it's his preferred choice. In other words, I met an axe murderer on the plane today. He stayed put, took off his shoes, slung a pair of Beats by Dre over his head, and claimed both armrests for the remainder of the flight. I looked over at Jeff to make sure he was catching it all, but he wasn't even paying attention. He looked *really* tired.

After take-off and drinks service I leaned forward, poked Jeff's knee, then he leaned forward too, and we chatted over Mr. Middle Seat's feet. I asked Jeff what was up and he told me he and Kate had been up arguing for most of last night. Turns out she's mad at us both, and has been for weeks, for spending too much time together. And other things.

"She didn't like what she walked into the other week when she picked me up for dinner with her parents. It really triggered something. That was not a good night." Damn, so she had noticed . . . whatever that was.

"Last night it came up again and she started asking me about our relationship — yours and mine — and what it really was. And I thought, *What is it?*"

Okay, while this was the single most exciting question I'd ever heard in my entire life, it also pissed me off. *What is it? What IS IT?* I've been over here pining like a sucker with non-stop butterflies and a tingling vagina for months, and this is the first time he's thought about us? I took an irritated swig from my tiny plastic cup of V8 juice and spilled some on my T-shirt.

"And then," Jeff continued, "I made things worse. I was so tired that instead of saying, 'nothing' I accidentally said, 'I don't know.' I didn't even realize I had said it out loud until I noticed Katie's eyes had gone wide and glassy. It was a really bad night."

As Sigmund Freud and Bubbe Bobby Grace used to say, "There is no such thing as an accident."

I tried my best to be sympathetic and I truly was sorry about the rough times they've been going through, even though I'm also obviously someone who stands to benefit greatly from those exact same problems!

Jeff is now sleeping, and I am now spinning.

HOW CAN HE SLEEP AT A TIME LIKE THIS?

1 a.m.

When we landed in Vancouver it was overcast and drizzly. We checked into our modest hotel and the desk clerk handed us our welcome bags and itineraries spelling out what was to happen over the next couple of days of the competition. We spent the afternoon shopping for our ingredients with the rest of the students at the Silver Platter's host supermarket, Save-a-Way. Tomorrow, there is a morning of press events (radio, digital, print, and TV), some sort of dinner at the convention centre, and then it's full steam ahead with the competition! Yipes! I get nauseous just thinking about it! But overall, I feel good. I think we have a solid game plan and, barring any unforeseen circumstances, Jeff and I should put out some pretty amazing food. I'm not usually a competitive person, but I really want to win this thing for Chef Antoine and the school. And for me and Jeff.

Inheritance Update:

Expenses: decided to crack down and keep to a strict budget, except for an impulse purchase of a windowsill herb garden $75 (figured it's school-related and brings my kitchen a pop of freshness).

Balance remaining: $46,729.45.

November

NOVEMBER 1

10 a.m.

While some of the competitors had to wake up super early for their promo appearances on TV morning shows and morning drive talk radio interviews, Jeff and I got lucky and were booked for the short "What's Cookin'?" segment on a lifestyle show called *Vancouver Today*, that's on right after the local news. Early, but not criminal. In segment five we were supposed to chat with host Candy Feldman about tomorrow's competition while doing a mini cooking demonstration.

A food stylist hired by the TV station had prepared some cooked crème brûlées for us, plus a batch of the crème base, so all we had to do was explain what we did to make it and then divide the liquid mixture into three smaller batches, adding some vanilla bean to one part, raspberries to another and melted chocolate to the third for three different flavours. A nice little twist for home cooks to try, we figured. After that, all that was left to do was switch the liquid custards for some cooked and cooled ones, top them with sugar, and brûlée them with a torch. Easy stuff. Or so I thought.

I told Jeff he should take care of the first part: charm Candy and get things off to a good start. I figured I'd have stage fright and might not be able to speak or breathe. Besides, Jeff's past life in the Wet Paint means he thrives in the spotlight and, as expected, he got the segment going with aplomb. He flavoured the custard base while charming the panties off Candy: "Oooh, it looks good, but so fattening," she chirped.

"Candy Feldman, you don't seem like the type to deny herself of earthly pleasures," said Jeff. *Yikes.*

Hating to break up the lovefest, I was nevertheless pushed into the fray by an 18-year-old intern so that I could put the filled ramekins into a bain-marie while explaining the importance of this hot-water-bath cooking method to the invisible home audience.

"Jeff, which one is your favourite?" asked Candy as I shakily poured boiling water into the corner of the baking dish, being careful not to splash any into the custard-filled ramekins.

"I'm not sure," said Jeff, "but I wish we were making a candy-flavoured one." (*Oh god, Jeff.*)

We swapped a batch of cooked crème brûlées for the liquid ones, and then Jeff sprinkled a tablespoon of unrefined sugar on top of each cooked and cooled ramekin while I sparked up the industrial propane torch.

So, here's the thing. The show had supplied us with a torch similar to the ones we use at school, but not exactly. And so when the giant propane torch starts spewing its flame, it's as if I'm holding a special-effects flame-thrower (I later learn the intern had borrowed it from the building's maintenance worker who had been working on plumbing repairs). Not only did I singe Candy's hair, but I also set all of the crème brûlées on fire, which set off the fire alarm.

I'm not going to say it was a five-alarm blaze or anything, but Candy panicked and started screeching, "My extensions — save my hair extensions!" So the young intern shot her in the face with the fire extinguisher before spraying the crème brûlées with the white fire retardant spew. The desserts sputtered before dying.

With the flames extinguished and Candy having run off the set, Jeff and I were left alone with the smoldering brûlées. It might have been the shock of the situation or the sight of the flames licking my once beautiful brûlées, but I instinctively started singing "Happy Birthday" and Jeff gamely joined in. And so did the intern. And so did the rest of the TV crew. And that's how we turned a fiery televised culinary disaster into a fun "blooper" clip for that night's six-o'clock news.

10 p.m.
Nobody in the competition seems to be particularly fun, so Jeff and I decided to make our own fun tonight. After the opening night dinner, we walked around Robson and then down to Georgia Street, eventually making our way to the Towne & Country Hotel to partake in some fine local wines at its new restaurant and wine bar called Seasons. (All part of our culinary education, obviously).

The place was nice. Too nice for us, really. It's a West Coast design statement in earth, wood, and fire (there's a focal point fireplace that divides the room) where after-work revelers-turned-dinner guests were drinking straight-up classic cocktails and bottles of B.C. wine along with modern retro-chic food, like pork belly and kimchi sliders and lemony lobster rolls. We were perched on our stools around the high-top tables, elbow-to-elbow with the well-dressed crowd in the bar lounge. The sommelier said they've got an extensive wine list that features hard to find local favourites like Tantalus Vineyards' Syrah, as well as more substantial wine experiences, such as bottles of Tenuta San Guido Sassicaia Bolgheri. And the best part was that "any wine can be selected by the glass, as long as a minimum of two glasses are ordered," added our flirty waitress sent by the sommelier to take our order.

"Would you rather drink a half cup of pus or a whole cup of blood," I asked Jeff as we sipped from our bottle of JoieFarm Winery's delectable A Noble Blend (from the nearby Naramata Bench, we learned). I loved it; very Riesling-forward.

"Would it be my own pus and blood?" he asked.

"Nope," I said. "A stranger's."

"In that case, the blood."

"Jeff, let me ask you something," I started. "Why would it make a difference if it was someone else's pus? Pus is an infection; it's disgusting. The correct answer is always blood." The wine had gone straight to my head.

"I don't think there's necessarily a right or wrong answer here," he countered. "I was thinking of doing the pus as a shot, in which case, drinking a long, thick, slow glass of blood would be much worse, don't you think?"

"Nope." Though he does make a good point. "You're never going to change my mind about pus." We were really classing up the joint.

"Okay, my turn," he said. "Would you rather give or receive . . ."

"Oh, me likey. Jeffy's getting deep."

"Wait, you didn't let me finish. Would you rather give or receive" — he looked around, put his hand on my shoulder, then leaned in closer — "would you rather give or receive . . . down there?"

Here we go. Sexy Jeff.

But then this happened: Jeff knew one of the servers, disappeared to go say hi, and returned 17 minutes later looking flushed and anxious. I was about to give him a mild piece of my mind about how rude it was to leave me for nearly 20 minutes alone at the table (I mean, who does that?!) but there was something off about him, so I aimed for a concerned yet gently passive aggressive tone.

"You've been gone for ages, I was about to file a missing person report. Hah. Are you okay?"

"Sorry, all good," he said. Motioning a different server over, he quickly ordered another glass of wine.

"Okay, then," I said, still annoyed but dropping it. *Here I thought we were headed towards a sexy conversation. Maybe he's just nervous about the competition. I know I am.*

NOVEMBER 2, COMPETITION DAY
Lunch Break
Competition morning arrived sooner than I liked. Aside from all the good luck calls this morning, Jeff called my hotel room. He wanted to know if I felt like going for coffee at 49th Parallel (great coffee and they do incredible latte art). But I declined. I wanted to have the last few moments of peace to myself, floating in a lavender-scented bath

and going over what we had to do to win today's competition. Besides, I wasn't up for any more isolated one-on-one time with Jeff before the competition. Didn't want to stir the pot (so to speak). Instead, I sank deeper into the tub, loving the scent but wishing for bubbles, while trying to put last night's events out of my mind.

An hour before the competition began, I got suited up in my whites, pulled my hair up into a topknot, grabbed my knife kit, met Jeff in the lobby of our hotel, and we began walking over to the International Culinary School together.

"What's up, boychick? Feeling good?" I asked while being taken aback by how hot his lanky body looked in his gleaming chef's whites under the full light of the morning sun. I never get sick of seeing him in his whites. It's like he's a sailor waiting to scoop me up into his arms and take me away to some unknown but perfect destination. Perfect, because he'd be there.

"Feeling fine, Ruthie. We're going to win this thing." He winked.

"Do you really think so?" (I did.)

"I do." (But I could tell that he didn't. And I wondered why.)

Yesterday afternoon we were allowed three hours of kitchen time to get our mise en place . . . in place and prepare some of the elements of each dish (without actually completing any of them) ahead of today's competition. Because three hours isn't nearly enough time to cook and chill and bake and get all of the sauces together for the many courses of the various rounds. Jeff was in fine spirits and on top of his game while I was actually feeling a little jet-lagged. He saved my ass a couple of times by jumping in and preventing some minor catastrophes: I almost over-whipped the cream, and my brunoise job on the carrots was lousy. But now a day later, it seemed as if the toque was on the other tête.

"Is everything okay, Jeff?" I asked. "You seem a little . . . preoccupied." I need him today. I really need him to be on his game today.

"I had another shitty conversation with Katie this morning," he said.

"Nothing that can't be fixed," I chirped, not wanting to get into a whole conversation about this, seeing as were on the way to a very important competition. Well, that, and the fact that I was the last person who should be giving him relationship advice, seeing as I happened to be a person who wanted his relationship to take its natural course by ending, so that I could finally jump his bones.

"Katie and I are really rocky," he said. "She's just so insecure even though she's a knockout and I tell her that all the time," I feel I should mention yet again that Kate's the most gorgeous girl I know. She almost looks like a grown-up angel. Literally every head turns when she walks down the street — it's truly something to behold. I know looks aren't everything, but there's no denying that they're a lot. I will admit, I'm not half bad, either, but let's just say 100% of heads don't turn for me. Maybe 27% at best. So, their recent issues couldn't be about attraction, but perhaps something deeper.

Jeff continued as we started walking down a pretty tree-lined street. "I guess beauty like that is a kind of a curse. People expect you to look perfect all the time — you should see how long it takes her to get ready in the morning. But that's not really our main issue. It's ... Me. Her. Us. It ... the relationship ... it's all become so ... boring."

Oh no! Boring is Jeff's greatest enemy! I mean, the dude was in a band, he lives for fun, partying, the zest of life! I didn't know what to say. On the one hand, this is pretty private stuff. In fact, he shouldn't be telling me any of this. And yet, I love that he did. He's confiding in me like a ~~true friend~~ future lover. Kate and Jeff are on the rocks! Can't wait to tell Trish and Lilly! Wait. Am I allowed to tell them? I should have asked Jeff if this was a secret. Of course it's a secret! Oy, it's just such great gossip. But he's sad, and I feel bad for Kate. But the fact that their relationship is in trouble is probably good news for me.

"Do you have any advice, I mean, in terms of Katie?" He stopped walking and turned towards me. "What do you think I should do? What do you *want* me to do?" Time stopped. My heart fluttered. And he was giving me such an intense look that it caught me off-guard and made my knees go weak. I stumbled, blamed the sidewalk, and he shook his head at me and chuckled.

Still, something was decidedly off. I had hoped for this moment for so long, and now that it was sort of here, I should've been over the moon. Yet this wasn't how I imagined it happening at all. For starters, where's my bouquet of ranunculus and the pint of coffee Häagen-Dazs ice cream? It was as if Jeff wanted *me* to be the one to say what I think *he* wanted to say — but won't. He wanted *me* to be the one who made the first move because *he* was too chicken. In other words, he wanted to have his cake and eat me, too.

I wouldn't do it. If he wanted me, he had to *want me*. Not just a solution to something boring. Instead, I said, "Like my Bubbe Bobby Grace used to say, 'You can teach a duck to swim, but it won't help if there isn't any water.'"

Then we continued walking down the street towards the competition, come what may.

7:30 p.m.
(I think? I left my phone across the room and I'm too zonked to check.)
It was tight, but we finished! When the bell sounded, signalling the end of the competition, I was sweaty, tired, pumped, and exhausted. And my feet were absolutely killing me — even worse than that time I tried speed skating. But I was also happy. Jeff and I made a great team. We did what we came to do, and for the most part I was pleased with what we put out. But sheesh, I can't believe how fast the whole thing flew by.

At the gleaming new culinary school where the competition was happening, we had the best set-up possible, all of the finest equipment, workspace galore, and all the pots and pans we could ever need. That is, all the pots we could ever need except for the large ones, which the Italian duo from a cooking school in Niagara had decided to hoard as a team tactic.

Not even kidding. They rushed in, collected all the large pots, and then literally announced to everyone, "We're not going to make things easy for you, so we're taking all the large pots and we'll be guarding them so that none of you can steal them."

"Hey, ladies," Jeff then called over to our nasty Italian-Niagarian competitors. "Bring over two large pots and you can use the ice cream machine as soon as we're done."

"We can only spare one pot," said the tall one.

"Jeff, I actually think we've got time to make a second flavour," I wickedly chimed in. "Let's start brainstorming."

"Okay, okay, two pots," says the short one.

Jeff and I were finding our groove in the competition kitchen, chopping, whisking, tasting and stirring like a scene out of my favourite food film, *Big Night*.

You know, the more I think about it, the more I realize what a fantastic job Chef had done in preparing Jeff and me for the competition, especially during the final few days before we left for Vancouver, when we had to make all the finicky last-minute decisions regarding plating and such.

At the same time, he instilled in us the importance of all the little details. "Everything must be perfect," he kept saying. "If you think it is perfect, it is not. Look closer and you'll see that it is not."

He also never stopped reminding us that everything is about timing. One evening, when we were working on a frisée salad with lardons and fried croutons, Jeff dressed the salad with the warm vinaigrette a titch too early and when Chef tasted it, he declared, "If this is exam: Fail!" Another night, Chef pointed out that we should sear our steak on the stovetop and then finish it in the oven. This way, we'd have the use of another burner and would also have 12 minutes to do a million other things rather than watch the ribeye cook to medium rare. Seemingly logical stuff, but I'm telling you, sometimes you just have to be flat-out told these things.

While comparing French and Italian food is like comparing John Cusack to Dev Patel (both highly marketable but decidedly different), the judges still had to pick a winner, and I really wanted it to be us. Still, those Italian-Niagarians, who we had immediately pegged as our biggest competition, were putting together some pretty impressive-looking plates. I spotted a duo of pouchy handmade raviolis: spinach and ricotta with fresh tomato sauce, and porcini in sage butter. Their fish dish was salmon with a skin so crispy it looked like crackling and their handmade pappardelle was tossed with braised rabbit. They went even more rustic with their desserts, albeit with elevated flavour combinations, like an orange flower torte with pine nuts, and a honey semifreddo with apricot lime sauce.

The Montreal team of Claudine and Patrice was also doing well but began to lose it after the second round when they both started making stupid mistakes. Soon after, they started to bicker, their bickering quickly escalated to shouting, and then things took a real turn when Claudine dumped a bowl of flour on Patrice's head, and Patrice retaliated by cracking an egg on Claudine's beak-like nose. Claudine then upped the ante by kicking Patrice in the nuts.

"Jeff," I said, once the hoopla had died down. "Whatever happens today, I promise not to square you in the crotch."

Here's how *our* menu went down:

First round: Three Individual Plated Appetizers. We did broiled, stuffed mushroom caps (filled with a Cognac-spiked duxelles), fried soft-shelled crabs with a tarragon-lemon aioli, and a take on Chef Luc Roy's insane poutine, but we topped our twice-fried frites with shredded short ribs and lots of fresh herbs instead of foie gras. Everything turned out well, I think, except the judges found the crabs to be a little oily.

"You sure that oil is up to temp?" Jeff had asked.

"It's just about there," I said. "Should be fine." I knew it wasn't hot enough but had panicked. The clock was ticking. Such an avoidable mistake. (I felt a phantom tomato hitting me, hurled by Chef Antoine.)

Round two: Two Individual Plated Entrées. In this round, we had to prepare two proteins using two different methods of preparation. We did lobster Thermidor and a grilled rib-eye with marchand de vin butter.

We decided Jeff would be Team Turf and I would be Team Surf, but, as always, we worked in tandem to ensure our two classics were both modern day winners.

He slapped an extra-large pot of water on the stove to boil: "Water on."

I started reducing red wine for the marchand de vin butter: "Reduction on."

He chopped veg and seasoned steaks while I incorporated the slightly cooled crimson wine reduction into the salted butter.

"Pan on," he said, putting the cast iron over the flame.

"Lobsters in," I said, dropping two 1.5 pound PEI lobsters into the big pot of now-boiling water.

"Steaks on," he said, and I heard a terrific sizzle.

We were in the zone, speaking in monosyllabic sentences. Nothing was going to stop us now.

On to round three: a Three-Course Formal Lunch Menu for Two People. We prepared a cream of mussel soup with saffron (elegant, rich, and flavourful with a touch of exotica), and then grilled red snapper with anchovy butter (light and lively), and a finishing dish of the apple pecan bread pudding with cognac butter sauce. While the judges also liked these dishes, they found our dessert to be "too simple." Agree to disagree, judges!

Finally, round four: a Platter of Desserts. One cake, one tart, one fruit, one type of cookie, one ice cream. Jeff fully took the lead on this one.

And when it was time to make the Sachertorte — I tried to rush it by pouring the warmed, strained jam only on the centre layer, as opposed to the centre layer and then all over the cake, as tradition dictates. Well, let me tell you, Mr. Perfection was not having it.

"Come on, Ruthie, you know that's not how it's done," said Jeff. "Do you think chef Franz Sacher became famous for creating this cake in 1832 by doing a half-assed job?" (Jeff had clearly been studying the syllabus.) "It takes no extra time to do it right than it does to do it wrong."

Apparently when it comes to famed Austrian cakes, Jeff is the new Chef Antoine. I felt scolded. (Also, it does take more time: 2 minutes and 14 seconds to be exact, as we had learned in our practice sessions.)

"Don't be mad," he said, noticing my huff. "What would Bubbe Bobby Grace have to say?"

"Well," I answered, instantly softened by the mention of her name, "She'd say, 'Dollface, Jeff is number one here and you're number two. So do what he tells ya, even though you're number one in my books!'"

"'Dollface,'" said Jeff with a smile. "That's cute. Well, you're number one in my books, too."

I smiled extra wide as I spread the apricot jam all over the cooled cake. Just as Franz Sacher's recipe had dictated.

Besides the Sachertorte, we also made sugar pear clafouti, prunes poached in white wine, almond macaroons, and iced orange soufflé with almond cigarettes. That's a lot, right? And as we know, pastries aren't my strong suit, which is why we chose recipes that were on the simpler side. Still, most of the desserts on our platter turned out well, although the prunes weren't a big hit. (I know, big shocker.)

"We nailed it, Ruthie," he said as he pulled off his chef's cap and wiped his brow with his surprisingly muscular forearm (must be all of the guitar-playing and whisking). Then he pulled me in for a collegial hug and we clung to each other for just a moment too long, the sweet smell of sugar still hanging in the air.

1 a.m.
What. A. Day. I have quite literally never been this physically exhausted. (Except for that time I tried water polo.) After my last entry I quickly showered and got gussied up for the splashy awards dinner where they would be announcing the winners. I thought about how Jeff had said it takes Kate hours to get ready, but even as I was trying to look my fanciest in a brand-new dress and heels, the longest I could stretch it out to was 20 minutes. What was she doing? And what was I missing?

Throughout the evening of better-than-average conference centre food and free-flowing local wine, the judges awarded the bottom five teams bronze medallions of participation, and then worked their way up from there, heading north from team number five to the top pair. I knew we weren't going to be in the bottom five because we weren't disqualified like Claudine and Patrice, and we didn't have any disasters like some of the other teams, including the sad-sack duo from Saskatoon whose ice cream never froze, whose soup scorched, and whose roast leg of lamb ended up being raw because they forgot to turn on the oven. (Talk about crumbling under pressure, *yikes*.)

By the time the culinary school chef judges and the MC (the glamorous Candy Feldman from *Vancouver Today*, wearing repaired hair extensions) were down to the final two teams, it was Jeff and me versus the Italian-Niagarians. My heart was pounding so loudly I could no longer hear what Candy was saying and was seriously hoping she didn't hold my lighting her on fire against us. Instead, I stared at Jeff while trying to glean the necessary information from his facial expressions and body language. He was looking anxiously at the stage.

". . . from Toronto . . ." I heard the announcer say.

Jeff was half-standing with his arm cocked for a celebratory fist-pump . . . eeep! . . .

"At first glance, the points indicated . . ."

Then Jeff was sitting down again and looking kind of glum . . . aww . . . fuck . . . but then he was on his feet again! And he was jumping up! And he grabbed my hand! A roar erupted from the audience as I suddenly had my hearing back, and there was clapping and hollering. He pulled me towards the stage with him as I teetered on borrowed heels.

"I can't believe we beat them by one point!" he shouted as we walked towards the stage. "On a technicality!"

The judges handed us our silver platter and shook our hands. Candy gave Jeff a big hug and then turned stiffly to me, awkwardly holding out her hand. We turned towards the applause, and Jeff pulled me in for a kiss on the cheek, which turned into a kiss on both cheeks, a beautiful la bise, followed by a surprise *third* kiss DANGEROUSLY CLOSE TO MY MOUTH. Dear Diary, this moment couldn't have been any sweeter had I scripted it myself. Or more confusing! I almost tipped over in my heels, but instead embraced Jeff, the exciting, hard-fought win, and this culinary feather in my toque. We really *are* the perfect team — confirmed, verified, award winning.

We called Chef Antoine right away. He was over "la lune" and said he wants to take us to his favourite wine bar after school on Tuesday to celebrate. But for now, we have one day left in Vancouver to be free and have fun and do whatever we want, which may include some walking and eating, and will definitely involve no cooking whatsoever.

NOVEMBER 3

"Now what?" asked Jeff when we met up in the lobby of our hotel for our 24 hours of freedom before returning to Toronto.

I knew just what he meant.

School has been so busy that it's been weeks since we've had any free time to do anything at all, let alone do exactly as we pleased. And now we found ourselves overwhelmed by choice. It was a feeling I had every fall when I showed up for the breaking of the fast after sundown on Yom Kippur. Getting out of synagogue so parched and plagued by pious hunger, you didn't really know what it was that you should eat first. Not that there wasn't enough choice: from the blintzes and gefilte fish, to the lox and herring, to the kugels and the salads, and a whole other table loaded down with fruit and cakes. Still, you were so hungry you couldn't decide, so you noshed on a half bagel with a schmear of cream cheese, drank some orange juice, and called it a night.

"This reminds me of Yom Kippur," I shared with Jeff.

"That's the one where you fast for 24 hours, right?"

"Good boy, Jeffy, you do listen."

"I do," he said, as we sat down on the couch in the hotel lobby. "But I guess what I don't understand is, why would 24 hours with me remind you of a day spent fasting and repenting for your sins?"

"Well, the day is still young," I answered coyly. (Zinger!) "So, what I was thinking," I continued, as if I wasn't suddenly flirting my ass off, "is that we should go to Silverman's and start the day off right with the best bagels in town."

"Bagels. What a surprise. I suppose you've researched this?" he said.

"I have."

We walked over to Kitsilano as a light drizzle fell. "You'll find these bagels are a winning cross between a Montreal style and a New York style," I started to explain. "They're kettle boiled and then baked, but they don't have the sweetness and density of a Montreal bagel. At the same time, they're not puffy and overblown like a New York bagel." We arrived, crossed the checkerboard floor, and joined the line to place our orders." To be quite honest, I think they may just be the perfect bagel," I continued. "I've heard they're also very generous with the cream cheese here, so, there's also that."

Within minutes my research was rewarded. As promised, the toasted bagel was at once warm, soft, and chewy. But Jeff had smelled the cinnamon buns even before we had walked through the door, so ordered one of those instead. I'm not going to lie — it kind of felt like a slap in the face. That is, until I tasted it. If bagels have a perfect cousin, it is these rich, gooey, caramelized buns.

"Yum," said Jeff simply. And I had to agree. We got a couple of chocolate babka buns to snack on later, and then we made our way to stop #2 on our *Ferris Bueller* day: Stanley Park.

Stanley Park is big and beautiful. Like Central Park, it's often referred to as "a city within a city," owing, I guess, to all the people and places and things going on in there. It's really quite huge. We made our way into the park through the main entrance at the west end of Georgia Street, because we were pretty confident we'd be able to find our way back by using the downtown skyscrapers as landmarks.

There we were, strolling away without a care in the world. The sun had started peeking through the autumn clouds, the bikers and joggers and dog walkers and skateboarders and Rollerbladers (and a couple of other wheel-related sports that were new to me) were going along their merry ways, just same old, same old along the Seawall in this green urban setting.

We continued along the seaside promenade, which apparently snakes around the park for nine kilometres. It was easy to see why people fall hard for this city, with its mountains and ocean and redwoods and temperate climes. We made our way to the Lost Lagoon, just because we liked the sound of it, and were rewarded with great weeping trees, a spouting fountain, and tons of geese and ducks and even some elegant swans, which I think are always an unexpected treat. (I wonder why it is that you always find swans in secluded lagoons, usually congregated under a weeping willow.) We cut off the regular path and ventured into the forest trails — the old-growth rainforest now padding our walk. There were lots of rustling sounds in the leaves and amidst the trees, mostly squirrels and chipmunks scurrying about. We saw the famous statue of the girl in the wetsuit on the rock. We looked up and up and up in awe at the Hollow Tree, a mammoth redwood so big that cars used to drive through its trunk. We looked at each other and we smiled. We walked and we walked and we talked and we talked and our hands sometimes brushed together, and that was my absolute favourite part. We lost our way and then found it again. Then we trundled down to English Bay and sat on the sand and leaned up against one of the giant logs scattered along the beach, and we ate our babka bun snacks. And for a while, we didn't talk and we didn't test each other. We were just quiet and still. It was so peaceful with the salt air in our noses and the sun on our faces and the sounds of the gulls. And . . . it was just so nice to be there. With him.

Stop #3 on our *Ferris Bueller's Day Off* day brought us to Matinee, a small, independently owned retro-style DVD store that specializes in hard-to-find films and also makes terrific espresso-based drinks using a vintage Elektra machine. Jeff and I ordered flat whites and perused the shelves. "*Grosse Pointe Blank*," said Jeff minutes later, between sips. "One of the best movie soundtracks ever."

"And a great movie, too," I said. And then I found myself delving into my recent yet almost-forgotten TelecorpMedia past: "*Grosse Pointe Blank*," I started. "Neurotic professional assassin Martin Blank (John Cusack) returns home to carry out an assigned hit while also trying to rekindle the flame with his long-lost love (Minnie Driver) at their ten-year high school reunion. Bullets fly as the Clash play on. Director: George Armitage. Cast: John Cusack, Minnie Driver, Dan Aykroyd, Jeremy Piven. 1997. 107 minutes."

"That's actually amazing," said Jeff, giving me a high-five for my movie capsule review skills, "but, have you ever noticed how often you mention John Cusack in day-to-day conversation? Is there anything you'd like to tell me? Anything I should know?"

"Nothing really," I said, "except for the fact that John Cusack has been in a lot of my favourite films of all time — *Sixteen Candles, Say Anything, The Grifters, Bullets over Broadway, Being John Malkovich, High Fidelity* —"

"*High Fidelity* — another truly great movie soundtrack," added Jeff.

"Totally. But just think about that list for a second. And that's just a fraction of them. Do you see what I'm getting at?"

"Not really."

Guys just don't understand. "Jeff, John Cusack may just be the most underappreciated actor of a generation! I used to bring this up all the time at TelecorpMedia because I thought we should launch a campaign to get him the recognition he so richly deserves. I mean, the guy has never even been nominated for an Oscar — how is that possible? Did the Academy not see him play Lloyd Dobler in *Say Anything*? I, for one, think that particular movie should be required viewing for every high school student; teach today's youth how to treat a gal."

Jeff nodded. "Lloyd did have some pretty righteous moves."

"If only life were like the movies," I sighed.

Jeff looked me in the eyes, and he didn't look away. It was ~~thrilling~~ terrifying. And then I suddenly spotted what I'd been looking for, right behind him.

"*Goodfellas*," I said. "There may be better films out there, but for my money there's no Mob movie more enjoyable than this one. *Goodfellas*: Brutally violent and rib-ticklingly funny at the same time. Based on the book by Nicholas Pileggi, it covers 30 years in the life of a New York Mafia family. The fast pacing and excellent cast suck you right in. And the scene where the gang stops off for a bite at Joe Pesci's mom's house (actually Martin Scorsese's real-life mama) is utterly delectable. Director: Martin Scorsese. Cast: Robert De Niro, Joe Pesci, Ray Liotta, Lorraine Bracco, Paul Sorvino. 1990. 148 minutes."

He just shook his head (amused?) as we walked over to rent it.

Back at our hotel, Jeff popped the DVD into the machine in my room. (It's a funny hotel — no Netflix or pay-per-view, but DVD machines and pour-over coffee setups with third-wave grounds in every room.) And then I collected all the pillows and fluffed them up against the headboard. And we leaned on those pillows and ate up the rest of the now-rainy day by enjoying the movie, which turned out to be just as good as it was the first time I saw it, whereupon I gave it a spontaneous 9.3 out of 10 while Trish and Lilly and I were still watching it. I remember we went for pizza straight after, even though we weren't really hungry. It was the first time I ever ate a sausage-topped pizza.

The credits started rolling and we sat in awkward silence. Oh god. "Ahem — I need to eat Italian food," I said to Jeff to break the tension. "I need to eat Italian food right now."

Understand this, dear diary, food was the absolute last thing on my mind after I had SPENT HOURS. IN BED. ALONE. WITH JEFF. Alas, food was the only thing either of us would be eating ~~for the time being~~.

"I'm with you," he said. Did I see him adjust his pants, or was it a trick of the light?

The desk clerk recommended a nearby place called Marco Polo's, a classic 40-year-old spaghetti joint with red and white checked tablecloths and drippy candles stuck into old Chianti bottles. I ordered the bucatini all'amatriciana. Jeff ordered veal Parmesan with a side of spaghetti and a litre of the house red. We inhaled the basket of warm garlic bread knots while we downed our first glasses of the Cabernet.

"This was a great day, and I want more days just like this one. Don't you feel like we really got to know each other better?" asked Jeff as he twirled saucy strands around his fork.

"Well, yeah," I said, momentarily putting down my fork so as to give him my undivided attention. "We've known each other for months, but I guess there's something to be said for being outside of school, away from home and the familiar — all of this time together . . . it's been sort of . . . perfect."

Out of nowhere, Billy Ocean's "Suddenly" played on the oldies radio station that the restaurant unwisely uses as its dining soundtrack. And it snapped me right out of my wine-and-possibly-love-induced reverie. Because, while this day has been one of the single best days in my life, it would inevitably end the same way my days with Jeff always ended. Because Jeff has a girlfriend. Even so, he was looking at me with that . . . *look*.

"We're not getting together while you and Kate are still together," I said softly while feeling my eyes going a little glassy. I didn't want the day to end on a sour note.

"I'm the one doing this, not you," said Jeff defensively.

"You've got to be kidding," I countered, now a little bit angry. (I was dying to say, "It takes two to tango" but didn't lower myself.) "You know, I can't believe your one major flaw is the fact that you'd cheat on your girlfriend."

"But it would be *my* flaw, not yours."

"Now you know that's not true," I said. "If I cheat with you, it becomes my problem too. I realize all of this award winning and pasta sucking and sauce licking has probably turned you on and that's what's pushing you to do something that goes against your moral fibre, because I know this isn't you."

"But it could be," he said. "Besides, I'm not exactly talking about cheating."

HOLD MY BEER!

"Jeff," I asked, "what do you consider cheating?" (Perhaps this was all a silly misunderstanding?) He was having trouble putting his non-cheating/cheating stance into actual sentences, so I decide to help (in my typically mature way) by asking a series of yes or no questions.

1. Is walking someone home from school cheating?
    NO
2. Is sending someone heart emojis cheating?
    NO
3. Is texting nonstop cheating?
    NO
4. Is buying someone family packs of Snickers cheating?
    NO
5. Has all of this, us, just been in my mind?
    NO

His answer to #5, the fact that he actually said it out loud, caught me off-guard, and I let out a little involuntary gasp.

"I'm just trying to be honest. Start us off on a clean slate," he said. "But for the record, I only consider sex as cheating."

("Start!" "Us!" ... "Sex?")

"This is seriously messed up," I said as I leaned back into my chair with a huff. And then I got to thinking that this is a conversation that has probably played itself out a million times by a million people trying to convince a million other not-awful people (but people who can nevertheless be swayed) to cheat with them on their significant others. First, Lilly's Craig, one of the all-time sweetest people you could ever meet. And now Jeff, who, while not exactly pure as the driven snow, I always felt was pure of heart.

It's the type of scenario in which there are no winners — just short-term gains. It's sad, really, and yet everyone thinks their situation unique. "There's no such thing as a love triangle," Bubbe Bobby Grace used to say. "They all just end up being heptagons — the worst shape of them all!" I know that's how I was feeling. Like a big, dumb heptagon.

"We've both wanted this for months, whether we've admitted it out loud or not," he said. "Kate's my past. You know it, I know it, and Kate has been feeling it, too. And she'll know for sure as soon as I get back to Toronto. We're a match, me and you. Why can't you just let it happen?" He reached his open, upturned hand across the table, but I didn't take it.

"I like you so much," I said, while focusing on zipping and unzipping my fleece pullover. "But the bottom line is, I don't make out with other people's boyfriends. Case closed."

"I am breaking up with her, Ruthie, I swear."

"I believe you," I said, looking him dead in the eyes. "And when you do, you know where to find me."

YOU KNOW WHERE TO FIND ME?!!!!! Who do I think I am? A buxom 1940s screen siren?

NOVEMBER 5

As promised, Chef Antoine took Jeff and me out for celebratory drinks at LeFou, a Parisian-style bar near school that reminds him of home. I was excited about going out with Chef but even more excited to be out with Jeff. We have to lie low until he breaks up with Kate. ~~It's been torture.~~ It's been hard but I am calm, cool, and collected. We can't let on that anything has changed, or rather, is about to change, in front of Chef.

"I will suggest for us a nicely chilled bottle of Sancerre and perhaps for zee table a warm goat cheese salad, some bread, butter, and of course even more cheese!" said Chef Antoine. Jeff and I nod in agreement like kindergarten kids. Chef orders for the table, and then we give him a play-by-play of the competition. He's quite pleased but chides me for my Sacher torte shortcut. (For the record, Jeff didn't turn me in, I had been giving Chef examples of how Jeff had been great under pressure.)

"Ruthie, you must not rush things. You are always so hurry, hurry, worry. You will find things more difficult in zee next session if you do not take time and follow zee recipes to a tee." Jeff topped up my wine glass and I saw Chef taking note of the second nature of it all. A flash of concern washed over his face. "We are moving into terrines, aspics, and roulades and they take even more precision," he said.

"Awesome!" Jeff hooted. And then he and Chef launched into an intense discussion on the art of the aspic while I sipped my Sancerre and worried about zee future.

NOVEMBER 7

I hadn't even been away from my girls for a whole week but it felt like months, especially since I basically had a year's worth of gossip to share with them! Since I've already written down the key takeaways here, I'll just say that they loved that we won the competition (they had a bottle of sparkling waiting for me; we popped it), they liked the sound of our day off (but were not thrilled that we watched a movie in bed together), and they were proud of me for putting down my foot about not fooling around with Jeff. They also couldn't believe that Jeff only classified sex as fooling around: "Preposterous," said Lilly.

An equally incensed Trish pulled out her phone and pulled up the Merriam-Webster dictionary site. "Fooling around," she read. "To engage in casual sexual activity."

"See?" said Lilly.

"Wait, there's more," said Trish. "'She found out that her partner had been fooling around on her. [=having sex with someone else].'"

"Hmmm," we all agreed.

And then Trish asked, "What *is* this stuff?" with an upturned nose, as she firmly rejected the sweetbread terrine that had taken me the better part of two days to complete.

NOVEMBER 8

Okay, not cool and collected.

I can't stop thinking about him.

And I can't stop thinking about how we're on the verge of something.

And I can't stop thinking about how he's going to hurt Kate.

And I can't stop thinking about what happens if he doesn't hurt Kate.

But most of all I can't stop thinking about what happens ~~if~~ when Jeff and I finally happen.

NOVEMBER 9

Today I shaved all my bits to make sure I was ready. It feels imminent!

I bet gorgeous Kate shaves every day. What am I talking about? She's probably naturally hairless. Poreless, hairless gorgeous Kate.

She's going to be a lot to live up to.

NOVEMBER 10

IT.
HAPPENED.
IT.
FUCKING.
HAPPENED.
!!!!!

Last night Jeff appeared at my apartment. He had biked over right after he left Kate's place with a small backpack full of his belongings: some T-shirts, undies, socks, aprons, and a stack of l'École de la Cuisine Française–regulation kitchen towels. After I buzzed him in, he ran up the stairs, still sweaty and breathy from the speedy ride over, and he grabbed my hand, danced me across the hardwood floor and pulled me on top of him as he collapsed onto my puffy couch.

"Are you ready, Ruthie Cohen?" he asked, looking into my eyes and caressing my face, while simultaneously unhooking my bra and unbuttoning my jeans in one fluid movement so that I didn't really have any time to stop or think. That is, until I did and said, "Wait a minute, mister." Because it wasn't going to be as easy as that. Even though I was *aching* for it.

I liked that he held true to his word and broke up with Kate, so now I knew it wasn't the high of winning the culinary competition or the beauty of Vancouver or too much wine that was bringing us together: it was something he truly wanted to do. He really wanted to be with me. (Yay!)

Still, there was that nagging incident in the bathroom at Towne & Country in Vancouver when he vanished for ages. What the heck was he doing? And with *whom*? Also, I can't say I'm all that comfortable with the fact that he was ready to jump into bed with me right after (and let's face it, before) he had officially broken up with his long-term girlfriend. I don't exactly want him to pine for her *obviously*, but he sure "Thank-u-next"–ed pretty quickly. What was going on in that handsome little head of his? The detective in me needs a little more time to find out.

So, I suggested we slow things down before jumping into bed, and Jeff is (begrudgingly) okay with it. He excused himself to go to the bathroom (slightly hunched), I made us a big bowl of buttered popcorn, and when he returned, we snuggled together under the blankets on the couch and watched *Jiro Dreams of Sushi* for the rest of the night.

NOVEMBER 11

When I told Trish that Jeff and I were finally together, I would have thought and hoped she'd be over the moon for me. Instead, the good news totally got her shirt in a knot and she said: "Be careful. If he did it to Kate, he'll do it to you."

"Don't rain on my parade, Trish," I said.

"Don't say I didn't warn you," said Trish.

Pretty shitty attitude, right? I mean, she more than anyone knew how much I had wanted this, had dreamed of this, had yearned for this, and when it finally happens, I get a "don't say I didn't warn you"? She must be PMSing. In fact, I know she is. She follows my cycle.

NOVEMBER 12

Jeff has officially set out to prove his intentions are true. For the past two nights, he's come over after school and cooked me dinner, all of my favourites, the secret info gleaned by asking casual questions like "If you were a salad, what type of salad would you be?" while rinsing lettuce at school. (So far everything has been delicious!) We've talked a lot and I feel like we know each other even better. I told him more about Bubbe Bobby Grace and he said he wished he had met her IRL: "I'm glad that her inheritance sent you to school and that I met you because of it," he said. "She sounds like an awesome Bubbe."

"She really was," I said, suddenly smiling at a recollection of prom night.

"About a decade ago," I told Jeff, "Adam Kirby, my newish boyfriend, was taking me to prom. He had just arrived at the door in his tux, looking all nervous and pulling at his vest, when Bubbe Bobby Grace, who had recently landed back in town from Florida, swanned through the front door without even noticing him. She was excited to see me in the lace LBD she had helped pick out, and also wanted to take pictures.

"'Look at you, dollface!' she had beamed. 'I'm plotzing! Just bursting with pride! That said, I'd like to see you in a higher heel and a brighter lipstick.' Then, suddenly, she sniffed the air: 'Is someone wearing Deep Woods Off?' She had been struck, as I had, by the strong odour emanating from the front door. It was my date, Adam, and I had never seen someone's face go so red."

"Ouch! You Cohens are a tough crowd," laughed Jeff.

"It's not our fault," I protested. "We all have a heightened sense of smell. It's a blessing and a curse!"

"Lesson #791," said Jeff as he drew in a little closer, brushing my bangs from my eyes. "Make sure the male musk is gentler on the nose than a prom night body spray."

He was making it really, really hard not to sleep with him.

NOVEMBER 16

The charm offensive is strong with this one. So far this week we've hit Cry Ducky Gallery, went to a matinee, and he booked concert tickets for three months from now. THREE MONTHS FROM NOW!!! He even came to my parents with me yesterday and made them his "secret recipe" fried chicken. "Shazamo!" shouted Dad after his first crunchy, juicy bites. Needless to say, like daughter like parents, they have fallen for Jeff, too.

NOVEMBER 18

Even though things are going great, I've stayed strong, held firm, and Jeff and I have only cuddled. He did ask me what my timeline was looking like, and fair enough, I thought, but I said I didn't have an answer for him just yet. It's only been eight days — I'm not ready.

NOVEMBER 19
9:15 a.m.
I GUESS I WAS READY!! A lot can change in a day. And regardless of what Trish and Lilly may think, I almost waited a full ten days, and I don't think I have too much to feel guilty about.

Last night, which will henceforth be known as THE NIGHT in these chronicles, Jeff made me paella. And after that, I pulled off my shirt and kissed his sweet, long eyelashes, and before too long was marvelling at the feeling of my warm chest pressed against his warm chest. Face to face. Heart to heart. For the very first time.

And then we did it. I mean, we *really* did it.

Things started off all rushed and fumbly, but once we finished round one, we slowed it down and started to enjoy each other even more, Jeff running his tongue over most of my body, me running my fingers over his. The heat between us was so intense I felt like I was running a fever. Beads of sweat trickled down my back and under my breasts and I noticed more than a few droplets falling from under Jeff's chin. There were even flashes of lightning and rumbles of thunder as an unseasonable (read: climate change) weather bomb rolled in around midnight. It was definitely the sexiest thing that has ever happened to me. Not a bad start!

12:30 p.m.
Okay, mildly rough start. Bumped into Kate! She wasn't too happy when she discovered Jeff and I had become a couple mere hours after they were finished. I do feel badly about that. But she wasn't supposed to find out. I mean, who would have thought she'd be at the exact same

bagel shop at the exact same time that Jeff and I decided we needed hot sesame bagels and cream cheese so badly? Honestly, what were the chances? And to say it was awkward is an understatement.

"Hi Kate," I said, upon sensing her long, blond shadow cast over me, "buying some bagels?"

"Hello Jeffrey," she said coolly.

"Hi Katie," said Jeff, looking at his feet.

"We, uh, just bumped into each other on the street and decided to surprise our class with bagels," I lied badly. "I'm just going over there to get a couple of tubs of veggie cream cheese and . . ." I wandered away and let them talk while I read orange juice and yogurt labels in the nearby refrigerator case. They chatted calmly, she cried, he rubbed her back, and a few moments later she headed to the door, sniffling, "Bye, Ruthie," on her way out, which made me feel like a total heel and definitely helped me understand what Trish and Lilly were talking about a little better.

NOVEMBER 21

GOOD MORNING, BEAUTIFUL WORLD! I haven't felt this way since Dean in Thailand. Textbook honeymoon phase with Jeff for sure, but my newfound happiness has been somewhat tempered by some big news from Trish.

She called last night and asked me to meet her for drinks at the Ossie. Then, when she ordered our first round of drinks, she insisted we needed "something extra strong" and bought us each double gin martinis — dirty, with extra olives.

"Oh geez," I said.

"I've got some news," she said, after taking three big gulps.

"Oh geez," I repeated.

"It's not bad news," she said, but she said it with one of the weirdest facial expressions that I've ever seen. It was a look that said, "I've got gas, but am inexplicably happy about it."

"Trish," I asked, "Have you got gas?"

"No, Ruthie." Another couple of gulps. Long dramatic pause: "I'm gay."

"No, you're not," I replied without hesitation.

"Excuse me?"

"You're not gay. You're not suddenly my friend Trish, the gay lesbian." I know. Bad stuff. But I was stunned!

"I know this is hard for you to understa—"

"Trish, I know you may think you're gay, but I'm telling you, you're just not gay," I insisted, while giving her no concrete evidence as to how I knew this to be true.

She started to get choked up and accused me of being unsupportive, and there's no doubt about it, she had me on that count. What the hell was I doing? Why was I being such a bad friend? Don't I want my friends to also follow their bliss? Even if it does lead them down a rabbit hole of hoo-hahs? Trish was getting so drunk on the extra-strong drink she ordered that my denial washed away like a sudden rain shower and was replaced by love.

"Oh god. I'm so sorry. I'm such a bitch." I gave her a hug. "I don't know why I said any of that. I think I was just surprised."

"Yeah, you and me both." She sniffed.

And then she told me how it all began . . .

During the past few years, Trish has become fairly famous at her open-concept office space for the massive furry mukluks she wears that reach straight up to her thighs, in the colder months. They're quite the work of art, but hot as Hades, so she always takes them off when she gets to work, leaving them in the common boot area and transferring her feet into more appropriate indoor moccasins, Mr. Rogers style.

One day, just over a week ago at the end of her workday, Trish went to put on her mukluks and was surprised to find the right boot stuffed with a white envelope with her name on it. She looked around the office to see if anyone was watching her, but nobody was. Then she opened the envelope and inside was a ticket to the Springsteen concert that was happening that night, along with a note typed all in caps that said: *I'VE GOT THE OTHER TICKET. HOPE TO SEE YOU THERE. — ANDY.*

Exciting, right? Total "things like this don't happen in real life," and "oh my god she's going to Springsteen!" and "holy smokes, it's a total blind date with someone who's been watching her at work," and "is that creepy? I hope he's not a psycho," and "who could it be?" etc. Well, the weird part is, Trish didn't tell me, or Lilly, or anyone about this mystery date. Forget the fact that we could have helped her choose the perfect outfit, but I think it was also kind of dangerous that she was meeting some stranger, and quite possibly going to a second location, and we didn't know who she was with or where she was going. That evening she simply told Lilly that she was going out for the night, and then disappeared for the next eight hours.

Okay, I'll cut to the chase and will let you know, as I have recently learned, that she went out with Andy. And Andy isn't short for Andrew. Andy is short for Andrea.

"So, you're a lesbian now." I was playing it cool but was totally shocked.

"Please don't be weird about this," she warned. "And I'm not exactly sure what I am, though if I had to label it, I'd say I'm probably a lesbian. Or maybe bi?"

Trish said for now all I needed to know was that she likes Andy "a lot."

As we sipped our second round of dirty martinis, Trish explained that this was different for her, that she was super attracted to the whole of Andy: her personality, her looks, her vibe and how she makes Trish feel. And I honestly love that for her. I'm still thrown, but I love it for her.

"Maybe it's all a numbers game," said Trish. "Maybe we're all up to 50% gay and then meeting the right person, whatever their gender may be, can tip you over to the other side."

"I think you mean team," I said unhelpfully.

"I don't know. But Andy just feels right. She also happened to give me multiple orgasms after the Springsteen concert, so there's that."

Just to be clear, even though I was surprised, I truly am happy for Trish, BUT IF I MAY... I get in trouble with the girls when I wait almost ten days to sleep with Jeff who I'd been lusting after for months, but she's allowed to jump into bed with a complete stranger on day one? Is there some sort of loophole I don't know about because Andy is a woman? I decided to let it go. This was about Trish and her newfound queer happiness.

"I'm sorry how I reacted at first," I said. "I was just caught off-guard. I can't wait to meet Andy. To know you is to love you. Lucky he, she, they or them."

Trish laughed. "Well, in this case 'she.' And I can't wait for you guys to meet her too, and for what it's worth, I'm just as surprised about all of this as you are. But you can't help who you fall for."

"I guess you're right about that," I agreed with a sigh. "You really can't."

NOVEMBER 23
1 p.m.
I can't believe school ends in just a few weeks.

And I can't believe I'm finally with Jeff.

And I can't believe that Trish is gay.

And I can't believe we have to make a full plated meal of grilled steak (côte de boeuf grillée) with garnishes of watercress, pommes mignonnettes, and tomatoes Provençal, along with a steak topper of beurre Colbert (a compound butter), all within the next two hours.

What I *can* believe is that I can do this. For any other mere mortal, this would be a daunting task. Not for Ruthie Cohen, super chef!

Wait. That sounds gross. But what's wrong with being proud of myself? I've worked hard, improved like crazy, and I'm finally really great at something! I want to shout it from the rooftops. In fact, along with Jeff, I'm the best student in the entire country at something, and I even have the silver platter to prove it!

It's not like I walk down College Street wearing my chef's toque, toting my shiny new award in one hand while whipping egg whites with the other. Still, anytime I bump into someone I haven't seen in a while and they ask me what's new, I tell them I bravely left the mind-numbing world of TelecorpMedia and have recently become a chef.

That's right; I'm already calling myself a chef. Because I honestly already *feel* like a chef. And I can't help but notice that my friends and acquaintances seem more than a little impressed by it all.

"Cool," they'll say, or "I've always wanted to become a chef," or "I still remember those spinach balls you used to make at your wine and cheese parties at McGill."

I haven't felt this proud since that time I made breakfast for Mom and Dad and Bubbe Bobby Grace when I was maybe six years old and barely able to see over the kitchen counter.

It was a rainy day in September, and Bubbe was getting ready to hit the road back to Florida. She came by our house to say one last goodbye, to have one last coffee klatch with my parents before she left. After a few minutes I got bored of just sitting there in my little pink nightie and fuzzy slippers, so I told them I'd make us all some breakfast.

Dad said, "Go get 'em, kiddo!"

Mom said, "That would be lovely, Ruthie."

Bubbe Bobby Grace said, "One fried egg, over easy. Brown toast, buttered."

My parents started chuckling, knowing that when my six-year-old self said I was making breakfast, what it really meant was getting out the spoons and the bowls and the milk and the box of Cap'n Crunch cereal, putting them all on the table, and then only pouring my own.

Bubbe Bobby Grace saw everyone as her equal, even her tiny granddaughter — she was funny that way. Which meant that if Bubbe could fry an egg, anyone could fry an egg. And so, it was that from her swivel chair at the round kitchen table, cigarette dangling from her perfectly manicured fingers, she coached me through making my first-ever fried egg while Mom anxiously looked on.

"Get out a small pan, Ruthie..."

"Bottom cupboard on the left," said Mom.

"Get an egg and the butter from the fridge..."

"Make two trips if you need to, sweetie," advised Mom.

"Put the pan on the element — that black coil thing — and then turn the knob on the left to seven. You know your numbers, right?"

"Bubbe! I can already count to 250!"

"Good stuff, dollface. Now, you need a spatula and a butter knife. I should have mentioned that before. I'm sorry. Go get them now." Dad grabbed the necessary utensils for me, handing them over with a wink.

"I'm going to want that toast hot and ready at the same time as my egg, Ruthie, so go pop two slices of the brown bread in the toaster, will ya? You'll smell when the toast is done," she assured me. "Trust that adorable schnoz of yours."

I methodically did everything that Bubbe Bobby Grace said, remaining calm, all the while feeling that more than anything else in the world, these three people, in this sunshine yellow kitchen, were rooting for me.

The butter sizzled the egg fried, and I flipped it with ease. The toast popped, I spread it with butter and then carefully brought my Bubbe's breakfast over to her. I remember being so full of pride at that moment that I thought my chest would explode. Cooking wasn't that difficult. I was good at it. And I did it all by myself.

"Look at our little chef!" cheered Dad.

"Nice job, honey," said Mom.

"Needs a little salt," said Bubbe Bobby Grace.

I hadn't had that feeling, a warm feeling of pride, until this year at cooking school.

Anyhow, it's amazing how far we've all come since those first weeks at l'École de la Cuisine Française, when we spent entire three-hour pratique classes working on nothing but our knife skills as Chef Antoine barked, "Non. Again! Non. It is not perfect. Do it again!" And again, and again, and then some more after that. And again.

But now look at us all, running around like it's a quick-fire challenge on *Top Chef*! I am thriving!

Which brings me back to today's leçon 33: Griller et Gratiner. This meal wasn't overly complicated — what it was, was a test of time: with everything timed just right, I figured in ten steps I'd be presenting Chef with a pretty plate of perfectly cooked and properly seasoned and rested meat, a pat of beurre Colbert sexily melting down its sides, along with some nice veg accompaniments, all on a gently warmed plate. At least that was the plan.

1. I started by grabbing the nicest looking rib steak I could find from the refrigerator, sliced it clean off the bone with my freshly sharpened butcher's knife and set it aside to come up to room temperature.

2. I got to work on phase one of the pommes mignonnettes. I peeled and cut several potatoes into quarters (lengthwise), sliced off their ends, and used my paring knife, attempting to turn them into perfect mini footballs. I really struggle with my "turning" skills. Jeff is so much better at this than me, so I give him a nudge and he effortlessly finishes off my last few while Chef wasn't watching. (I'm not proud of this.)

3. I took a big, fat tomato and cut it in half, clear across the centre, then sliced a bit off the bottoms so that each half sat flat. I squeezed some of the seeds from the tomatoes, but I did this gently, as if one was fondling a gentleman's balls. To make the crumb topping for my tomatoes Provençal, I chopped up two garlic cloves, scooped a couple of handfuls of fresh breadcrumbs over the garlic on my cutting board, and mixed the two together. I chopped up some parsley and threw that into the mix. I minced them all together until they formed a uniform, fine crumb, then scooped my breadcrumb topping into a bowl and added a generous amount of olive oil, black pepper, and salt. I tasted for seasoning. Good stuff. I did a time check: 45 minutes had passed.

4. The beurre Colbert needed some time to set, so that was my next task. Easy enough: to my softened butter I added lemon juice, salt, and pepper, plus a whisper of cayenne, some minced parsley, and some melted and cooled glace de viande, or meat glaze, to add a uniquely rich beefy flavour to the beurre Colbert. In went some freshly chopped tarragon, one last stir, and then I spooned my soft butter mixture onto a sheet of plastic wrap and carefully rolled it into a tube, twisting the ends to force it into a sausage shape. Into the fridge went the compound butter to firm up a bit.

And that's when I noticed Jeff went missing.

At some point within the past half-hour, Jeff had up and left the kitchen. Plum disappeared! I stepped in to cover his station, making sure his rib steak came out of the oven at the right time, and I finished off his potatoes while I did mine, tossing all of the parboiled little footballs in clarified butter before roasting them in the 400 degree Fahrenheit oven, keeping a sharp eye on them. Then I drained them on paper towel and salted them while they were still screaming hot. Jeff's tomatoes were already prepped, so I put them in the oven along with mine, about five minutes after I'd taken our steaks out to rest.

Jeff returned with ten minutes to spare. He reclaimed his station and his recipes, warmed up our plates in the oven, and washed and dried the watercress, never missing a beat. His finished dish looked lovely. But he did not. He looked weird. I don't really know how to explain it other than to say that he looked different from how he looked before he left class ten minutes earlier. It was almost as if he'd been drinking, yet I didn't smell any alcohol on his breath.

"What's wrong with you?" I asked.

"What do you mean? I'm fine."

"You left class."

"Just for a bit."

"If you don't want to tell me what's going on, that's fine, but just so you know, those turned potatoes didn't turn golden brown all by themselves."

"Look, I said I was fine," he snapped. Then Jeff looked down at his workstation, paused, and regrouped. "Sorry. I'm just a little tired today."

"But where did you go?" I pressed. "It's not exactly normal to leave your station in the middle of class for ten minutes without telling anybody."

"You mean, without telling *you*," he said as he gave the stainless-steel countertop a final spray and wipe. "I told Chef Antoine I wasn't feeling well and had to go out to get some air."

"Oh! Sorry. Well, are you feeling any better? Your eyes are actually pretty bloodshot. Is it allergies? I think I may have allergies." I felt like a heel for not believing him, so rather than admitting I was wrong I decided to keep asking him annoying questions.

"Yeah, maybe allergies," he said, sniffling. "Or maybe a cold. Not sure. But I'm fine. Honestly."

NOVEMBER 24

Jeff made us steak sandwiches for lunch today using yesterday's leftovers. All is forgiven.

NOVEMBER 26
5:20 p.m.
I'm waiting for the girls to get ready. Since Trish met Andy, she's been putting more effort into her looks. She even got professional eyelash extensions yesterday. We're getting all dressed up because after dinner we're all going to a fancy bash at Bar Magma to celebrate Jeff's pal Christopher's inclusion on the World's 50 Best Bars list.

"So does this make you a lipstick lesbian?" I asked Trish, as she carefully applied a scarlet colour to her puckered mouth, followed by a quick swat to the back of my head. I was at Trish and Lilly's, primping for a big night out.

"Ouch! What?" I protested, then readjusted my now-ruined updo. "I've seriously never understood what that term means! I'm trying to understand our new reality. I'm trying to be a better friend!" Trish and Lilly rolled their eyes at one another, and I suddenly felt left out. (Isn't it amazing, the devastating power of a well-placed eye roll?)

"Okay, I'm sorry," I grovelled. "I'm looking forward to meeting Andy at dinner tonight. I'm sure she'll be a wonderful guest. And you guys are going to love what Jeff and I have been cooking up all day." I catch them smirking into their bathroom mirror and with that I was off the hook. (I looked it up later and a lipstick lesbian is in fact a lesbian "who has glamorously feminine characteristics, as opposed to the stereotypically masculine lesbian." Of course, there was no way I was going to share my findings with the girls since I knew this politically incorrect–sounding yet Wikipedia-approved information would somehow earn me another swat. I learned it could also mean "a woman who only acts gay for show," and even though that is 100% not what I meant, I knew it could earn me more swats.)

But getting back to tonight: when Lilly and Craig broke up, she threw herself into even more work at the hospital by picking up extra shifts and then filled any remaining bits of spare time with a plethora of clubs, classes, and causes. It was as if she didn't want one free moment to herself — no time at all to think about Craig and her broken heart. Trish and I didn't think this was healthy so had several interventions with Lilly, none of them successful, including the time we cornered her after her belly dance recital.

"You can't jiggle away your troubles!" I insisted.

But Lilly said that belly dancing and Big Sisters were making her happy, and it did seem like for now, they were.

"You guys look hot," I said to my best gal pals as I sat on the edge of their bathtub, pulling on my black sheer stockings.

"That style is super flattering on you," said Lilly, nodding at my new red jersey wrap dress. (The second new dress I've bought this month. Saw it in the window at Kizmet and had to have it. Jeff was the instigator.)

"That necklace makes you look like you could be from Paris," said Trish of Lilly's interlocking silver loops.

"That colour makes your lips look just like a pretty rosebud," I told Trish. We're so good to each other.

Anyways, if anyone should have been smirking into a mirror it should have been me, because Dear Diary, I HAD AN R-RATED DAY TODAY! (Not to mention, an instant classic). I don't want to get too off track here, so will quickly describe how Jeff and I had woken up in a tangle (after a GREAT night), showered and headed over to the St. Lawrence Market. It was just mild enough out to stay bundled up while getting caffeinated over lattes and croissants at a picnic table on Market Street. As he sipped, Jeff tucked his spare hand between my thighs to keep warm. (I love when he does that).

"So, you say that on your Newfoundland trip a while back Lilly tried a donair for the first time?"

"And LOVED it. We should make donair spring rolls, with that weird sweet, garlicky mayo dipping sauce," I said.

"Totally!" said Jeff. "And we should also kill zee lobster and make some buttery lobster rolls."

"YES. She would love that!! With lots of dill."

Then we picked up our dinner party provisions: some beef for our spring rolls, a lobster, butter, garlic, Martin's Famous Potato Rolls, dill, eggs, cream cheese, blueberries, and some wine. Then we walked back to Jeff's, unpacked our groceries . . . but quickly got distracted! I was about to start browning the ground beef and washing the dill (Jeff was going to get started on the lobster and garlic), when he hugged me from behind, leaned in close and whispered, "Before we get our hands dirty, let's get filthy." And then he coaxed me to the floor, pulled off my sweatpants, pulled my sweatshirt over my head, and opened the fridge. He pulled out just about everything he could quickly grab, a jar of Chili Crunch, sour dills, red pepper jelly . . . and the next thing I knew I was totally naked with my tush on the floor and my back arched as if I was Kim Basinger having honey licked off of my titties by Mickey Rourke. (No blindfold though). And I loved it!! (But I told Jeff to be careful with the Chili Crunch). After we finished, I laid on the floor exhausted, with a flushed Jeff laying right beside me. Then I leaned my head on my hand, munched on a pickle spear and said:

"*9 ½ Weeks*: An erotic romance for the masses, this explicit big-budget film sees a purely sexual relationship taken to the edge in delicious turns. Dir: Adrian Lyne. Cast: Mickey Rourke, Kim Basinger, Margaret Whitton, David Margulies. 1986. 117 min."

Should I have told the girls we had sex *three times* and showered twice while preparing their dinner? Or that Jeff cracked open the lobster while he had a giant hard-on? Probably not.

We built the menu around some of Lilly's favourite Newfoundland-inspired dishes — she's going to freak out. Lilly and I took to Newfoundland a few years ago, and that week remains one of my all-time favourite trips.

We had flown into Gander for a week-long road trip along the winding coastal roads to the city of St. John's and its jellybean-coloured row houses. Gander was an hour and a half drive to a place called Twillingate, which we had heard was our best bet (50/50) for seeing icebergs in the summertime. We signed up for the two-hour boat tour with Skipper Doug Decker aboard the *M.V. Sunrise* out of Twillingate Harbour, and sure enough, after a half-hour of cruising we spotted the first of two icebergs in Horney Head Cove — all icy white with baby blue oxygen lines veining its façade.

"This one will be gone in two weeks," figured Skipper Doug. You'd think after so many years at the helm of a tourist boat the Skipper would grow tired of all the whales, birds, and 'bergs. But it wasn't so. "I could stay here all day following those beautiful beasts around," he said. "That's just the type of man I am."

The whole trip was magic — a winning combo of nice people, breathtaking surroundings, a relaxed pace, and an overall sense of peace. But it wasn't until the final day that Lilly fell for the Atlantic puffins.

She had started thumbing through brochures at the front desk after we had stumbled back to our B&B from a cuckoo night out on George

Street (think Vegas, but with no showgirls and a lot more Screech rum). Yet even in her drunken state she discovered that the Witless Bay Ecological Reserve, just a half-hour away, was North America's largest Atlantic puffin colony, and "How can we pass up an opportunity like this?" she reasoned, waving the colourful pamphlet in my face.

"Puffins are for suckers," I said, swatting her hand away.

Nevertheless, the next morning I found myself aboard the second boat in as many days, this time the *M.V. Iceman*, in the tiny community of Bay Bulls.

"Hey Lilly, why don't we ever do stuff like this at home?" I asked as we walked the gangplank on wobbly legs. "Why don't we do day boat tours? Why don't we get back to nature? Why are we almost never at one with the animals and the trees?"

"Well, you're always at work or away and I'm always at the hospital or with Craig," she sighed, resting her arms on the white steel railing as the *M.V. Iceman* launched from the docks into the great beyond. "We're city girls with no time."

Well tonight we've got plenty of time and I was going to use most of mine helping Lilly get happy again. Dinner was also about letting iceberg-sized prejudgements melt away as we make room for new friends ... even though Lilly and I don't really have high hopes because in the less than five days Andy's been in our orbit, she's proven herself to be a bit rude (she told Lilly it was weird that she kept her hair so long when she met her at their apartment the other night), flakey (Trish let it slip that Andy was late for their second *and* third date), unapologetic (see aforementioned lateness), and worse, didn't seem enthused by this dinner and isn't showing any interest in getting to know us (or meeting me!), which means she clearly has terrible taste. Well, besides her interest in Trish. I mean, I love that Trish is all a-flutter and excited but ... I don't really get it?

6:15 p.m.

Journalling from the toilet at Jeff's while the girls chatter in the kitchen with him ... it warms my heart hearing them all getting along. Anyways, when we arrived at Jeff's, he was outside looking totally hot in his trim black suit and Converse while smoking a cigarette. But Jeff doesn't smoke? He spotted us, tossed the butt onto the sidewalk, popped a piece of gum in his mouth, and slapped on a big old smile.

"Looking good, ladies," said Jeff with a wink.

"Is Andy here yet?" Trish asked hopefully. (She hadn't heard from her in over an hour. Weird.)

"Nope," said Jeff. "You look really nice, Trish. You all look great. And Ruthie, baby, you smell awesome," he said, nuzzling his nose into my neck. He put his arm around my shoulders and kissed me on the lips, just like a real boyfriend would. Because Jeff is finally my boyfriend. Sometimes I still can't believe it's true.

Shit — Jeff is calling for me. I didn't realize how long I've been sitting on the toilet lid writing. He's totally going to think I have a bladder infection.

7:48 p.m.

I had to step away again to make note of the fact that Andy didn't show up and I'm *fucking furious*. Dinner was called on the early side, for 6 p.m., because we have to eat and clean up then get to Magma before they hit capacity. We waited for Andy for an hour, then Trish asked if we could wait just 30 minutes more. That was 18 minutes ago. Andy just texted to say she'll meet us at the party at Magma instead, and let's just say Trish the newbie lesbian is a lot more forgiving than Trish the no-nonsense bestie.

9:10 p.m.

Touching up my eyeliner and wanted to update today's entry by saying a great time was had by all at dinner, even without Andy. Actually, *especially* without Andy. Even with the pre-cooking coitus and late start time it was super delicious. And let's just say Jeff's Shazamo! was off the charts. He serenaded Lilly with his guitar and kept serving Trish extra helpings of my no-bake blueberry cheesecake trifle with crisp meringues. I'd probably be jealous if Trish wasn't a lesbian and Lilly wasn't grieving Craig, and both of them weren't my best friends in the entire world.

But wait, there's more! After dessert I kept catching Lilly texting someone and giggling. Is she already secretly dating?! Is it someone at the hospital? She looks so happy!

Do Trish and I need to plan another stakeout?

NOVEMBER 27
11:30 a.m.
When drinking Iceberg vodka martinis starts to feel like drinking tall, cool glasses of water, the chances are pretty good that you're going to spend the latter part of the night puking into a toilet bowl and then laying your head upon the cold hard, tile floor, the thought of which would normally be disgusting, but given the fact that the bathroom is spinning and the bed is in a whole other room, it is just about the best feeling in the entire world. (If someone could bottle that feeling they'd be rich beyond their wildest dreams.) Anyway, this was my thinking late last night. Ugh.

And I mean *ugh*.

In a hilarious twist of fate, a Newfoundland-based vodka brand called Iceberg sponsored the event at Magma. I love a solid, branded event. The bar looked amazing. There were delicate origami paper puffins — Lilly's beloved puffins! — in various states of flight throughout the room, swinging awkwardly from dozens of schoolhouse pendant fixtures. An Instagram activation was set up in the far corner, where you could get a nice shot of yourself and your friends aboard a fake sightseeing boat, with breaching whales and giant icebergs as a backdrop. The photographer's assistant was also handing out comment bubbles on sticks that said things like "I doubt vodka is the answer but it's worth a shot!" In the middle of the bar they even created a dance floor covered in huge vinyl decals of ice cubes. The place was packed belly-to-belly and back-to-back, as trays of espresso martinis, cosmos, and something clear with foam on top were held aloft by servers wearing black fisherman-style toques, the trays seemingly floating through air. This isn't our usual scene — so see and be seen — but we were in for a good time.

I immediately started drinking the free-flowing dirty Iceberg martinis and I danced with Jeff, and I danced with Lilly and Trish (Lilly's modern jazz lessons are really paying off), and I drank another Iceberg martini (branding really does work!), and I danced with strangers, and I made out with Jeff, and I lost an earring, and I found my earring (or at least I hope it was my earring).

"Let's celebrate with more martinis," I cheered, spilling a big splash from my glass onto the floor.

"She's not here," said Trish, who had sidled up beside us.

"Who's not here?" I asked.

"Andy."

This was getting hard to watch. I was in a tough spot because I was pretty trashed, and the more I learned about Andy the less I liked her for sundry reasons . . .

1. She is incredibly mean and judgemental (horrible)
2. She is always late to everything (selfish)
3. She doesn't care about Trish's friends (ridiculous)
4. I know she is going to break Trish's prickly pear heart (boooo!)

And 5. She DIDN'T SHOW UP FOR DINNER TONIGHT! So, even though we had timed everything perfectly, dinner could have been ruined while we sat and waited for Andy to NOT show up.

I know this situation isn't all about me, and Andy potentially ruining dinner, but this *is* my diary, so there.

In other words, for these reasons and more I was afraid I was going to say something to Trish that was going to further upset her.

"Have you checked your cell? No missed messages?" Jeff asked Trish.

"No missed calls. No texts. And I've tried her half a dozen times and she's not answering," said Trish.

"That's weird," said Jeff. "Is she usually this unpredictable?"

"So-so. But she's been doing this a lot. Just not fucking showing up," said Trish, her anger finally arriving to the party.

"Hey, I guess dating a woman is a lot like..." Jeff covered my mouth to stop me from finishing my brilliant observation. I licked his palm. He kept it clasped over my mouth.

"Anyway," said Trish, who had diverted her eyes away from mine and back to Jeff's. "I'm getting sick of it. I'm so over this crap. Do you think this is normal behaviour?" she asked Jeff.

"Do you want my honest opinion?" Jeff replied.

"No," sighed Trish. "Besides, tonight's about Lilly."

I smacked Jeff's hand away.

"To Lilly and the puffins!" I shouted, victoriously hoisting an Iceberg-fuelled martini glass towards the puffin-filled ceiling.

The next thing I remember I was in an Uber on the ride home, slumped into Jeff's lap. He was stroking my hair and I was enjoying the ride while sobering up a bit. Lights flashed against the blackness of the night — mostly streaks of red and white and thankfully, a lot of green. And then a thought occurred to me.

"Jeff," I said, lifting my head and looking up at him, "I saw you smoking by the door when we first arrived. Since when do you smoke?"

"You must have been seeing things, Ruthie," he said looking straight ahead. "It wasn't me."

"Alright," I yawned, laying my head back into his lap and closing my eyes.

Except, it *was* him.

But I don't want to think about it, because otherwise, Jeff was super sweet. He held back my hair for the first half hour of my barfing, put a damp washcloth on my forehead in the most caring way, and strategically placed a bag-lined garbage can beside my bed. I'm telling you, he thought of everything. He even had orange juice waiting for me this morning (with extra pulp, of course). It's like he's Saint Jeff of the Perpetual Vomit.

"So, should I be embarrassed?" I asked him as I rubbed my eyes with my knuckles, trying to will myself awake.

"Define embarrassed," said Jeff, putting down his book and snuggling in a little closer.

"For instance, did I expose myself in public?" (Always my first and main concern following an evening such as this.)

"Define exposed."

"Come on, Jeff, it's seriously all a blur," I whined, poking around for pieces of dried puke in my hair.

"Okay, in all honesty it wasn't pretty, but it wasn't a total mess, either," he started. "You're just lucky you're a cute drunk."

I don't know about cute, but I do know I'm a particular brand of funny when I drink. I can't tell you how many people have told me this. They say, "Ruthie, you're funnier than Sarah Silverman when you're drunk," or "You should drink more often," and even "I like you better when you're drunk." But I don't make a habit of getting plastered all the time. In fact, since I started at l'École de la Cuisine Française, this has been my only knock-down-drag-out night of boozing it up.

Jeff crawled out of bed and went to make himself some coffee and breakfast (I took a gaggy pass) while I stayed put and nursed my hangover. He continued recounting the night's sordid details from down the hall in the kitchen as I shouted back follow-up questions from beneath the duvet.

". . . and did we dance together?" (Yes, he said. Lots.)

". . . and did Andy ever show up?" (He said no.)

". . . and why is there a new scab on my knee?" (Origin: Unknown.)

Twenty minutes later and I had to hand it to him, Jeff did a very admirable recap of the entire evening, from the fact that they ordered 30 Maker pizzas to the party just as we were leaving (damn!), to Jeff carrying me up several flights of stairs after the Uber dropped us off at my place — and it sounds like everyone had fun and I'm not in trouble so, all I can say is *phew*.

Jeff returned to the bedroom eating a half-finished fluffy Gruyère and mushroom omelette (he's very comfortable in my kitchen — even stores some of his own secret seasonings here) then sat back down with me in bed for a few minutes more.

"Some additional things to note," he said while taking in the last hungry bites. "After Andy stood her up, Trish was talking to some guy she seemed into ... and Craig — that's Lilly's ex-boyfriend, right! He showed up when I was getting our coats. Lilly seemed totally stoked to see him, but Trish gave him the cold shoulder."

I was suddenly nauseous, sad, and happy. I hadn't had such mixed emotions since that time I went bungee jumping in Switzerland! But I needed a shower to clear my head and come back to life before I could call Lilly and ask what the hell is going on.

And it is only when I finally kick off the cocoony comfort of my down duvet that I realized I was wearing my favourite red bikini.

"What the ... ?"

"Oh yeah, and you insisted on putting on a bathing suit and doing handstands and splits on the bed when we got home," said a chuckling Jeff as he kissed my bare belly.

Oh god. It all came back to me in horror-filled flashes: Did I really stuff 11 olives into my mouth at once for a crowd? Did I actually challenge Lilly to a "puffin taking flight" competition during the sponsor's brief speech? Did I dream about giving Jeff a handjob in the back seat of the Uber, or did that really happen? And what the heck, Jeff?

"That was all real, baby," he said, lying back down and putting his hands behind his head with a satisfied smile.

I pulled the duvet back over my face and momentarily wished I were dead. But Jeff had to leave. He slid into his dress pants and buttoned up his dress shirt and pulled on his socks and laced up his Converse and grabbed his coat and headed out the door to practise the civet de lapin à la Française recipe he's been struggling with from leçon 35.

"Call me if you need any help," I yawned as I shuffled off to the bathroom in my bright red bikini.

1 p.m.
The shower worked its magic, and I've made a surprising recovery. I'm even feeling well enough to eat something. But not the usual morning-after-the-night-before fried or poached or scrambled eggs or even my new favourite egg preparation — oeufs cocotte à la crème (eggs slowly cooked in a bain-marie then topped with heavy cream — delicious).

Instead, I whipped up a post-bender blender cure-all: my frozen banana and peanut butter smoothie. It's like a meal replacement for times like these when you don't even have the strength to chew. (*Exhausting.*)

I'm finally ready to start the day. Time to call Lilly.

1:10 p.m.
"Okay, toots," I said before she'd even had time to say hello. "Start talking!"

"How are you feeling, Ruthie?"

"Well, I just about barfed up a lung last night, but don't worry about me, I want to hear about *you*!" I said, kind of screaming the word "you!" back at her because I was just too excited about this whole Craig business, even if he did kiss a redheaded floozy in a bar a few months ago.

"Um, do you mind if we talk a little later?" she asked.

"Yeesh, sorry, I didn't mean to wake you."

"It's not that. I'm up. But . . . Craig's still sleeping."

"Lilly!"

"Bye, Ruthie, I'll call you back soon, I promise," she said with a happy spring in her voice.

"Lilly!"

Click. "Lilly?"

Exciting! Gotta call Trish and dish.

1:12 p.m.
"Trish! I just called Lilly and she hung up on me because . . ."

"Hey, Ruthie," said a groggy-sounding Trish, "can I call you back a bit later? I'm kind of in the middle of something."

"But we've got to discuss Lilly! Did you hear her come in last night? Because you won't believe . . ." Just then I heard a muffled voice in the background. A muffled *male* voice. Trish giggled and told the voice to "Shhh!"

"Trish! What's going on over there? Who does that muffled male voice belong to? Put Lilly on the phone! Are you still a lesbian . . . ?"

"We'll call you later to debrief. Bye-bye!" Click.

Aaargh! I hate my friends so much! What on Earth happened last night?! It's like we were all bridesmaids hooking up at the end of some magical puffin wedding. So exciting! But what's the use of having all of this freshly brewed gossip if there's no one around to drink it with? Feh!

Okay. I need to busy myself. I think I feel well enough to do some light housework while I wait for those jerks to call back.

1:45 p.m.
I did the kitchen, Swiffered some coffee grounds that Jeff had missed on the floor, washed the dishes, dried the blender, and made some tea. They still haven't called. Washroom?

1:55 p.m.
I attacked the washroom. The toilet needed a good scrubbing, that's for sure. I squirted in some Toilet Duck and let the vibrant blue cleansing gel trickle down the bowl and work its magic before getting out the brush and lazily swooshing it around. Flush and done. I'm such a productive hungover person. They still haven't called.

2:10 p.m.
Had to stop cleaning. Too woozy. Will never drink Iceberg vodka again. Where the heck are the girls? I have practically nothing left to clean!

NOVEMBER 30

Huge news! Craig and Lilly are basically back together! Trish dumped Andy and has decided she's probably bi! And I aced the éclairs in class today! Also, is it possible that I'm still a little hungover?

The girls came over to hang last night and we had a proper debrief. So much has changed in a mere 24 hours I can hardly believe it. Trish said she was already pissed at Andy and was getting sick of waiting around for her, her thoughtlessness, the bad outweighing the good.

"But you know how it is in a new relationship," she said. "I was starry-eyed and super into her. And the fooling around with a woman was so awesome and different, I felt a little drugged."

"And then the drug wore off?" I asked.

"Listen, I can take a lot of crap," she said. "I'm friends with you, after all." I gave her a friendly shoulder punch. "But after she missed the dinner *and* the party and then admitted she had been out with friends all along, I just thought, *fuck this*. Fuck her. Life's too short."

"Hooking up with Chad after the party certainly helped too," added Lilly.

"Chad again?!"

"Chad again," said Lilly with a laugh.

"I took it as a sign that he was at the party and Andy wasn't," said Trish.

"So, are you and Chad a thing now?" I asked

"Hardly," said Trish.

"When I overheard her saying goodbye to him at the door," said Lilly, "Trish said, 'I guess I'll see you again in a year or two.'"

Trish is back.

And so is Craig!

I was a bit hesitant at first — I mean, cheating is unforgiveable — but if I'm honest, I knew in my heart they'd get back together at some point because they are the definition of soulmates, so Trish and I have been careful not to trash-talk him even though we were spying on him. Besides, Craig is also our friend, so it was hard to write him off as just another douchebag.

Lilly said that after he explained his side of the story, how he had been feeling — ignored, anxious, depressed — and how he was getting professional help, and how incredibly sorry he was, and how stupid he felt, and how much he loved her, and how nothing happened with the redhead other than that drunken public make-out session, Lilly cautiously let him back into her life. Plus, she loves him too. Based on her explanation, they're not fully back together (even though they basically are), but they're committed to working on things and moving forward.

Inheritance Update:

Expenses: *airport cabs $83, bike rental in Stanley Park $50, drinks at Seasons bar $120, treats, video rental and dinner during Bueller day off $237. Here in Vancouver for school, so obviously all purchases count as school-related . . . even a last-minute purchase of kickass black cocktail dress for competition ceremony $270.*

Balance remaining: *$45,969.45*

December

DECEMBER 1

We're in the final throes of intensive pastry classes at l'École de la Cuisine Française, and let's just say it's not my strong suit. At all. Pastry class is why I'm a cook and not a baker, and the way I see it you're either on one team or the other and you've got to choose sides.

Much like love, cooking is all about taste, smell, and sound — a last-minute touch of white pepper, a satisfying sear — while I find pastry far more clinical. It's about the weighing and the adding and the subtracting and the multiplying and the dividing up of ingredients, all in precisely measured scientifically relevant, totally important proportions. (Turns out Dad *was* right — I would need math one day.)

Making matters worse, Chef Antoine isn't our teacher for the final weeks of practique classes because he isn't one of the school's pastry specialists. "I do love it," he told us. "But in France there are a great many people who are a great deal better at this than me. These people rise very, very early to make zee baguettes and croissants that my countrymen rely on to get us through each day. Alors, this pastry life is not zee life for me. I like to hit zee snooze button many times," he said while casually stirring a half-cup of heavy cream into his coffee mug.

This was Chef Antoine's typically unemotional way of bidding us all a fond adieu while also informing us that the school's early rising pastry instructor, Chef Bertrand, would be taking it from here. Chef Antoine would still be around for the remainder of the course before we all headed out on our work placements to finish off our diplomas. But for the most part he would be leaving our kitchen, and us. And this doesn't bode well for me because Chef Bertrand doesn't exactly share the same semi-fond feelings Chef Antoine has towards me.

I get it. I'm not for everyone.

DECEMBER 4

Our whole class was invited to the home of the president of l'École de la Cuisine Française to welcome prospective new students and their parents. Each graduating student was asked to bring a dessert for the sweets table to illustrate how much and how well we had all learned this term. We could choose to either use a classic recipe from the school's syllabus or one of our own creations that incorporates some of the French techniques we'd mastered.

The table looked amazing. Everyone did such a great job! There were elephant's ears and angel wings, baba au rhum and crème brûlée, a lofty croquembouche, and perfect kouign-aman.

As for my contribution, even though I have long lived by the personal motto "If it ain't chocolate it ain't dessert," I decided to make a moist gâteau aux carottes with a crème fraîche and cream cheese frosting because I know for a fact that everyone in the entire world loves carrot cake with a rich, tart frosting. As expected, it went over like gangbusters. The crowd was really enjoying it — maybe even a bit too much. After finishing his tasty slice, President Johnson came over to congratulate me and in doing so crushed my hand while also almost shaking my arm from its socket with his overly enthusiastic greeting. Meanwhile after her slice, his wife Adele started firing off coasters as if she were dealing a hand of long-distance blackjack to the roomful of guests. "No water marks on the antiques, please! Respect the wood! Use coasters!" She yelped, hitting one woman in the back of her coiffed head.

The buzz in the room kept getting louder — and jumpier. This was more than just a sugar high.

Some of the middle-aged parents had taken to sitting cross-legged on the finely woven Turkish rugs and were rocking back and forth, while others had become enamored by the oversized tassels holding back the red velvet curtains. I stood in a corner and took it all in: the strangers dancing like lovers to the music being played by a lone harpist, a loud argument down the adjoining hall, someone wearing plaid pants and a mustard-coloured sweater was throwing up into the potted Ficus beside the baby grand piano. I made my way over to the table, and prospective students were physically fighting over the last slice of carrot cake.

What the hell was going on here?

Jeff wandered in with his stunning St. Honoré. He quickly took in the scene and spotted me by the table looking more confused than a virgin on prom night. He made his way over to me and whispered in my ear, "What the hell?"

"I know. It's bizarre. But on the plus side, before this broke out, everyone was *loving* my cake! They ate it all up," I said. Jeff's face fell.

"Oh fuck. I fucked up. Listen, Ruthie, I was just picking up some of my seasonings from your place. Did you happen to use any of the icing sugar from that little jam jar I brought over this week?"

"Yeah," I answered, "all of it. Sorry. But don't worry, I'll replace it. I was just a bit short."

"We've got a problem," said Jeff.

And that's how I found out Jeff does cocaine.

DECEMBER 5

Dear Diary,
   Just to quickly recap, in the last 24 hours I:
   + Accidentally iced a carrot cake with *cocaine*.
   + Had to frantically explain to President Johnson that it wasn't intentional, and that I am *not* trying to make a political statement on why *all* drugs should be legalized.
   + Got dumped. Yes. Dumped.

After my last entry, Jeff called to say he was coming over. I paced my apartment for the better part of an hour before he got here and couldn't believe how nervous I was to see him. How could so much have changed so quickly?

In walked Jeff and for some reason he didn't look like the same old Jeff I knew (and loved) from a few hours earlier. He looked broken. And nervous, too.

We sat down on the couch, and he explained that he hadn't been altogether truthful with me (duh), that he has a bit of a drug problem (you think?), and that he does indeed smoke (I knew it!). He'd been in touch with Chef Antoine and President Johnson. Everyone from the party was okay, thank god, and I'm not in trouble. But . . . he is.

Then Jeff said that early tomorrow morning his parents were coming to take him to get help at a rehab clinic in upstate New York.

It was a lot to take in.

But the overwhelming emotion I was feeling was anger. So I stood firm. I stayed strong. I told him I had thrown out anything I had found in canisters or jars that he had stored in my kitchen cupboards — but had washed the containers and saved them for recycling. (I'm not a monster.)

"I guess that was the right thing to do," he sighed. "Ruthie, I'm sorry about everything. All of it."

I nodded and smiled. *Lump growing in throat . . . Lip starting to quiver . . . Tears welling . . . Don't cry. Don't cry . . .* "What did I do wrong?" I started to blubber. "We were having such fun together. We were finally a real thing, weren't we?"

"We were," he said. "We are. Look, I've totally fallen for you," he said, rubbing my back. (It felt good.) "I'm crazy about you, you know that."

"Well then what changed?" I sniffled. "What drove you to drugs? Am I already boring?"

"You're the opposite of boring! Nothing changed," said Jeff. "Listen — I've got big problems. I have for a while. But these are my problems, and they have nothing to do with you or how I feel about you. I thought I had it all under control, but I relapsed — that damn server at the wine bar in Vancouver gave me my first hit of coke in years. And once I fall off the wagon everything goes to shit."

Jeff said the drugs were all a carryover from his bad old band days.

"I should have told you everything, Ruthie," he said, now covering his sweet eyes with his manly hands so that I couldn't see him cry. "I fucked up big-time. I don't know why it happened, maybe the stress of school, or not knowing what comes next. But I do love you."

"You do?" This took my breath away because it was the first time he'd said it.

"I really do."

And then stupid old me, we headed to my bedroom and got undressed, and we started making out like it was the end of the world, because for us, it truly felt like it was. But then I put a stop to it because it wasn't right. This man in my bed had just gotten kicked out of school for drug possession and nearly causing the cake-related drug overdoses of a house full of people. So instead of making love we both lay there crying, and then morning came and Jeff had to leave. But before he did, he broke up with me.

"I don't want you waiting around for me," he said, sniffling.

"I don't think we should break up," I said, dumbfounded.

"I don't know how long I'll be away for."

"I don't care how long you're away for."

"It's too much pressure on me. It's just not a good idea."

"But I don't want to be with anyone else," I said. "Do you?"

"You don't get it, baby. I can't be with anyone. I can hardly take care of myself right now."

"But..."

"I'm sorry," he said, hugging me tight. Then he swung his legs over the side of the bed, pulled on his jeans, laced up his Converse, and headed out the door.

I stood there staring at it, wiping my eyes in disbelief, hoping it had all just been a bad dream.

DECEMBER 6

Jeff really took off for rehab.

I am numb.

DECEMBER 7

This is the second saddest I've ever been in my entire life. The first saddest was when Bubbe Bobby Grace died (obviously). I hate that this is all happening in the *same year*. Not cool, universe.

When I was crying at her funeral, I thought of the advice she gave me when I was around ten years old. My first childhood pet had died and I was wearing my bravest face as I lowered the shoebox into a hole in the ground that I had dug in the backyard of our old house. Lucy had led a good life, a happy life, a long life for a hamster (a solid four years), though at the time it didn't feel like nearly enough.

At Lucy's graveside ceremony, Bubbe said, "Let the tears flow, dollface," as she dumped a shovel of earth over Lucy's Adidas box casket. "Pain needs an outlet and tears help us heal. Lucy deserves your tears, so let 'em rip."

DECEMBER 9

Those are just a few of my tears. (Can still kind of see the stains.)

DECEMBER 10

Claire called today to see how I was doing. Claire is the best. I don't know why we never really hung out outside of school. I think I can only handle two besties, even though Claire and Jeff and I were a bit of a trio at school. Claire was worried about me, and about Jeff. I should be thinking about Claire and others. And my final exams. But for now, I can only think about me.

DECEMBER 11

Boy, did I ever take Bubbe's advice. Here's my schedule lately:
- Go to school, where every day everyone asks how Jeff is doing. (For the record, I have no idea.)
- Come home, lie on the couch and cry.
- Lie around in bed and cry.
- Lie in the bath and cry.
- Consider climbing up a tree and crying to mix things up.

DECEMBER 15

I have zero appetite. Nothing tastes good anymore. I can't stomach anything but my old breakup standards of frozen peas and mashed bananas and applesauce.

My parents call often to check up on me, and Lilly and Trish come by almost every day as shoulders to cry on, bringing all of my favourite snacks, too. But I can't touch any of it.

"I think I have a tapeworm," I told Lilly.

"You don't have a tapeworm," said Lilly.

"Then maybe it's ringworm," I said.

"Ruthie, you don't have ringworm," said Lilly.

"It might be an ulcer," I said.

"It's not an ulcer," said Lilly.

"Well then it must be indigestion," I said.

"It's not indigestion," said Lilly.

"Well then what's wrong with me?"

And then Lilly said nothing but gave me a big old hug. And then I cried some more like a big old baby.

Was it possible that just as I was about to start my new career as a chef, that I'd lost my love of food?

Or even worse — the love of my life?

DECEMBER 18

Lists are about all I have the energy for these days, so let's go over my most recent one, shall we?

- Almost killed my entire graduating class along with a group of prospective new students and most of their parents with a cocaine-laced carrot cake
- Lost boyfriend to rehab

- Barely passing advanced baking classes
- Newly single

Not that I mind being single. It's just that if I had the choice between being single or being with Jeff, I would definitely choose Jeff. Even after everything.

Anyways, he started writing me from rehab — nice, long letters that say nothing, really. Jeff says his letters are an important part of his therapy and recovery (they're not allowed to call, text, or use the internet) and he basically writes about himself and his past and what the counsellors are teaching him and how he's feeling and what he's been eating (the food sounds gross — I had no idea that they still made green Jell-O). It's basically as boring as it sounds because he's stuck at a clinic in the middle of the Adirondacks. I try to muster up the will to care even though my disappointment and anger usually get in the way. I will say, he has written a few funny stories about some of the other inmates (er, patients?), but that's pretty confidential stuff so I shouldn't write it down here just in case someone with nefarious intentions stumbles across this notebook. But I did snort-laugh at his description of the guy with the sex addiction and the curious case of the missing beets (that particular story is even worse than it sounds).

Jeff told me not to write him back, so I don't, even though it's sort of unfair that he broke up with me but is staying in touch, yet I'm not allowed to reply? While this may be helpful for *his* recovery, hearing from him isn't really helping in *my* recovery.

That being said, not having him in town for the couple weeks following the breakup has been kind of freeing: no calls, no chance of bumping into him at the grocery store or the bagel shop or the YMCA or our favourite café, even though now and then I see someone from behind or from afar who I'm convinced is Jeff and my heart stops for a couple of beats. I'm not going to say "out of sight, out of mind" or anything like that, but it's amazing what a little distance can do for a broken heart. It helps to put it all behind you. If only for a moment.

DECEMBER 23

I'm starting to get back on my feet. Or, as Trish helpfully pointed out while I was attempting to make eye contact with a cute guy at a bar: "Ruthie C's got her groove back!"

"How do you know?" I asked.

"For starters," said Trish, "you've washed your hair."

"Thanks for noticing."

"Also, you're not being boring anymore."

"Um, hello? Trish, I was never boring. It was called *depression*."

"Depression for you, boring for me," she said with a shrug and a sip of her martini. I love Trish. She's just like me.

And she was right, of course. The worst seems to be over. For instance, I am eating ice cream again, instead of applesauce. I am wearing red again, instead of grey. And I've been thinking, with ever-helpful insights from Trish and Lilly, of course, that being single again allows me to pursue my passions more fully. Not just food, but also travel — I've barely been anywhere since starting at school and am seriously getting itchy feet. *Maybe I can convince Trish to come too.* If there was ever a time in the history of our lives to go on a spontaneous, inspiring trip, this is it. Last time, we ended up in Thailand — and look how great that turned out!

But first, it was time to start thinking about my friends. They've been so amazing this past sad little while, so patient and understanding. Next level stuff, to be honest. Food in the fridge, non-stop memes to try to make me laugh, and last week, from the couch, I spotted a new bottle of Dawn beside the sink and wondered how it got there. Then I heard a couple of sharp snaps and Lilly popped out of the kitchen wearing a new pair of yellow dishwashing gloves.

"I'm just going to clean these up for you," she said. "I know how yucky it feels to have a sink full of dishes." She came to clean my kitchen on her one afternoon off, and I hadn't even noticed her arrive.

But now, as if emerging from a fog, I was off the couch, at a bar, and asking Trish about her life again. She confirmed that Andy is totally out of the picture and that she's decided to take both a lesbian and a heterosexual break. Meanwhile, she says Craig is totally back *in* the picture, and that he and Lil have taken to feeding each other while cooing.

"Like babies. I'm happy for them, but it's gross," said Trish.

"It sounds gross," I said. "By the way, what did I do to deserve you two?"

"It's okay Ruthie C., we've all had our ups and downs. It was just your turn."

DECEMBER 24

Sometimes I'm single around the holidays and I don't mind it at all. This is new though, this is post-humiliating-breakup single. But a Christmas Eve spent at Legendary Asian in Chinatown sure wasn't new.

We've had a standing reservation for 14 family members in one of the shabby private rooms in the basement of Legendary Asian every Christmas Eve for the past decade. This is Christmastime for the Jews. It mostly involves fighting over what size of wonton soup to order, how heavy to go on the appetizers, and then trying to appease everyone's tastes by ordering way too much food — the lemon chicken, the sauteed snow pea shoots, the spare ribs, the Shanghai-style fried noodles, the moo shu beef with pancakes, steamed rice, fried rice, sweet and sour chicken balls, the tofu with garlic sauce — and then racing to serve yourself as if there won't be enough for everyone. This year, however, there was something new on the menu: my disastrous love life. Mom had obviously confided in Auntie Brenda, because when cousin Kenny innocently asked, "What's new, Ruthie?" Auntie Brenda almost tore his head off.

"Enough!" she shouted while slamming her hands on the round, red-clothed table. "Leave your poor cousin alone!" A confused Kenny shrugged and returned to his moo shu.

Mom shot Auntie Brenda a look.

Like the days of our lives, so turned the giant lazy Susan.

Teapots were refilled and gossip revealed: the mood at the table took a turn after Kenny's question, so with a simple nod I gave Dad the go-ahead to explain. This is how Cohens deal with their dirty laundry, they let it air dry. Dad stood up as if he was about to give a toast at a wedding. "Ruthie met a wonderful boy," he said, as he held his Chinese teacup aloft. "This kid has Shazamo! like you wouldn't believe. But there were problems. And Jeffy's away now, getting the help he needs. We're all rooting for him." Dad sat back down, looking a little downcast. "And we'll leave it at that."

A kind but somewhat wanting explanation of the sordid events. But that didn't matter to the Cohen Crew. Because they knew that at some point during the car ride home, they could expect an incoming call from Auntie Brenda with all of the juicy details.

I busted open my fortune cookie: "A passionate new romance will appear in your life when you least expect it." LOL.

There was the usual full-body wrestling match over the bill, Auntie Brenda "won," and then we left. "Always such a kibitz," said Dad, jabbing at his teeth with a toothpick as the three of us walked back to the car. "Damn spare ribs. Every time!"

DECEMBER 26

Before I left my soul-sucking job at TelecorpMedia, I spent most of my extra cash and all of my extra time travelling. Some people like to spend their disposable income on leather jackets and whisper-thin TVs with custom-designed surround sound systems. But me? Give me a roundtrip ticket, throw a beach towel or a Eurail Pass into the mix, and you've got yourself a deal.

And even though culinary school didn't end on a high note — *actually*, it did, haha (see, I am clearly better because I am funny again) — I'm still in Chef Antoine's good books, so it seems like I may just have a burgeoning culinary career after all.

I know this because after the final class, Chef invited a small group of us (the crème de la crème, including Claire, and minus Jeff, for obvious reasons) out for drinks and the excellent charcuterie boards served at la Gaffe, where he pulled me aside.

"Bonjour, Ruthie," he said, sipping his flute of Pol Roger.

"Bonjour, Chef," I said, sipping mine.

"You had a very unusual semester, did you not?"

"I did, Chef Antoine," I said, nodding. "I sure did."

"You go up, you go down, like an airplane. But I think you will be a very good chef."

"Do you still think so?" I asked, somewhat surprised but mostly relieved. "Because I really did screw up there at the end."

That said, I screwed up because we ended on pastry with my official nemesis Chef Bertrand, and pastry is obviously my weak spot. Also, I didn't realize how much I had depended on Jeff in pastry class until he was gone. Before he went to rehab, I'd be fretting over failed pastries, like my first batch of baked choux for chocolate éclairs, wondering why they all had soggy bottoms. After some quick troubleshooting, Jeff often had the answers. "It's not your dough," he deduced after giving my failed batch the once-over. "It's your angle. Try piping at 45 degrees and try exerting constant pressure so the éclairs don't bulge in the middle," he said.

"That's what she said," I said.

He was so good at this. And he liked my jokes.

During intensive pastry I was also obviously going through a breakup, which only made matters worse. I should have earned extra marks for simply getting out of bed, brushing my teeth, and actually showing up for class.

"Ah, Chef Bertrand," said Chef Antoine with a dismissive wave of the hand. "Zut alors, Ruthie, zee pastry is not for everyone. I have even told you this many times before. It's your timing, your instincts, your sense of taste — this is what will make you a great chef one day. So, I am curious, what are your plans?"

Had Chef asked me that same question a week earlier I wouldn't have had a clue, so deep was I in my woes about Jeff. Certainly, cooking is what I want to do — school has furthered my skill set in leaps as well as bounds, and being told that I'm officially good at it by professionals makes me want to be a chef even more. I'm so happy to finally be passionate about something. And I'm that much closer to realizing my dream of opening a bistro and watching guests enjoy my style of food.

The other night, being at my favourite Chinese spot with my family helped me better understand what I was looking for. It's more of a feeling right now than a solid vision. I'll need investors for sure... although Bubbe Bobby Grace's inheritance could be the seed money to help get this started. I want to wow them with décor! Dazzle them with technique! (And maybe a soft serve machine?) I want to open up a perfect little spot that would mark my arrival on the city's culinary scene. But... maybe not just yet. I need to take a break first — a little time out to unwind before my school-capping job placement begins.

DECEMBER 27

As luck would have it, turns out Trish needs a break, too.

Trish and I had met for dinner at Café Roma and were eating arugula salad, mushroom-gorgonzola toasts, and pan-fried gnocchi (as per usual), when out of the blue she brought up the fact that she was bored at work, was feeling stifled, and was thinking about changing jobs, or at least ad agencies.

"You're not just saying that for my benefit, are you?" I asked.

"And how, exactly, would my job dissatisfaction benefit you?" asked Trish.

"I guess I was jumping ahead. It's just that it sounds an awful lot to me like you could use a little getaway," I said with a coy cock of the head.

"You think so, do you?" she said with a wry smile, which was all it took for me to know that we were in the exact same headspace. (The fish was on the hook. Time to reel her in.)

"Look, Trish. I just went through some shit, and you just went through some shit. Put us together and we're like a half-finished roll of toilet paper," I said, miming the action of throwing a wad of paper into a toilet and flushing it, followed by some bonus miming of washing my hands with hot soapy water and then using a wall-mounted hand dryer.

"Go on," she said with undeniable interest.

"I just got dumped by an amazing guy who caused me to drug my entire class," I continued. "And you just dumped an unreliable lesbian who turned out to be a total dick... Hey, isn't it funny how women can be dicks, just like men?" I realized aloud.

"No, not so funny," said Trish. "And Andy wasn't exactly a dick. She definitely had her issues, but I think she was also confused."

"Confused about what?" I asked.

"Confused about me." I didn't dare bring up the fact that Trish had slept with her annual hookup at the Magma party before she and Andy had officially called it quits, but Trish made good sense, since as far as I could tell, Trish was a little confused about Trish as well.

"Do you want to talk about it?" I asked.

"I'm fine, honest," she said in her usual independent Trish way. "I just want to have fun."

The more I thought about it and the more we talked about it, the more having an adventure together made total sense. The stars were aligned. The timing was spot on. It will all be fine perfect.

"Have you got any money saved?" I asked.

"I sure do," said Trish, offering up a rare high-five.

And so, over the course of a dependable Italian meal, we talked each other into taking an eight-day trip to refresh our souls and cleanse our palates. The answer to all of our problems is clear. The answer is France.

DECEMBER 28

Two noteworthy things to report today:
1. Trish and I booked our tickets!
2. FUCKING JEFF STOLE MY FUCKING MONEY!

I tried to book my tickets to Paris, but the credit card attached to my new inheritance account was frozen, so Trish paid for them both, and today I went to the bank to find out what was up so I could transfer her the money. I walked down College Street to my bank.

"Good afternoon," chirped the friendly teller in the purple polyester blouse when it was finally my turn. "How can I help you today?"

"Something is up with my new credit card, and I need it unfrozen so I can go to France, please," I said, squeezing one of the stuffed charity fundraising bears sitting on the counter.

"Fun stuff!" she said, clicking away at her terminal. And then, "Wow, fourth big withdrawal for you lately."

I stopped fiddling with the bear. "What do you mean?"

"These three $10,000 withdrawals from your savings account earlier this month," she said, swinging her screen around so that I could see my recent transaction history, followed by my horror-filled reflection. A wave of nausea washed over me. My legs felt shaky. I clutched the stuffed teddy.

A few minutes later I was sitting in a forest green chair in the office of my regular bank guy, Trevor Jones, drinking a glass of cold water. (I didn't pass out, but it was close.) I like Trevor. He's got a straightforward personality with a buzz cut to match. But I mostly like Trevor because he agreed to give me a $15,000 line of credit when I asked for one, but only if I started an RRSP account first. (Trevor really cares about my future.)

"Do you know of anyone who would have access to your computer and your online password?" he asked in the most sympathetic voice imaginable.

I did. I instantly recalled that not so long-ago day, the word "Snickers" now coming back to haunt me like a bad shawarma.

Jeff and I had returned from an enjoyable afternoon spent taking in a live show (the Whipper Snappers at the Simpleton on Dundas) and were hanging out at my place while I tried to get some Sunday chores done: returning calls, doing the laundry, paying bills, et cetera. I was online at my banking site when Jeff snuck up behind me, started rubbing my earlobes, and casually asked me what my password was.

"Do I look like a moron to you?" I answered while enjoying the gentle massage.

"Don't you trust me, baby?"

"Trust ain't got nothin' to do with it, buddy," I said. "This is business." (Which just happens to be Lesson #487 from Bubbe Bobby Grace.)

"I'll bet I can guess your password," he taunted.

"In your dreams," I said, as I paid off my Visa bill with a couple of clicks.

"Three guesses or less," said Jeff.

"*Fine.*"

His first guess was "1, 2, 3, 4," and I scoffed.

His second guess was "1, 1, 1, 1," and I chortled.

His third guess was "Snickers," and all I could do was look down and say nothing.

"Oh Ruthie, you really are a thief's wet dream," he laughed, and now in my memory I have him greedily rubbing his palms together and licking his lips as he said that.

In my defense, I really did mean to change my password after Jeff had figured it out, but then things got busy with school, and then the breakup happened, and I forgot. Besides — and I don't want to play the victim here or anything — but how could I have possibly known then what I now know about Jeff? Honestly, during that first week after Jeff and I finally got together, I thought we had tried every position in the book. Yet somehow this guy keeps finding new and inventive ways to screw me!

"This is fraud on a pretty sizable scale, Ruthie," Trevor Jones told me as he got up to shut the door of his glassed-in office. "Your boyfriend could face serious jail time for this."

"Ex-boyfriend," I said, feeling the need to correct him.

"Sorry, of course."

Trevor explained that, without knowing it, I couldn't have made things easier for Jeff. All he had to do was go to my bookmarked bank site and my saved access card digits when I wasn't home, enter my online password, and then he could transfer all of the money he wanted straight into his personal account. Especially since he knew I rarely looked at this new account.

"But shouldn't there also be a security question?" I protested.

"Looks like he was able to answer that, too," said Trevor, swinging the screen around so I could see the correct answer: DOLLFACE.

Sigh. At least Jeff listened.

The good news is he didn't completely clean me out. There is still $15,969.45 of Bubbe Bobby Grace's inheritance left in the account, so even if my dream of opening a restaurant or café had evaporated overnight, there was still some hope for Jeff, right? He didn't leave me destitute, after all.

Trevor said he'd get in touch with the bank's fraud squad to see what, if anything, he could do about getting my money back, but he also said that it would take a while before he'd know anything for sure, and advised me to go away to France, as planned, if my heart was still in it.

"Where's your ex-boyfriend now?" he asked, looking as though he'd like to punch Jeff in the face.

"Rehab," I said with a defeated shrug.

"Are you in touch with him?"

"Sort of." And then I wondered how many more letters Jeff was going to write me before he got around to mentioning the little fact that he had bilked me out of $30K!

"Do you want to press charges, Ruthie?"

"Let me think about it," I sighed while getting up to leave Trevor Jones's office. "I'll let you know in a couple of weeks."

DECEMBER 29
3:27 a.m.
(Technically it is December 30 but I haven't slept yet, so it doesn't count.) I'm just lying here staring at the ceiling, marinating in my feelings, wondering what to call all of this. Is it a humiliation or something even more sinister — something so deeply hurtful you don't know which way is up anymore? I mean, what do you call having your heart ripped

out, your money stolen, and your future highjacked all in one fell swoop by one of your favourite people in the world? So here I am, eyes wide open, wondering if it was all a lie: every kiss, every laugh, every lightly toasted sesame seed bagel. I think I'm still in shock. In a million years I never would have considered myself the type of person who could be an easy mark. I've always felt savvy and confident with a good head on my shoulders and a nice dose of Nancy Drew running through my veins. How could I have been tricked in so many ways?

My parents and Lilly say it has nothing to do with me. That I wasn't wrong about Jeff. That he has a disease. That he may have been deceitful, but he has a good heart. That it's all part of his addiction. But how do they know? What do any of us really know? Trish isn't being quite as generous about Jeff, and I appreciate that about her. She's saying everything I want to hear, like, "Next time I see that guy he's getting a punch in the throat."

This evening, Trish was comforting me during a sudden crying jag while we were going through our packed itinerary: "We're going to France, Ruthie. You've got lots to look forward to. It's all going to be alright. In fact, it's going to be magnifique." And while some people may have cancelled an expensive trip once they realized they'd been robbed of $30,000, I remain an optimist and am certain that somehow, some way, I'm going to get at least some of my money back. Besides, Bubbe Bobby Grace would have wanted me to go on with the show. "You only live once, dollface," she'd always say, "so may as well live it up while you can!"

DECEMBER 30

Even though he said not to, I wrote Jeff a letter. This isn't about what Jeff wants anymore. Trevor Jones said it was a necessary first step in retrieving my money — figuring out where it was and how much (if any) was left. He said that we needed to create a paper trail as part of the investigation and to keep the letter simple. So, I did:

> Dear Jeffrey,
>
> It has come to my attention that you have stolen $30,000 from my bank account. I was wondering when and how you planned on returning it.
> — Ruth Cohen

DECEMBER 31

It's New Year's Eve for most, but for Trish and me it's takeoff time to France! I'm glad I'll be on a dark plane at the stroke of midnight instead of looking around for someone to kiss once the ball drops. Is it crazy that I still want to kiss Jeff? I feel like such a fool! Thankfully, for the next ten days, I'll be concentrating on things other than Jeff. Namely, incredible Michelin-starred restaurants from the French Alps to Lyon to Paris. Chef Antoine was nice enough to reach out to his culinary contacts and we got last-minute reservations at a handful of the best restaurants in the country. And we're so excited! This trip will cost me a good chunk of the remainder of my inheritance, but it will be worth it: a grand eating adventure before I start working as a chef at my second-term placement, and then part two of my new life!

So, here I go, unencumbered, with my bestie Trish along for the ride. Tonight we may be stepping onto a transatlantic flight, but tomorrow morning we'll be landing in a new year, in a new country — in the culinary capital of the world! We'll be eating at old guard, new guard, and everything in between. I've heard so many of Chef Antoine's amazing stories about the good old days in France. Now, the plan is to make our own memories.

Inheritance Update: I don't want to talk about it.

Balance remaining: $15,969.45

January

JANUARY 1

We landed at Charles de Gaulle, booted it to Paris Gare de Lyon, and then took the train to Saint-Gervais-les-Bains-Le Fayet. After another half-hour bus ride from the train station (thanks to Trish for having navigated all of this — she has the gift), we were in the shadow of Mont Blanc, where the horse-drawn calèches trundle après-skiers along cobblestone streets in the mountainside resort of Megève. We came to this specific town because it's a glamorous base camp for Haute-Savoie cuisine, so much so that the lure of the restaurants has started eclipsing the soft-pack moguls of the famous ski hills. Trish grabbed us cups of mulled wine from one of the fireside al fresco bars, and we stood there, sipping while taking it all in.

"Is this place for real?" asked Trish, struck, as I was, by the storybook perfection of it all.

"It seems to be, but I can't quite believe it myself," I responded, eyes wide to the winter wonderment on view. We are smitten, charmed, giddy even. And we had only been in Megève for 20 minutes.

Trish and I continued on, mulled wine in hand, trudging through the snowy town, beholding the bell tower and skating rink, the fur hats and designer ski suits, the twinkly lights and the grand Christmas tree in the middle of the square. Apparently, the honour of lighting the tree this year went to local hero Chef Romaine Renault, whose restaurant, Sel et Poivre, a pilgrimage for alpine gourmands such as Trish and me, had just earned its third Michelin star. And we're eating there tomorrow night! Exhausted (Trish suddenly looks cross-eyed), tonight we'll sleep. But tomorrow, we'll eat!

JANUARY 2
10 a.m.
This morning, I woke up with a giant lump in my throat.

"Uh oh," I told Trish. "I think I'm getting sick." But when I told her my one symptom (the giant lump in my throat), she said, "It's okay to be sad, you know. I don't mind."

"I'm not sad anymore," I said. "I've mourned. And now I'm in France with you. In Megève! I'm good."

"Jeff wasn't who you thought he was. That's a new wound that needs licking."

"Trish, I know you're all self-evolved now, but please..."

"No jokes, Ruthie C. Let's talk about this."

She handed over the latte she had picked up for me on the way home from her morning run. (Can you imagine going for a run while on vacation in FRANCE?)

"Okay," I started (I hate when the girls make me do this). "I think I was in love with Jeff, and I hadn't felt that way since my instant connection with Dean in Thailand. But then Jeff, this person I thought I knew really well, turned out to be some sort of gorgeous illusion. So now I feel dumped and duped. And I don't know where to put the love."

"Atta girl. Let down those walls." She tore apart a flakey croissant. I liked her nonchalant half-focus. Trish knows that props and feigned disinterest always make me feel freer to talk.

"I'm also afraid I don't know how to have a real relationship because I keep attracting or choosing the wrong type of guy: coworkers, world travellers, addicts . . . I think my instincts are off."

"You definitely have a type. Let's call it 'unavailable.' The 'what-ifs,'" she said with air quotes. "But let's let Lilly delve into that part of the equation a little deeper when we get home. Her psych placement last summer usually comes in handy." (We all have our roles in this friendship.)

"I also don't think I know how to maintain a lasting relationship," I worried.

"Excuse me?" she said, full attention now directly on me. "What are me and Lilly? Chopped liver?"

"That's different," I said. "You're my girls."

"It's not different," she said, picking croissant shards from my bed. "You just need to find someone who loves you as much as we do. Even when you're being annoying."

I suddenly felt much better. Though the lump in my throat had tripled in size.

Midnight
WHAT A NIGHT!

Sel et Poivre's grand yet woodsy alpine room! The feature wall studded with 14 cuckoo clocks! Pea-size red cabbage and turnip gnocchi in a horseradish broth! This place turns humble ingredients into dishes that are as dazzling as an Oscar-night Valentino.

"I love that we're in a Michelin-starred restaurant and people are wearing woolen sweaters and toques," said Trish, as we nervously took our seats.

"Literally the first time in our lives that we're not underdressed. Only, our sweaters are Zara, not handmade macrame cashmere Brunello Cucinellis," I said, tipping my head to my right so that Trish would check out the glamazon two tables over. "I just read about her sweater in the inflight magazine. It costs $15,000."

We then realized that we were, in fact, underdressed as usual.

During the fish course, Chef Romaine Renault came out to chat up the tables and told Trish and me that Michelin stars no longer gave chefs immunity when it comes to sustainable cooking, not even in France. "We used to put a tiny perfect square of sea bass in the centre of the plate, but we no longer do that," he said. Instead, there's white flaky fera fish from Lake Geneva, decked out in lemon meringues and citrusy buttered broth. "We used all the parts of the fera, all the trimmings," explained Chef Renault. "I like to do the technique, but you don't know that I've done the technique." He reminded me of Chef Antoine in all the best ways.

Next came the rib-sticking Savoie charm you expect of the French Alps: veal shanks, carved tableside and served with shared crusty pots of potatoes au gratin burbling with reblochon. Trish appeared to be levitating above her leather bucket seat. "Ruthie! These potatoes!" she practically screamed.

"Cuckoo!" went one of the clocks, as if in agreement.

Tonight was the perfect expression of the type of French hospitality Chef Antoine has always talked about. From the food on the plate to the wine in the glass to the cuckoos on the wall to the kindness of Chef Renault. I don't think I'll ever forget it.

JANUARY 3

"Morning, Ruthie," said Trish, handing me today's latte in bed (a new tradition I could really get used to). Trish is a morning person. I am not.

"Sorry about all of the farting last night," she said.

"That's okay," I lied. "The cheese?"

"*The cheese.* You've got ten minutes to get packed and ready before we head to Lyon," she said.

Four hours and two train transfers later, thanks again to Trish's navigational prowess, we dropped our bags at our petite hotel, Ici, in the centre of town. Most people consider Paris the culinary capital of France, but Chef Antoine says it's actually Lyon. We came to find out why.

And he said our first stop should be les Halles Bocuse. ~~Yes~~ Oui, Chef!

Named after Chef Paul Bocuse, Lyon's favourite son, les Halles is a lovely food hall full of restaurants and shops where you can sip Champagne and suck back oysters for breakfast while picking up some specialty ingredients. The food is amazing, but it turns out the people manning the stalls and restaurants are the real MVPs. At la Mère Ripert, the owner has been making and serving cheeses with a smile for decades. You can tell watching us ooh and ahh over her oozing stinky cheeses brings her as much joy as it does Trish and me. Everyone is so kind, talented, and passionate that we've started questioning our personalities. "Are we jerks?" I asked Trish, at Colette Charcuterie Traiteur, a mecca for homespun sausages and pâtés, where the 80-year-old owner, Colette Ricci, has been working for 63 years and told us she had actually *been* a close friend of Paul Bocuse. Trish made her pose for a picture with me, then Colette snapped her fingers and suddenly there was an impromptu indoor picnic before us, crusty country bread, great slabs of pâté, and bottles of Mâcon-Villages Paul Bocuse wine. Honestly, I don't know why everyone says the French are so rude.

JANUARY 4
10:30 a.m.

We just finished FaceTiming with Lilly and Craig while eating gloriously stinky oozing cheeses and red wine in bed. Bear in mind, this was our brunch, and we were "morning tipsy."

"Are you guys pacing yourselves?" asked a slightly concerned-looking Lilly.

"Have you *tried* the cheeses in France?" Trish responded.

"Touché," said Lilly.

Craig, who was shuffling by in the background in slippers and a white robe, leaned in to give us a big "Bonjour!" We're all so happy to have Craig back in the fold. We just can't help ourselves.

Lilly and Craig are on a little weekend getaway of their own at a new luxury retreat on the outskirts of Algonquin Park. You bunk in a small prefab cabin on the shores of a snowy lake, and all of your activities, classes, and wholesome organic food are included. Craig gave us a quick tour of the cabin and it looks super cozy. They had already been cross-country skiing to watch the sunrise and were going to go sound bathing soon, whatever that is. Seeing them happy makes me happy. And it gives me hope. They were able to figure things out after a massive curveball...

2 p.m.

We hit the cobblestone around 11. I had warned Trish that today wouldn't be nearly as fancy of a food day, as we'd be visiting a bouchon or two. We had learned all about them in school and I was anxious to see them IRL.

As I explained to Trish, found only in Lyon, bouchons are a specific type of restaurant, born of the need for 18th-century horse groomers, coach drivers, and the city's famed silk workers to have hot, hearty meals, like tripe stew, as early as 4 a.m. There used to be many but today, there are only 20 true bouchons left in the city, according to l'Association de défense des bouchons Lyonnais, which certifies restaurants as "authentic" each year.

"Well thank you, Professor Cohen," said Trish, after my bouchon primer.

We were told to stop by our first bouchon to meet Chef Antoine's friend Yves Roblienne, because not only does he own an authentic bouchon, but Chef had sent me to France with a very heavy one-litre tin of Canadian grade A amber maple syrup for him that I was thrilled to finally unload. Yves greeted us at his handsome and historic restaurant with a communard, the Lyonnais Kir made from red wine and black currant liqueur. (It tastes just like Manischewitz.) Yves explained that though the hours and menus have changed — these days people aren't hankering for tripe stew in the wee hours of the morning — the unique "atmosphere and spirit" remain. Yves's bouchon wasn't open for the day yet, so he encouraged us to check out Daniel & Pierre for lunch. He told us he was going home to make crêpes to go along with his Canadian maple syrup.

"This is just the best trip ever," said Trish as we hobbled down the cobblestone streets of Vieux Lyon (a UNESCO World Heritage Site), on our way to the next bouchon. "And I'll say it again: if I'm loving it this much, I can't imagine how your head is still attached to your shoulders."

"Because my mind is blown?" I asked.

"Correct," said Trish. "I'll bet you're already feeling pretty inspired."

"One hundred percent inspired," I answered. "One thousand percent grateful." (Thanks for the awesome trip, Bubbe Bobby Grace!) "And one million percent hungry."

7:40 p.m.
I just woke up from the most decadent food coma/nap in the history of the world. I feel like I may have even been dead for a little while, my sleep was so deep. Here's what caused it . . .

"I'm not eating tripe — or sweetbreads," Trish had warned when we arrived at Daniel & Pierre around noon. She still wasn't over the fact that I had tricked her into eating the thymus gland of a cow during school.

The cafeteria-style lighting made for an inauspicious welcome. Long shared tables were crammed with diners who looked to be part of a football team, digging into plates piled high with saucisson, calf brains, and sautéed tripe. The room itself was steamy, rowdy, and if I'm being honest, a little stinky. (Damned me and my heightened sense of smell.) At first, Trish was taken aback by the raucous scene but rallied once she read the menu and eventually relaxed into the jolly atmosphere. We grabbed the last two seats at a communal table near the front. Our bow-tied waiter plopped down a basket of bread on the checked tablecloth, and glasses of house wine were poured as soon as we had answered the question "red or white?" We wanted to try just about everything on the menu. We didn't, but we came close: pâté en croûte (foie gras, sausage, and jellée wrapped in a buttery crust), AOC Bresse chicken — "the best in the world," said a seatmate. It came jacked with morels and a woodsy, winey cream sauce. Incredible! Sides of Lyonnais (fried) potatoes and gooey mac and cheese instantly rocketed their way into Trish's "best-of" territory.

"Do you think someone can actually be addicted to potatoes?" wondered Trish.

"Absolutely not," I answered, even though if such a thing was possible, she was coming dangerously close. "Keep shovelling."

Meanwhile, old-fashioned desserts like crème brûlée and floating islands proved that they're classics for a reason. "A Lyonnais customer is a difficult customer because he has such a refined palate," offered a proud local to my left before letting out a satisfied belch.

Trish and I belched right back.

JANUARY 5
9 a.m.

Trish went out for her run and while I'm lying here waiting for her to return with my morning latte, I'm thinking about Jeff. I'm thinking about all of the dishes we made together in class that I had experienced in Lyon so far. I'm thinking about how he would have loved Megève and Chef Renault, and all the cuckoos on the wall. I'm thinking about how comfortable this bed is, and how fluffy the feather duvet is, and I'm thinking about how we could have had some amazing times in this hotel room together. Too bad he had to blow it with blow.

5 p.m.

The weather has been gorgeous, and Lyon is such an easy city to get around. In addition to all of our truly memorable meals, we've been hitting cafés, going for long walks, checking out the galleries and museums, and Trish bought a forest green fedora that I think is going to be her new personality. We also went back to les Halles Bocuse because we simply cannot get enough of the place, and because we wanted to try the pink praline tart. I can't remember Chef Antoine talking about the pink pralines of Lyon, but shame on him, because they're a really big deal here. At first, we were put off by the garish pink colour of the candied almonds, but the more we walked around, the more we realized that pink pralines were a speciality of Lyon — all the patisseries looked like French Baker Barbie had set up shop.

"This is the best thing I've ever tasted," said Trish as she bit into a tender sable base with a pink praline caramel on top. *Fair enough*, I thought, but Trish has been saying that at every meal. The thing is, she's not wrong.

"You know who would have loved this?" she asked of the tart.

Bubbe Bobby Grace.

"Bubbe Bobby Grace," she said. "Can you please make this when we get home?"

"Of course," I answered, while buying a 500 gram bag of the pink candied almonds. "But don't mention home just yet."

"Sorry. I know some not-so-great-stuff is waiting for you when we get back. But remember, we're having the best time and I can't wait for you to take all of this inspiration back to Toronto. Imagine, my friend Ruthie Cohen, opening a bistro featuring roast chicken with a booze sauce, cheesy potatoes, and pink Lyonnaise tarts? You'll be the toast of the town!"

"That actually sounds perfect . . ." I agreed.

JANUARY 6

Tonight, we got another two Michelin stars under our belts at one of Lyon's oldest and most famous restaurants, la Mère Brazier.

"Well, I guess they all can't be the best meal ever after all," said Trish before heading off to wash up for bed.

Once again, thanks to Chef Antoine's connections we snagged a coveted reservation for la Mère Brazier's famous chicken, AND the handsome executive chef (Laurent LeBlanc) came out to meet us. All sexy stubble with a lick of grey in his slicked-back hair. "We are eating very well in France," he bragged, with a flourish of his hand. "You will not find this dish anywhere else, not even the Alps." He was describing the restaurant's 100-year-old recipe for poularde de Bresse demi-deuil that we — and every other table — had ordered. He said the chicken, with its slate blue legs, from nearby Bresse, was cooked for four and a half hours at 162°F in a fragrant poaching liquid with sliced black truffles tucked under its skin. The chicken is then carved tableside and covered in a white port cream sauce. I love thinking about the fact that two other pals, just like Trish and me, probably enjoyed this exact same chicken dish in this exact some room, over a hundred years ago.

"I hope the chicken is as yummy as him," said Trish as soon as he had headed back to the kitchen.

"I can't wait to taste *his* creamy sauce," I added.

"RUTHIE!" yelped Trish. Then we both started laughing and I got the hiccups from my aperitif. Long story short, he *did* turn out to be yummier than the meal.

"Is it wrong that I liked the chicken at the bouchon more than the one at a Michelin-starred restaurant?" asked Trish.

"No, it *was* better," I confirmed. "In fact, it was twice as good, and a tenth of the price."

"The way tonight's chicken was cooked just seemed bizarre to me," she said. "The meat was overdone and mushy and the skin was flabby." It's true. At the bouchon, not only was it perfectly cooked, but they had also added truffle under the crisped skin of the rotisseried Bresse chicken, and had served it with a gravy boat of a similar luscious white port cream sauce. I think it's possible to improve upon tradition without breaking with it. A little bit of improvisation — an updated cooking method, a different cook time, a lighter sauce, or even serving the sauce on the side to retain a crisped skin — shouldn't be against the rules. It should be encouraged. Celebrated, even! Imagine if every chef stuck to the exact same old recipes? Nothing new would ever happen. We'd still be eating medieval recipes like nettle pudding and bone broth. (Wait a minute...)

Rules, rules, there are so many rules!

1. No fish or seafood with cheese: Well then, say goodbye to one of the best sandwiches there is: the tuna melt. Or yummy crab dip. Or the lobster Thermidor that helped win us the Silver Platter.
2. Patience is a virtue: Sometimes I think the French make recipes so long and intricate just to kill spontaneity. There's more than one way to get to the finish line, Pierre!
3. Always follow the recipe: That's how you get a dish like the poularde de Bresse demi-deuil, served in modern times but stuck in the distant past.

In fact, the 100-year-old Bresse chicken recipe reminds me of the downside of tradition. Chef Antoine had brought this up in class on several occasions. He said while most French recipes cannot be improved upon, some can, and that's where critical thinking comes in. "We cannot blindly follow zee past," he said. "We should remain true to it, bien sûr, but we must also think for ourselves." (That was the day we found out he hated cassoulet.)

I wonder if this is what my cuisine could be ... rooted in the classics, but lighter and brighter — with a dash of me. It's like Bubbe Bobby Grace used to say, "Doing the footwork is important, but always follow your schnoz."

JANUARY 7

Paris, here we come! Trish obviously booked the train for us. (I asked if she minded being in charge of getting us everywhere and she said why would she mind doing her favourite thing?) She also mentioned it would take about two and a half hours to get there, so we should probably grab lunch at the station. I had done *my* research and knew there was a restaurant in Gare de Lyon called le Train Bleu, famous for its ultra-luxurious décor. We took a peek — it looked like the Sistine Chapel, only even fancier! We weren't dressed for it (nor could we afford it), so we got baguette sandwiches from an artisan-minded grab-and-go chain called Picto instead.

JANUARY 8

One of the things I love about this city is that you can walk 27,320 steps in a single day and not even notice because your eyes, your mind, and your soul are too busy focusing on all the gorgeousness of everything around you. And then there's the food. THE FOOD. We've found some major French culinary rules being (lovingly) broken in Paris. Take tonight's dinner for example.

I had read about ChaYum in a travel story in the *New York Times* and was immediately intrigued because it fuses two of my faves — French and Chinese — to make, in my mind, a perfect choice for our last meal. Chef Simone Alline and her Hong Kong–born husband, Ken Chi Chan (the restaurant's tea steward), are doing something truly unique for France. Butter and cream are almost non-existent (zut alors!), French enamel and copper pots are swapped out for steam heat and fast frying in woks. It also wasn't stuffy like a lot of the traditional places. The timber ceiling, curved stone-and-grass entrance, and pretty watercolour lily-pad mural whispered feng shui, not Michelin star. (But guess what? They have one of those, too.) No starched tablecloths on the eight tables, just bare wood and smooth chopsticks . . . Ugh, it's *so* cool. Chef Simone is clearly inspired by classical French cooking but she's totally making it her own. SHE's so cool.

For instance, her "half-cooked" potatoes are shredded, poached in oil, drained, and tossed with a lip-smacking homemade XO sauce, and then topped with a perfect piece of steamed turbot. It's not your traditional, beautifully plated French meal, but I swear it has raw sex appeal and it's so good.

"These potatoes!" moaned Trish (as per usual).

Next we had Franco-Chinoise seared sea scallops with spinach and Chinese herbs lolling in a vaguely Thai broth, and they were paired with an orange wine from Alsace. Ying/yang, baby! But the kicker was the steamed Chinese "brioche" buns in lieu of baguettes that came with the dish, which, taking a cue from the tables around us, we ripped and dipped into every last drop of that broth. Honestly, it tasted like the future of French food to me.

"Hey Trish," I said, catching her in the act of licking her chopsticks. "Could you see me working in a place like this?"

"Maybe. But probably not."

What. "Why not?"

"Well, even though this place is comfortably casual, it's still pretty precise: one piece of fried spinach on each scallop, a fancy tea service," she whispered. "It doesn't seem very you."

"But I think I could learn a lot from a higher-end spot. Everything is still so new to me."

"That's true," she agreed. "I don't really know how this all works. I think when you see it, you'll know it's a fit. It may be a trial-and-error sort of thing, but it sounds like you're fully inspired, so that's a great start."

"I sure am," I said, as I looked past the curved stone entrance and out onto the streets of Paris.

Suddenly, I couldn't wait to get home and start cooking.

JANUARY 11

Just got home from Friday night dinner at Mom and Dad's. I am still jet-lagged so found Mom and Dad a little more annoying than usual tonight. Mom had just set down the brisket, noodle kugel, and tzimmes: "Honey," she said, continuing an earlier conversation about Jeff stealing $30,000 from her beloved daughter. "Don't let money get in the way of your wonderful dreams. How is Jeffrey doing anyway?"

I don't know about Jeff, but I'll tell you how I'm doing: reality has hit *me* like an open-handed slap to the face. (Think: Chris Rock at the Oscars.) BUT, my parents felt so bad about Jeff stealing the majority of my remaining inheritance from Bubbe Bobby Grace, that they topped off my savings account as a surprise consolation gift when I returned home from Paris.

"Just enough to get you past that emotional barrier," said Dad, thoughtfully rubbing his five o'clock shadow. "I'm not sure what it is, kiddo, but there's just something about that 10K mark — ten thousand dollars really means something. Like a sink full of dishes."

Dad is being great; super sympathetic without making me feel like a total loser for being taken to the cleaners by Jeff. And Mom is being pretty cool about it, too.

"Now Jeff-o is what you'd call a man's man," said Dad as he passed the brisket. Eye roll. The term "man's man" makes me want to spew my carrot tzimmes. "He's got Shazamo! It's not something you can learn, this Shazamo! You've got to be born with it," he said between bites, as if I was hearing about Shazamo! for the very first time.

"So, you think that Jeff was born with it, do you?" I asked, trying hard not to let my rising anger get the best of me. "Then let me ask you this, wise parents of mine: Is breaking my heart part of his great Shazamo! appeal? Or the fact that Jeff is a drug addict and a liar and a thief, not to mention a complete failure when it comes to cooking tender rabbit dishes? Is that all normal and okay in your wonderful world of Shazamo!?" Okay fine, I didn't exactly get my rising anger under control. But come ON.

"Okay, honey, simmer down," said Mom. "We didn't mean to upset you. You two seemed so well suited for each other that we couldn't help but like Jeffrey. Besides, what have we always taught you about forgiveness?"

"That Jeff isn't a bad person, he just did a bad thing," I grumbled into my kugel.

"That's right, honey," said Mom. "Jeffrey did some truly horrible things, but he's not beyond redemption is he? Haven't we all made mistakes? Don't we all deserve a second chance? Ruthie, all we want is for him to get the help he needs so that he can get back to his life. You kids worked so hard this semester."

"I don't know about rabbit," added Dad, "but I'll never forget the fried chicken Jeff-o made for us that time. Remember that?" he said, turning to Mom, who nodded and smiled as if she was reminiscing about her wedding night. "Listen, kiddo," Dad continued, forking more brisket onto his plate. "You've brought a few boys around here in your time, and some of them have been jerks and some have been wimps and some have been perfectly nice. But your mom and I had never seen you happier than when you were with Jeff, and as far as I'm concerned that's got to count for something." Dad took a few moments to chew his slightly tough meat. "Yes, he acted like a total schmuck. He did drugs, he lied, he thieved. But you know what? He was in a bad way. Wasn't right in the head. *Unwell.*" Dad was right. Drug addiction is a sickness. But still . . . "Remember your cousin Eric?" he asked. "Remember how sick with worry Annie and Stan were over him? That whole mess lasted for years. *Years.* The hell that family went through."

"Such hell," said Mom, shaking her head while sopping up brisket sauce with another slice of challah. "And now, ten years later, he's perfectly fine," she added. "Married, with four healthy children."

"People can turn themselves around is all we're saying, kiddo," said Dad. "But remember the Cohen family 'two strike' rule, Ruthie. I don't want my little girl being put through the ringer. You understand what I'm saying? Two strikes, and Jeff's out." Why didn't my parents understand that Jeff was already out? "It's one thing to be fair," Dad continued, "but it's another to be a fool. And things can get especially tricky when Shazamo! is involved."

And just like that he finished his sermon as quickly as it had begun, having spotted the blueberry crumble pie I made as a thank-you gift, sitting on the sideboard. It's his absolute favourite — it has an amazingly crispy, almost salty crust, a sweet, buttery crumble topping, and is totally jammed with berries.

Deep sigh. I guess I can't really blame my parents for being on Team Jeff. After all, they've clearly fallen for him, and I know how that feels (and Jeff's fried chicken truly is great). There was just something about Jeff that got everyone and their mothers (and apparently fathers) hot under the collar.

Still, are my parents right? Does Jeff have something other than a killer fried chicken recipe up his sleeve? Could redemption be in the cards?

Only my banker knows for sure.

JANUARY 14

Damn Officer Yonkers. Damn you to HELL!

After thanking me for the pretty box of (slightly crushed) pistachio macarons that I had bought for him at the Charles de Gaulle airport gift shop, Trevor Jones motioned for me to take a seat in his glassed-in office. And then he got down to business, explaining that each bank has a "corporate security" team that is made up of ex-cops and former RCMP officers who work with police to launch investigations such as mine.

"I've been liaising with Officer Yonkers on your case," said Trevor.

"And?" I was literally on the edge of my seat.

"Whether the case is considered fraud or not hinges on if you actually shared your password with Jeff," he said, casually removing his glasses and wiping the lenses clean with a silky blue cloth.

Noting that my facial expression had no doubt changed from jovial to one of deep sadness, Trevor went into a bit more detail. "Now, I understand the whole online banking story as you told it to me, Ruthie, but I'm afraid there could be some personal responsibility on your part."

"But it was just a lucky guess!" I protested. "How could I have possibly known that Jeff was some sort of secret genius code breaker?"

"No offense — and believe me I'm not trying to blame you for what happened. You know I've been working hard at getting you your money back, but let's be honest. Jeff knows you a whole lot better than I do, and 'Snickers' would have been *my* second guess for your password."

"Well then," I said, slightly defeated, "you would have beaten Jeff by one guess. But how did you know?"

Trevor looked me dead in the eyes and said, "I have never met with you when you have not been eating — or have not mentioned eating — a Snickers bar. At the end of the day, Ruthie, if Jeff simply guessed right and broke into your account..."

"Which is exactly what happened."

"... which you *say* is exactly what happened, most banks, including this bank, would guarantee that you get all your money back. It's our policy," he said. "You can even read the 'online fraud guarantee' on our website."

"This is great news, Trevor. Yay! I'm relieved. And excited!... You don't seem happy."

"It's that darned password of yours, Ruthie. It was just so guessable that I'm afraid it might come back to haunt you."

"Meaning?"

"Officer Yonkers is not at all happy that your password was 'Snickers.'"

JANUARY 15

I got a letter from Jeff. A super long letter about stealing my money. The letter arrived while Trish and I were in France, but I just got the courage to open it now. In it, he came clean about everything and said at the time he truly believed his life was at risk owing to a depraved drug dealer, blah, blah, blah. But Jeff also said that, with the help of his rehab counsellors, he would be in touch with the bank and would tell them he was completely to blame, was going to try to repay them in full, and he planned to beg the bank to give me my money back for now, because it would take him a while to do so on his own, blah, blah, blah. Seriously, has anyone ever told this guy that Shazamo! doesn't work on LARGE FINANCIAL INSTITUTIONS?

JANUARY 16
11 a.m.

I can't really tell if it's good news or bad news for the restaurant industry, but ever since I got back from France, just about every place I've reached out to for a stage to finish off my diploma has said yes, sight unseen. Claire also got hired right away at Practique, the bakery in Yorkville she'd been coveting.

Part of it is because I went to a great school and graduated at the top of my class (thanks to Jeff dropping out and bumping me into his slot), but it also didn't hurt that Chef Antoine gave me a glowing letter of recommendation, not to mention the fact that I happened to win a national cooking competition. Within a few days of being home, I had my pick of a dozen of the best restaurants in town.

And today, I started my very first job as a real-life chef at my top pick. Sort of! I lasted exactly 17 minutes, but I swear it wasn't my fault...

I chose the hottest spot in Toronto right now, EchoEcho — a whitewashed temple of molecular gastronomy in a high-rise room cantilevered out over King Street. The young executive chef is a former student of Chef Antoine's, and Chef cautioned me that while Chef Nick Zane is truly a talent, Chef Antoine wasn't so sure his particular style of cooking was the right fit for me.

"It is all of that fuddy-duddy-muddy business," said Chef Antoine.

"I know we didn't learn much about molecular gastronomy in school, Chef," I said, accurately deciphering his sentiment. "But I think some of the techniques are really interesting. It's sort of like the first new thing to happen to cooking since, well, the creation of French cuisine."

"You torch zee crème brûlée: this is molecular gastronomy. You poach a chicken: this is molecular gastronomy. You reduce a sauce: this is molecular gastronomy. This 'new' cuisine that you are talking about is nothing new. Think of the cuisine we have been making in class. Escoffier. Paul Bocuse. Authentic French food has few ingredients. We know this. Where zee magic lies, is in zee *technique*. Once upon a time a creative chef dreamed up topping custard with torched sugar. Do you understand what I am saying? Only now, instead of using classic technique and time, they use zee super-fast chemicals and machinery to impress zee diners with no tastebuds," said Chef, with more disdain than really seemed necessary.

"But Chef, don't you feel that thinking about food in a new way and moving things forward is a good thing? Remember how I told you about ChaYum?"

"Ahh, but you don't seem to understand what I am saying. That was not molecular cooking, those chefs were cooking fresh ideas based on French technique. There is a new generation of French chefs who are taking their heritage and beliefs and infusing them into dishes that are familiar but with a new interpretation. This, I think, is wonderful. Magnifique! This is what I see for you. Like zee dish you made with the rösti potatoes, caramelized apples, and crème fraiche." Chef said there's always a well-tested recipe one can follow, but nothing beats the magique of experimenting and making it perfect for you. He said the problem with molecular cooking is that it goes too far. "It wants to take everything that we know and make it go poof! — like zee bad magic. It is too much up here," he said pointing to his noggin, "when it should be right here," he continued, placing the same hand over his heart.

"Can't it be both?" I asked.

"Non."

Hrmph. So, if I listened to what I thought Chef was saying, I should probably trust myself when it comes to the Jeff predicament, too. But which to trust, my heart or my head?

Anyways, enough of Jeff. I was giddy with excitement as Nick Zane walked me through his gleaming white dining room this morning, and then into his kitchen.

His kitchen was unlike anything I had seen before, as bright and clinical as a hospital operating room, but instead of heart monitors and scalpels, it was full of induction burners, anti-griddles, and thermal circulators. I immediately sensed I was in trouble. But charming Chef Zane, famous for manipulating ingredients into dishes where taste, aroma, texture, mouthfeel, appearance, and presentation all contribute to the overall sensory experience of the food, somehow made me feel at home. "I want to duplicate the scents of fond food memories in my kitchen." I was intrigued by what he was saying. So, I pushed my fears aside and tried to keep an open mind.

He showed me one dish (in a series of 22 intricate courses that amount to a foodie tour of never-never land) that the team had been working on. They had fashioned a skewer out of a 15-centimetre oak branch, complete with dead leaves, and threaded it with marinated pigeon breast, candy apple, and a cube of sage-flecked cider gelatinized with agar-agar. The skewered delicacies were then tempura-battered and fried, and the branch's dead leaves were torched and then snuffed just before serving, so that the dish arrived tableside still smouldering. As Chef Zane explained it, people immediately connect the nostalgic smell with raking leaves. "It's a very powerful thing when you use aromas in cooking," he said. "The sense of smell is a potent memory trigger." Yes! So important!

No two ways about it, it *was* interesting. But within moments I also realized it was perhaps *too interesting* for me. Looking around I noticed there were no flames, just the sous-vide cookers. There was no lively banter, no yelling or tomato throwing, no hustle, and definitely no bustle. Just an eerie silence broken by the odd beep from one of the many timers set to remind the stable of young, meticulously groomed male chefs who were weighing out food chemicals on electronic scales when to retrieve the vacuum-sealed plastic bags filled with lobster, lamb, pork, and beef from their perfectly calibrated water baths. I felt like I had gotten off the wrong train in a foreign country (yet again). Or maybe even off the wrong planet this time! We hadn't learned any of this in school. I literally didn't know how to work a single thing in the entire kitchen, and the chefs around me with their pockets full of tweezers, didn't seem eager to help me either. (Where are Jeff and *his* tweezers when you need them?)

Chef Antoine was right. I was lost there. This wasn't where I belonged. I explained to Chef Zane that as much as I admired his work it was all just too mathy for me.

He understood. "It's not for everyone." He smiled as he ushered me through the kitchen and out the back door.

Current Situation
- Jobless because am too dumb to even work the hand dryer in the EchoEcho bathroom
- Boyfriendless
- Hopeless?

Calm down, Ruthie. You just had a bad start. It wasn't a fit. Chef even warned you about that. Tomorrow will be better.

JANUARY 17

This morning, I met up with Lilly for a much-needed coffee talk. I have to regroup, rethink. Lilly was post-call from her duties at the hospital, so was free to hang with her soul-searching pal.

We met at our usual coffee spot, at the corner of Dundas and Ossington, but then Lilly suggested we walk in the opposite direction from our usual haunt.

"It sure is a hard time being Ruthie Cohen these days," said Lilly, stating the obvious. "So, I figure if left doesn't work, go right."

"Hey, good idea," I agreed. "Maybe my new thing should be zigging instead of zagging."

"That's the spirit, Ruthie C."

Within ten minutes, our directional change brought us to a brand-new coffee shop called Rick Slone Coffee Stop. It's about the size of a shoebox, and just as efficient. There's a checkerboard floor and a blackboard behind the counter detailing coffee beans for sale as well as the various types of beverages on offer, among them, old school espressos and Americanos.

And then there's the siphoned coffee, which is both old and new — and totally cool. Lilly and I watched as the enthusiastic coffee guy gave a quick aroma test to a couple wanting to try this particularly brewed coffee. They chose their beans based on which "flavour notes" they liked best, like wine in France, and then the coffee guy whooshed around performing, basically, magic, and we all watched as the brew gurgled, was removed from the heat, and moments later the bottom vessel's brewed coffee shot up as air was drawn through the grounds to release the built-up vacuum. Seven minutes later, the coffee was ready. The champion barista had the couple smell it before pouring it into two dainty teacups to drink. "Amazing!" they said, sipping away.

"What does it taste like?" I asked.

"Sort of like a really dark tea," the woman answered.

"Is that a positive?" asked Lilly.

"We like to try new things," she concluded, unhelpfully.

Lilly ordered a cappuccino and I got a latte. He made it the normal way. We plopped ourselves down on the café's wooden bench.

"You know, this place kind of reminds me of Chef Zane's kitchen, but obviously on a much smaller scale, and on a more approachable level," I told Lilly. "There's science at work here, but I understand it, and all of my senses are engaged."

"Even your sense of 'scent memory'?" asked Lilly. I flashed her a half-hearted frown. "Sorry, Ruthie, I couldn't resist," she giggled. "Trish and I were laughing about your ill-fated stage all last night. That restaurant is the polar opposite of the type of place that we picture you working at."

"Heyyyy. This is my troubled future you're mocking."

She couldn't help herself and continued, nonetheless. "Do you remember when it first opened, and I went there for a big internal medicine dinner?"

"Oh yeah!" I chuckled, "I had totally forgotten about that."

"Those awful plastic pillows filled with lavender-scented air that our bowls of freeze-dried yogurt and gelatinized honey were balancing on while the pillows slowly deflated, releasing a comforting lavender scent . . . ?" Lilly was working herself into a full-on laughing fit at the rehashed memory of it all. I couldn't help but laugh right along with her. ". . . but the poor waiters had overfilled the pillows so most of the bowls ended up toppling off of the pillows and smashing on the tables, and we were all covered in rehydrated yogurt and honey goo and ceramic chards!" sob-laughed Lilly, while dabbing the tears of laughter from her eyes.

God, I love when Lilly laughs. "Even if it's not my cup of tea," I said, still chuckling as I lapped up the foamy milk from my latte, "I think Chef Zane is a bit of a genius. But you know what? There's also something to be said for using really good products and sticking to the basics."

"I think you're onto something," said Lilly.

JANUARY 18

Freshly inspired by yesterday's freshly brewed coffee, today I headed out by my-unemployed-self, turning right again, and this time travelling even further afield. About 20 minutes later I found myself at Frankly Frankie's, a new bakery and sandwich shop specializing in long-fermented doughs using organic flours and Italian ingredients. I took a seat on a swivel stool at the blond wood bar and decided it was the perfect spot to get some deep thoughts down on paper. Looking around it immediately strikes me that this place is the polar opposite to the kitchen at EchoEcho, yet I am already making new scent memories here, thanks in part to the awesome aroma of baking bread.

Besides the giant stand mixers and dough rollers, there are at least ten back of house staff on view from the open kitchen, real-life humans doing real-life human tasks like hand cutting cookies, slicing fiore de latte, and grilling red peppers over an open flame on an actual gas range. There's also this big, weird coffee machine behind the wooden bar, a brushed aluminum apparatus with an upper shelf, a bottom shelf, and a drain out the back. How they brew the coffee here, as friendly Frankie frankly explains it to me, is by inserting a natural paper filter into one of the plastic cone filters stuck into one of the holes along the upper level, then scooping a tablespoon of freshly ground coffee (from the vintage Ditting Swiss burr grinder) into the waiting filter, and then slowly pouring about a cup of hot water overtop so that the coffee is slowly saturated.

"You don't want too much water and you don't want to do it too quickly because you want to evenly distribute it," said Frankie, in his tweed driver's cap. "See those bubbles? When it's truly fresh, coffee bubbles up like that." So old school, I love it!

And let me tell you, Frankie's coffee couldn't have been any fresher: ground five seconds earlier and poured a minute later, the mug waited patiently underneath to catch the rich liquid dripping out like sand through an hourglass. Perfect with a slice of their super moist pistachio olive oil pound cake. Pretty inspiring stuff.

JANUARY 19

Third time's the charm! Today, for day three of my winning inspiration streak, I strolled into yet another new spot along a burgeoning Dundas Street strip. It specializes in simple local and organic snacks and light meals, such as salads, sandwiches, and homemade chocolate chip cookies topped with a little fleur de sel.

I called Trish, who is happily back at work at the same old job following our big French adventure. Turns out she just needed a break.

"Can you meet me for lunch? Like, right now?"

"What's up?"

"I think I've found my mark," I said.

Trish zipped over and we took a table inside the Antler & Beavertail.

"What do you think?" I whispered.

"I think it looks really great, Ruthie," she whispered back.

Rustic, is what I'd call it. It has reclaimed wooden counters, hardwood floors, and a very cool art installation along the walls, using twigs and branches to form antlers and mini beaver dams. The floor-to-ceiling windows of the corner lot building lets the sun pour in, while the sidestreet patio with mismatched chairs and heaters offers even more direct

UV exposure — perfect during Toronto's long winters. The vintage front display case shows off what looks like an apothecary of baked goods, such as all-butter croissants, fudgy salted caramel brownies, and apple-cheddar-rosemary scones. Off in the corner I spotted a guy (who must be the chef) taking baguettes out of the Blodgett oven.

Trish took a seat while I ordered a date square, a croissant, a cappuccino, and a latte, and then I started asking the baguette baker some questions.

"We sell about 100 croissants every day," answered Peter, who isn't an "official" chef (he's self-taught) but appears to be just as talented as Chef Zane based on what I tasted. "People go nuts for them. Our croissants are a little bit darker, a little bit crunchier, and more misshapen than most."

"Yeah, I was going to ask about the wonky shapes. Thought maybe you had a cockeyed baker."

"It's all by design," said Peter (not really acknowledging my joke). He said he's just not a fan of that perfect French crescent shape. "These look more homemade," he said while readjusting his black baseball cap. "I also really like our pain au chocolat because it lets you have chocolate for breakfast without having too much sweet. That's 72% fair trade organic dark chocolate in there. Perfect with our medium roast."

"And what about your butter tarts?" I asked, pointing to the golden beauties before us. "I've never seen butter tarts so tall and quivery."

"I want lots of butter in them. No raisins," he said, holding out his hand in the "stop" position. "If I wanted raisins, I'd ask for a raisin tart. But then, I would never ask for a raisin tart."

"Me neither!" I sort of shouted, growing more excited by the minute.

Cookie sheets full of scones and squares were stacked up on the steel baking racks. The whole place smelled of butter and coffee. They roast their own beans, because, said Peter, "If you can, why wouldn't you? It's not that hard, and it means you can get the coffee you want, roast it exactly how you want it, and you don't have to have it shipped clear across the country." It took a little while to totally understand it all, he said, "But if you're selling coffee, you should probably understand it anyway."

And this is where things got really exciting. Peter went on to explain that, while they're a bustling café by day, people don't want sandwiches and pastries for dinner. "I close at 4 p.m. even though I'd love the Antler & Beavertail to stay open at night. I picture it turning into a bistro for dinner service. Unfortunately, I just don't have the money or manpower to make that happen right now." He sighed an exhausted sigh. "But hopefully one day."

"What do you think, Trish?" I asked once I'd finished pummelling Peter with even more questions. As she used her index finger to pick up the very last buttery crumbles of her oversized organic date square, she stopped for a moment and said, "I think it's great. Perfect, even. I see you in a place like this."

"Exactly like this?"

"*Exactly* like this."

Trish bought a blueberry brown sugar crumble muffin to go, and as he rung it up, told Peter, "You'll want our girl on your team. They don't make them better than Ruthie Cohen." Then she headed back to work while I stayed behind to chat with him some more.

I told Peter about my situation and my culinary training and my current need for a restaurant placement to finish off my diploma. And he, in turn, told me to come back early tomorrow morning for a trial day.

And with that, the Antler & Beavertail is now my new goal.

Are things finally turning around?!

JANUARY 20

So far, I'm loving what I'm seeing: Peter and I are on the same wavelength, though he is definitely more earnest than I'm used to. Possible problem? I don't think so. It's just different. Besides, I could probably stand to be more earnest.

At 6 a.m. this morning at the A&B, Peter filled me in even more on his general food philosophy, this time using a sandwich as an instructional device.

"Lucky for you, I took these baguettes out of the oven 20 minutes ago. They're still warm," he said as he sliced one open. "We bake them every morning using organic flour and a sourdough starter, so as we bake more throughout the day they become more sour, which is kind of fun. My thinking is, if you're not going to use good bread, don't bother making a sandwich at all. It makes me so mad." He briefly stopped to frown. "You want structure, you want a crust, but you've also got to be careful because you don't want lockjaw."

Peter's baguettes are elongated and slender, with a snappy white inside and a nutty brown crackled crust. He fetched some Quebec brie from the fridge (says it'll warm up in the sandwich) and an Ontario gala apple. He explained how a trio of carefully chosen olive varietals were pitted and chopped before going into the processor to make the tapenade, along with toasted walnuts, a clove of garlic, some grapeseed oil (so it doesn't thicken up in the fridge like olive oil would — clever!), and freshly cracked black pepper.

He said you want to taste every flavour in the sandwich: "The olives, the walnuts, the crispness of the apple — and you can't use just any apple — the greens, the dressing, the brie, and the bread. One component shouldn't overpower the other. I want every bite that you take of that sandwich to be perfectly balanced. If you have too much filling in there the balance will be off." *Yes! Balance is so important in sandwiches — and life!*

Peter thinly sliced a generous amount of brie and mounded it onto the bread. "It's really, really important that the brie goes on the bottom." Next, he sliced the apple whisper thin with a mandoline just before putting it on top of the brie and fanning it out like an extravagant peacock tail. "The apple is like a palate cleanser just before you hit the cheese," he joked. (At least I think he was joking?) "Today's salad is a mixture of leaf lettuce, watercress, dandelion, and arugula. Again, be careful about which leaves you choose — you don't want too much bitter in there." *Let not the bitterness overtaketh the sandwich, or the heart . . .*

Next, the greenery goes on top of the apple fan, then a drizzle of raspberry vinaigrette over top of that (a mix of grapeseed and extra virgin olive oils, mustard, shallot, salt and pepper, and a spoonful of organic raspberry preserves).

"So here I'm adding a bit of moisture," he said. "Every element of the sandwich should be very satisfying."

Peter gingerly spread some of the olive walnut tapenade over every inch of the top piece of baguette, before resting it over the bottom half of the sandwich, perpendicularly on a mottled ceramic plate. "Don't just smoosh it down — you want to see what you're eating before you dig in. Every ingredient must stand on its own. You want to be proud of the sandwich. You want it to be like a gift. Otherwise, why would you serve it to your customers, your community, your friends, your family?"

Yes, Peter, I get it. The sandwich is a metaphor for the human condition. Can I eat it yet?

My breakfast baguette was ready but the class wasn't quite over. While I scarfed down his just-prepared brie and apple sandwich, Peter filled me in on his café's commitment to being the greenest, most environmentally responsible restaurant in the city. "We put only one bag of garbage to the curb, every two weeks. When you do it right, when you reuse, reduce, and recycle, you'd be amazed at how little trash you produce," he explained. "It's the biggest little thing we can do for the Earth."

My mind was racing. On the one hand I was thinking, he's too earthy times two. But you know what? Best frigging baguette sandwich I've ever had, and let's not forget that I was just in France! Besides, what do I all of a sudden have against the planet Earth?

"I think I need to work here, Peter," I said.

"Well then, Ruthie, let's give it a try," he said.

And we officially shook on it.

JANUARY 22

Chef Antoine approved my stage at the Antler & Beavertail. After checking it out and talking to Peter, he thought it would be a good fit.

That said, he wasn't a fan of Peter's misshapen croissants. I think he called them blasphemy, but I'm not sure because all I heard was him mumbling something under his breath that sounded like "zut alors, blasphème." He said the baguettes were very good though, and he loved his sandwich. "Overall, it eez a charming place."

JANUARY 26

Why does the first day of a new job feel exactly like the first day of school? The excitement! The jitters! Choosing the perfect shirt! Learning on the fly! But it's also amazing how many things you don't realize you don't know until you suddenly have to know them. I did pretty well for a first day, though. I made some nice lattes and was even able to eke out a few milk foam hearts, which the guests appreciated. (I swear only three looked like saggy testicles.) My bakes went fine — though still not my strongest skill. I learned how to use the POS system no problem, which was a big relief because you know about me and numbers.

But then things got busy. Really busy. I have to say, Peter didn't appropriately warn me about the A&B's morning rush: it is *no joke*. In fact, now I understand why Peter was so quick to hire me and how he sells over 100 croissants a day. I've also come to realize that it has been quite some time since I've worked in a guest-facing position. I had to work fast, make all the hot beverages, bag our (still-warm) morning treats, and be nice — all at the same time and at the speed of light. In fact, I was so busy I decided that something had to give, so I decided to lose the nice.

Regulars rushed in, some introduced themselves and others started asking me questions about myself, but I simply didn't have time for it. So, I answered by saying things like, "Listen, Mr. Blueberry Muffin and Cappuccino, today I'm learning, tomorrow we'll chat." Some of them found it charming. But not all. Mrs. Lemon Poppyseed Loaf and Earl Grey with One Sugar, for instance, icily responded, "It's Dianne," and suggested my customer service could use some improvement. I felt a blush of embarrassment. Maybe I'm not as charming as I think I am? But then the next customer introduced herself as Miss Cheese Croissant and Americano, and I felt much better.

And I probably *am* as charming as I thought.

JANUARY 28

Even though I absolutely hate waking up so early and working my ass off, I couldn't be happier at the A&B. Hooray! Could it be the satisfaction of a job well done?

Peter prepares most of the doughs to ferment overnight and I do most of the prep work. And we've already had some exciting chats about opening the nighttime bistro, but before we hash that out, I've been rolling out of bed at 5 a.m. and heading over to the café to roll out the day's worth of Peter's puff pastry and bake the first batch of baguettes. Since I'm the first one there, I also grind the first batch of coffee beans, start baking off the croissants (thank God he prefers them misshapen), and get a lot of the mise en place done for our perfect sandwiches and salads so we don't get slammed when all the regulars start streaming in. Peter says he's grateful for my help and even cut out early today for the first time in months. (He went snowshoeing in High Park. Yes, apparently people do that.)

Knowing Peter was off this afternoon, Trish popped in to keep me company while I closed up for the day, and I suspect to see if there were any leftovers she could snatch.

"I put aside a morning glory muffin for Lilly and a slice of pink praline tart for you," I said.

"It seems to be going well here," said Trish, looking around the toasty café. "Look at you, my friend Ruthie C., baking up a storm and wiping down counters like a real pro." I playfully give the counter an extra couple of spritzes from the bottle of water and vinegar to prove her point. "I'm so glad you found this place."

Me, too.

JANUARY 29

Holy shit.
    Is Mercury finally out of retrograde? It sure feels that way, because not only am I loving my first week at work, but ... DEAN CALLED! Yes, THAT Dean. Thailand Dean. Totally out of the blue! He said an iPhone photo memory of us in Thailand popped up, he got a heart pang, and decided to call. And we had an actual meaningful conversation! We talked for over four-and-a-half hours, which must be some sort of world record for a first phone call?
    We talked about everything under the sun and over the moon and got to the bottom of what had gone wrong. Basically, we were both too busy, but also too scared to pursue a post-Thailand long-distance relationship. A sort of "why mess with perfection?" scenario. But by the end of the call we decided to give us a shot. Us! A shot! And right after I hung up, Dean booked a flight from Chicago and emailed me the details. He's coming in just a few days! I told Trish and Lilly and they're freaking out. I'm freaking out! I can't believe it! Dean from Thailand is coming to Toronto! (I'd better buy condoms.)

Inheritance Update: inspirational and empowering culinary tour through France, $7,500, still waiting to hear back from Trevor and Officer Yonkers.

Balance remaining: $10,000 (thanks for the top up, Dad!)

February

FEBRUARY 4

On Friday night Dean arrived at my door with the hugest smile I've ever seen and the biggest hug I've ever felt, plus a bouquet of gorgeous ranunculus, and a pint of coffee Häagen-Dazs ice cream he had somehow picked up on the way from the airport. He knew me for all of three weeks in Thailand months ago, yet still remembered all of my favourites. Now that's what I call a stand-up guy. *A good man.* After our quick hello he found my bedroom and by the time I'd put the ice cream in the freezer and the flowers in water, he was lying naked on my bed on top of the duvet. *A funny man.*

"Ruthie, I've been waiting a year for this," he said, after I had followed him in. "And I don't want to wait a minute longer." *Why did this scene suddenly seem so familiar?*

Looking at his big stiff eggplant emoji, he definitely seemed ready. So, I did a running leap onto the bed beside him, whereupon he slowly unbuttoned my jeans, gently pulled my sweatshirt off over my head, unclasped my bra, and asked me to just stay there for a minute while he took me in. He even stroked my cheek. *A sweet man.* Eventually, I flopped onto my back and lay down beside him while wondering how that huge schlong of his was going to fit inside of little old me. *A big man.*

FEBRUARY 6

So, I don't like to compare one partner to the next, and I'm certainly not about to do that now, especially since Dean just left and I'm dying to document our magical first weekend together as accurately as I can. Besides, how could Dean possibly be as good as say, Jeff, during our very first time? There had been a months-long build-up. In this case, contact had been lost and regained. Expectations were high. And you know what? The sex with Dean was fine. It was *fine*. No, it was better than fine. It was ~~satisfactory~~ wonderful. And afterwards, I felt so happy just lying here, watching him sleep, our naked legs slung together, knowing that Dean was finally in Toronto and in my bed. Dean and Ruthie. Ruthie and Dean. Together at last. Duthie. Rean? We'll work on that.

We ended up staying in my apartment, in my bedroom, all night, into the next morning, all afternoon, and into the evening, improving in leaps and boinks, stopping only for water and fruit (for him), Häagen-Dazs and chocolate (for me), and showers and pee breaks (for both of us). Sometimes we had to cool it because my legs got too shaky or Dean got a foot cramp, and then we'd conk out for a couple of hours. But then one of us would poke the other awake and it would start all over again.

Until this afternoon when Dean had to catch his flight back to Chicago.

"Holy shit, Ruthie," he said, freshly out of the shower and towel drying his curly mop top. "That was epic."

"Totally insane," I agreed, giving him a bear hug from behind. No doubt about it; a great few days.

"Can you come visit me next weekend?" he asked.

"I can't," I sighed. "Peter gave me this whole weekend off last minute because he knew you were coming. I can't ditch him again next weekend. But I'll come for a couple of days the week after next."

"Okay, and then I'll take you out to one of my favourite places," he said, brightening back up. "For our first real date."

Our first real date. "Can't wait."

FEBRUARY 7

I had a meeting with Trevor at the bank today and the news isn't good. I'd actually classify it as worst-case scenario. Officer Yonkers informed Trevor that since Jeff accessed my account on my personal computer in my own home, there was no way for them to verify that Jeff and I weren't in cahoots with a grand scheme to bilk the bank out of the $30,000.

"So, Officer Yonkers and the bank are saying that I stole my own money?" I asked Trevor.

"I'm so sorry, Ruthie," said Trevor, looking honestly sorry. "Of course, I defended your character and told them what a valued and responsible customer you've been over the years. But they've got some fairly strict guidelines when it comes to this sort of breach, and unfortunately, in your case, the law is siding with the bank." And then Trevor opened his top drawer and slid a Snickers bar across his desk to me. "Still your favourite right?"

"Not anymore," I whimpered, taking the chocolate bar nonetheless.

FEBRUARY 9

Suddenly my mornings just aren't the same if I don't hear that strange FaceTime ring from Dean first thing.

"Hello lover," he'll smile. Then we'll spend about five minutes having coffee and catching up before hurriedly carrying on. And it's the absolute best part of my day.

FEBRUARY 11

I've been developing and testing new recipes at home that I *think* Peter (and our customers) will like for the café. I'm excited about adding new dishes to the lunch menu, but also want to get him thinking about the possibility of a dinner service soon.

For my first sandwich, I think I want to bridge the gap between a foie gras pâté plate with baguette, and a lighter meatloaf. Like ... an organic meatloaf baguette sandwich with a spread of some sort and some lightly dressed greens ... or something ...

Meatloaf Test #1
- Add about a pound organic ground sirloin and a pound of ground ~~turkey~~ chicken into a bowl
- 2 beaten eggs
- ½ cup ~~toasted~~ breadcrumbs (USE STALE)
- About a tbsp Dijon
- Medium diced fresh tomato
- 2 minced shallots
- ~~3 sprigs~~ 1 tbsp fresh thyme
- Good pinch of kosher salt and pepper
- Mix, press into a parchment-lined loaf pan
- Bake at ~~350~~ 375°F for ~~50 mins~~ about an hour.

*Next time try making a day ahead and seeing how it is cold the following day.

Hmmm ... a couple months ago, Jeff and I had a friendly sandwich-making competition. He won, as usual, in part because of the delicious artichoke spread he made to go on his sandwich. So, I think I'll use his top-secret artichoke spread. (He steals $30K from me, I steal artichoke spread from him. HA.)

Artichoke Spread Test #1
- In a mini chopper add:
  - 2 small jars of drained marinated artichokes
  - tsp of Dijon
  - half tbsp mayo
  - 1 clove of garlic
  - 2 tbsp extra virgin olive oil
  - salt and pepper
- ~~Blitz until smooth~~ PULSE. (Leave a little texture in there.)
- Dress some ~~watercress~~ baby arugula with a squirt of lemon juice and some extra virgin olive oil

Full Sando Test #1
- Half a warmed halved baguette per sandy
- Generously spread artichoke on both sides
- Add a couple of (1/4-inch?) slices of the chilled meatloaf on the bottom
- Add dressed arugula on top
- Season arugula lightly and place top half on sandwich

FEBRUARY 13

Trish and Lilly came over to try the now-perfected meatloaf sandwich. "It tastes like a school lunch at the spa," said Lilly. (Lilly went to private school.)

The girls definitely miss the extreme level of freebie meals and pastries they had become accustomed to from the good ol' L'École de la Cuisine Française days, so they've been happy and willing A&B guinea pigs. Two thumbs up on this one. And two giant thumbs up on the news that Dean and I are officially a couple.

"This is really best-case scenario," offered Trish. "We know him, you trust him, he lives long-distance, so you won't get bored of him, and you'll still have lots of time to hang with us."

"An arrangement that's almost as good as this sandwich," added Lilly.

FEBRUARY 15

Well, that was fast. Lilly and Trish were so happy to hear that Dean and I were a couple, thrilled even, especially since they wanted me to get over Jeff. And now a couple of days later I'm already getting grilled?

"How long do you two figure you'll be able to keep up this long-distance thing?" asked Trish as she and Lilly and Craig slid into their favourite booth at the A&B. (Craig is addicted to our pain au chocolat.)

"I guess for as long as it takes," I answered, as I returned with three glasses and a recycled bottle full of Toronto's finest tap water. Trish and Lilly rolled their eyes and Craig asked, "What does that mean?"

"Really," said Trish. "Could you be any vaguer?"

"It means she doesn't know," Lilly explained to Craig. "Ruthie, haven't you two talked about next steps?"

"Yeah, it must have come up at some point during one of your hours-long talks," added Trish.

"Are you guys nuts? You said the long-distance was good!" I yelped. "PLUS, we've been together for like two weeks!"

"Two weeks plus about a year," corrected Trish.

"Thailand was a long time ago, Trish. We're basically starting from the bottom up."

"I thought you said no butt stuff," said Trish.

"Trish!" said Lilly, while covering Craig's ears.

All joking aside, what was the big rush? Dean and I are brand new and still getting to know each other in the real world. We're learning new things about each other every day. Like the fact that I'm a light sleeper and he, oddly, likes to sleep with a light on. And that he washes the tub after every use. And apparently before every use...

On that first night he was here, before he showered in the morning I heard a bit of a ruckus in the bathroom.

"You okay in there?" I asked.

"Perfect! Just looking for some paper towel. And, you wouldn't happen to have some Clorox, rubber gloves, and bottle of Scrubbing Bubbles, would you?"

"Oh my gosh, Dean, if you're cleaning, don't! I cleaned the whole place before you arrived. Wanted everything spick and span for my man."

"No, it's fine. It's sort of my thing," he said. "Or rather, sort of a thing I have to do. Bit of a neat freak, I'm afraid."

Oh. I see. Turns out Dean has mild OCD. I don't care. We all have our things, and he seems to have it under control. Meanwhile, my bathroom has never been cleaner.

But something did come up about Dean that I do mind. Something surprising. Something I think he may have been hiding from me, either consciously or unconsciously, because he wasn't sure how I'd react to it. I was nervous to tell the girls and Craig, but I had to.

"What's wrong, Ruthie?" asked Lilly, seeing the torn look on my face.

And then I sat and I sighed. I sighed a sigh bigger than any sigh I've sighed before. I sighed a sigh that was deep and loud and long and high. I sighed a sigh for the ages. And then I told them that we have a problem. A big fucking problem . . .

It's kind of weird that I hadn't noticed it in Thailand. In fact, it wasn't until this week that I finally started to put it all together. With the mostly vegetarian lifestyle we'd been living on Koh Tao, and then with my natural affinity for cooking with fresh vegetables and whole grains at home, it just hadn't occurred to me that . . .

"Oh my god," said Trish. "Is Dean a vegetarian?"

"Worse," I said.

"What could be worse?" asked Craig.

"Oh no," said Lilly, a giant smirk gathering at the corners of her mouth. "He can't be . . ."

"He can't be what?" asked Craig.

"Holy shit, Ruthie, he isn't . . ." cackled Trish.

"Isn't *what?!*" whined Craig.

"It's true," I said. "My worst nightmare has been realized." (Dramatic pause.) "Dean is a card-carrying vegan."

"Nooooo!" they all shouted in unison (even Craig) and then we all laughed together, even though I'm sort of dying inside. Because it's not a laughing matter. At all.

Here's why: I am a chef. I love raw milk cheeses and steak tartare and butter-poached lobster and chocolate mousse. This isn't just what I eat; it's what I do. It's my new life, and I love it.

And Dean loves raw mung bean sprouts. Maybe I'm just overreacting. (*Who? Moi?*)

I head to Chicago tomorrow, let's see how this goes...

FEBRUARY 18

Loving Chicago. Loving Dean. But today we went to a place called the Krishna Hut for lunch and I did not love it.

I ordered the Magical Bowl, which the menu described as a macrobiotic special composed of steamed vegetables on organic brown rice with miso gravy, chunks of firm tofu, peanut sauce, organic alfalfa sprouts, and shreds of toasted nori, and Dean looked right at home as he happily ordered the soup of the day, a chana mung bean dahl, followed by the Buddha's Feast, a dish of stir-fried veggies on more brown rice.

"This is my favourite place in the whole city," Dean volunteered to our earthy waitress as he handed her back our tea-stained menus.

I decided not to make any snap judgments. I've been to *great* vegan restaurants. Ones where instead of being served simply steamed, the beets were roasted and chopped into a tartare with shiso and toasted hazelnuts and served with fried gnocco dough, crisp, puffed and golden, like a clever tartare. Vegan restaurants where the waterier vegetables like zucchini and yellow squash are treated with even more care: chunks of grilled zucchini surrounded by a vibrant yellow squash purée with chili crunch, lime, and fresh mint, served with fresh-from-the-oven vegan barley bread for ripping and dipping. I've also had amazing vegan desserts. Once, in class, Claire made a chocolate cake layered with a creamy tofu mousse, rhubarb gelée, strawberry sauce, and fudge crunch, using no gross heavy olive oils or coconut cream. It was magnificent!

So, this place seemed like a throwback to 20 years ago. Hopefully it's just an anomaly, even though it appears to be Dean's favourite restaurant. It occurs to me that the vegan thing I can handle, but what happens if Dean has *no taste* when it comes to good food? Or even worse, what if he doesn't care about food at all?

I didn't feel that Dean belonged at the Krishna Hut because I sure didn't. And yet, I do think we belong together. So how exactly does that work?

When my heaping Magical Bowl arrived, along with cutlery rolled up in brown recycled napkins, there was a kaleidoscopic topping of sprouts, shredded raw carrot and shredded beets. Beneath it, the broccoli florets were emerald-green, the carrot chunks and cauliflower were also steamed to a turn; the sauce was warming with brown miso and peanuts making the rice all earthy and nutty. Even the marinated tofu chunks weren't entirely unpleasant.

"Looks good," encouraged Dean.

"Tastes healthy," said me.

FEBRUARY 19

11 a.m.

Dean brought me a latte in bed today! But it was made with oat milk, and I had to secretly plug my nose while I drank it because I hate oat milk. It made it hard to drink.

"Are you okay?" he asked while I gasped for air between sips.

He had to pop into the hospital for an hour or so to do his rounds this afternoon, and I took the opportunity to run out and get a Chicago-style hot dog.

Am I a horrible person?

6:30 p.m.

Okay, so we've been planning our first pop-up at A&B for a couple of weeks, and we finally pulled the trigger tonight and put the word out on Instagram — hoping for the best! Peter posted a pic of the menu and wrote in the caption:

POP-UP! ONE NIGHT ONLY. THIS FRIDAY. THREE COURSES, A GLASS OF WINE, AND A CUP OF COFFEE. $65, TAX AND TIP INCLUDED.

(Peter had gone to the liquor store to buy a one day "special event" liquor license.)

7:15 p.m.
Okay WHOA. I don't know if everyone loved the sound of the menu or that tax and tip were included, because let me tell you, it sold out in just 15 minutes. We're shocked! And excited! And nervous!

7:45 .pm.
And a bit annoyed!

"A nice response, but it could just be first-time excitement," said Dean as I was literally jumping for joy in his apartment.

I stopped jumping. "Dude..."

"I'm sorry, I'm sorry," he said. "I just want you to be realistic. Sometimes you're overly optimistic."

Isn't that a good thing?

"Excuse me, but I thought that was one of the traits you liked most about me?"

"I do. I love that about you. It's just that sometimes your ominous positivity can border on naïvety."

Ominous positivity? So, we sell out our pop-up in 15 minutes flat and I'm suddenly labelled a naïve optimist with leanings towards ominous positivity?

"Excuse me?"

"I'm sorry, I'm sorry," he said again, this time coming in for a hug. "Your pop-up is going to be a huge success. I'm just afraid if you're a big hit in Toronto, you won't bother being a big hit in Chicago. And I want you to be a big hit in Chicago."

"Oh... like, if I move here?"

193

"Yeah, I mean, we haven't really talked about that yet..."

"True. But didn't you say there weren't any infectious disease openings in Chicago for you anyways?"

"Yeah, I just think we keep our options open. But I'll look at Toronto hospitals too."

"Okay. Good! Well, my ominous positivity tells me that everything is going to work out just fine," I said, hugging him tighter and giving him a kiss on those plump perfect lips of his.

FEBRUARY 20
10 a.m.

Even though I'm not exactly thrilled about Dean's surprise veganism, at least he doesn't wear "Meat is Murder" T-shirts or anything like that. (I actually just checked his dresser drawers while he was scrubbing the shower to confirm. Side note: Jeff actually had a faded blue T-shirt that says, "Save a Cow, Eat a Vegan." *Sigh*.)

I appreciate the fact that he didn't judge me when I scarfed down an omelet at Ethel's Finer Diner, a great little spot a few blocks down from his place. And if I'm being totally honest, how can I judge him or his choices (even though I'm clearly totally judging him for his choices)? Dean is a vegan for environmental reasons: "Eat one cow or grow a field of soy," is how he broke it down for me over his oatmeal and fruit. He's trying to do right by the Earth and he's trying to do right by his fellow man. He's trying to do right by all the little lambs and cows and ducks and chickadees of the world.

"It's strictly an ethical decision," he explained.

Okay, ouch? I mean, I don't think he means that I'M unethical, but it still left me feeling a bit moody. It's his personal choice. That doesn't make me a bad person by default, does it? And look, I know I should be more like Dean. We should all be more like Dean. Dean is good, Dean is right. Dean is justice, Dean is light. Yet knowing all of this, why do I still want him to be more like me?

Anyway, after the initial ~~horror~~ shock of the situation — which Dean correctly predicted, which was why it took him a while to cop to the whole veganism thing — wore off, I decided to make his dietary constraints work within the framework of our relationship. Dean's veganism will force me to use some ingredients and techniques that are new to me, which is kind of fun. And I like making good things to eat for the people I care about.

10 p.m.
Just back from Chicago. Dean dragged me to the Orangutan Kitchen this afternoon and I started rethinking my whole veganism rethink.

The menu offers up vegan delicacies such as Zucchini "Alfredo," in which zucchini "noodles" (or "zoodles," so I guess we're all living in Whoville now) come tossed in a white cashew "cream sauce." The Great Ape, meanwhile, is a big tepid bowl of "mineral rich leafy green" veggies, almonds, veggie pâté, olives, chili, hempseed, and a "superfood" dressing. In other words, let's scoop a whole bunch of mismatched crap into a bowl and sell it for $28. Meals are complemented by tall glasses of colourful "power" juices. I went for the Green "Taco" lunch special, which is a spiced chili and walnut mix with some guacamole and salsa wrapped in romaine lettuce leaves. (It didn't sound great, but how bad could it be?)

After we placed our orders, Dean went off to wash his hands again, while I perused the surroundings. The furniture is second-hand and garage-sale cast-offs. Duct tape plays a major role in the restaurant's overall design scheme. The floor is unevenly laid fieldstone — I witnessed two people wiping out while Dean was in the washroom, which was worth the price of admission alone. The juicers were making a turbo-like racket as they went full torque during our entire meal. There are low ceilings and bad art decorating the yellowing walls. But it's the unmistakable scent of mildew that turned out to be the tipping point for me.

I mean, come on! There are vegan restaurants with Michelin stars all around the world, some of them even in this city. And I work at a place that also serves mostly organic, wholesome dishes, and I'll bet our décor cost about the same as this dive, or probably even less since foraged willow branches are a big part of our overall design. The difference is, when Peter found new chairs and tables at second-hand stores or contents sales or by the side of the road, he took the time to clean them. He'd usually strip them down, sand them and paint or stain them, too. But at the very least, he *cleaned* them. It's not that difficult. Anyone can do it. Even me. I don't understand how Dean, with his OCD issues, can eat at the Orangutan Kitchen, based on its unhygienic appearance alone. Not to mention the noise and stink and the fact that half of the menu is composed of made-up words that need quotation marks around them so that you aren't even more disappointed when your wet food finally arrives. How can't he see that veganism is a cop out for them. It allows places like this to seemingly bypass health codes and dress codes and especially the codes of good taste. And it literally goes against everything I believe in. So why were we there, again?

By the time Dean returned from the washroom I was furious. And then came the food. Dean's Zucchini Alfredo tasted of absolutely nothing, though he claimed he loved it, which made me *more* livid.

"You're lying!" I said, while choking down a taste of it. "There is absolutely no seasoning to it whatsoever. No salt, no pepper, no garlic, no fresh herbs, and it's swimming in water!"

"I like its subtle flare," he said as he continued happily slurping, not noticing that he was splashing me with "zoodles" water as he ate.

"That's right. Keep eating," I taunted. "You'll want to finish it while it's still tepid." And then Dean squeezed my knee, which is either his way of being affectionate or him telling me to shut up. I haven't figured out that odd little habit yet. I sat back and tried to relax sulk, while contemplating where the closest place to grab a quick slice of pizza may be.

FEBRUARY 23
12:10 a.m.
It's showtime, baby. Well, it was, earlier tonight. We had our pop-up!

Our plan to start slow was obviously shot to shit when we immediately hit our max of 30 people, even before Trish could get a ticket. (Lilly had to work, but I told Trish I'd squeeze her in at the bar, gratis.) Peter had said he wanted to test the waters before diving into the evening bistro concept, and if this pop-up was any indication, I'm pretty sure he's totally convinced. He seemed so pleased, almost Zen-like as he looked out over the warm glow of candlelight once everyone had been served coffee and dessert. "This is what it's all about." He smiled.

We did a simple set menu of salad Lyonnaise (we had previously poached the eggs then quickly reheated them in warm water before topping each dressed frisée salad serving with one), local trout quenelles with lobster sauce (along with hunks of crusty baguette for mopping up said luscious sauce), and slices of pink praline tart. Peter's cousin Phil — who was slowly coming out of his shell after he caught wind that we call him "Sad Phil" behind his back — was happy to help out by sidling up to each table with two bottles of wine and asking, "Red or white?" (The red was a pinot noir from the Okanagan and the white was an unoaked chardonnay from Niagara.) A single local greenhouse tulip in a bud vase on each table (vases helpfully sourced by Trish at Goodwill) added a splash of colour to the happy buzz in the room. *Was this actually happening?*

Trish was impressed that the quenelles tasted just like the ones from the bouchons of Lyon. Maybe even better. "I especially liked your use of local fish and the freshly snipped chives" she noted.

"And *I* like that you're using the occasion to finally debut your new hat," I said.

"Am I pulling it off?" she asked, adjusting the rim of her forest green fedora.

"Very Molly Ringwald," I said.

During dessert, when Peter and I were walking around asking guests for feedback, most said they really loved the food and the wine and the vibes — even Sad Phil got a couple of mentions. Meanwhile, the pink praline tart became the Insta darling of the evening. Also, a food critic from *Toronto Life* was there and asked if we planned on doing more pop-ups because she wants to write us up!

But best of all, a little later, when everyone was gone and we were washing up, Peter turned to me and said, "That went better than expected." Now, if you know anything at all about Peter, that's basically the equivalent of him shouting "Hallelujah!" from a mountaintop. Truly, everything was best case scenario.

I guess the only downer was that Dean didn't call to see how the pop-up went, even though I have been nervously talking about it constantly.

I get it. He's busy. He's literally saving lives over there.

FEBRUARY 25

Dear Diary, while things are going well with Dean, if I'm being honest (and of course I am) the veganism isn't the only problem. We both have insane schedules ... we're long distance, which is way more challenging than I had anticipated and I'm having trouble adjusting to all of the changes. Or maybe I just don't want to adjust.

But why should I? I just became a chef! I work at an amazing café! We just had a super successful pop-up! And I enjoy my food and my food choices. Our mismatched culinary views have been a bit of a sticking point in the relationship, but whenever I try to bring it up, Dean just says we can talk about it later.

"Tofu talk isn't conducive to sweet lovemaking, m'lady," he'll joke.

The other problem is, well, let's just say if you're talking about tofu in the middle of lovemaking, maybe the sweet love making isn't so sweet.

Could it be that Dean is better on paper than in real life?

Could it be that Dean and I should have let Thailand be a one-time thing?

No. Don't do this.

Dean is great. He's a wonderful, caring person, he's funny and charming. He thinks the world of me, and I think the world of him. Just stop this. I'm being ridiculous. "Dollface, you're lucky if tofu is the worst of your worries," Bubbe Bobby Grace would probably say. (Or would she?)

Besides, Dean is coming in two weeks and has a bunch more interviews lined up at Toronto hospitals. Things are good! I am ~~happy~~ optimistic. And things are getting *real*.

Inheritance Update: since school is over and am still awaiting the fate of my stolen inheritance, I'm now investing in me.

Expenses: return flight to Chicago $455.89, vegan restaurant meals $434.78, normal restaurant meals $259.

Balance remaining: $8,850.33.

March

MARCH 2

Had a much-needed girls' night out at SteakFrites with Trish and Lilly. It's a clever new restaurant concept on Queen West. For $67, you get a prix fixe meal that includes a 10 ounce NY striploin served with a side of Béarnaise, a crisp green salad, and endless shoestring French fries. The wine list is mostly red, approachable, and affordable. They ding you on the desserts, though. We had a grand old time, but mostly I was just excited to be eating steak with my besties. I've been so busy I hadn't realized how much I was missing them.

MARCH 5

Claire texted me this morning to ~~tell~~ warn me that Jeff is out of rehab and moving back to Toronto. She wasn't sure when. I won't tell the girls until there's actually something to tell.
    FFFUUUUUUCK.

MARCH 7

FUCK! FUCK! FUCKETY-FUCK!

MARCH 10

New plan. Forget about Jeff's imminent reappearance. Instead, focus on Dean. I, Chef Ruthie Cohen, am going to show Dean how his food can be done. How it *should* be done. I'll fix this. I'll fix him. (*I'll fix* us?)

I start with "cheese." After taste-testing a dozen brands of vegan cheeses, I stumble upon a product called Daiya that the online vegan community seems to love. It's mostly made from tapioca and other plant-based ingredients, yet the first time I served it to Dean, on top of a rustic rapini and "mozzarella" pizza, he thought I was lying and had served him real cheese. I actually had to dig the packaging out of the garbage to prove it was vegan before he would deign to eat it.

"The nerve!" I said as I waved the empty plastic wrapper in his face.

"Sorry, lady," he said, jumping up to hug me. "It just looked too good to believe. This cheese is a game changer!"

Next, I roasted some kale chips, which I hadn't made in a while but have totally loved for ages, even before I fell for a vegan. I barely had a chance to snag a handful before he inhaled them all.

With Dean loving the "cheese" pizza and kale "chips," I am really starting to believe that if we try doing things my way, maybe this vegan issue wouldn't be such a problem after all. It could actually be a good thing. My mind is racing ahead to future vegan meals: black bean sliders with pickled jalapenos and guacamole, roasted eggplant with tahini, pomegranate, and zhug. Cajun yam fries, a spicy chickpea and roasted-cauliflower curry with sweet mango chutney. From India to Israel, I can travel the world through vegan recipes and put out meals that both Dean and I would love. Fresh vegetables! Exciting flavours! This is going to be great. This is going to work!

MARCH 17

"You okay?" asked Dean from the other side of his bathroom door, several hours after our meal at One Luv last night. I was trying hard to conceal the fact that I'd just experienced yet another bout of explosive diarrhea, but I don't think I was doing a very good job at hiding it from Dr. Stein.

"I'm fine," I whimpered, "just a little thirsty from all the soy and miso. I think I'll just relax in here for a while; maybe take a bath, drink some water, read a good book."

"Are you sure? I can get you something to make you feel better."

"I'm fine," I lied.

Nope, this isn't going to work. I'm usually a pretty healthy eater, but this much plant-based protein and fibre is just too much for my dainty digestive tract. I swear, sometimes I'm even clenching during dessert — usually an avocado "mousse" or beet-infused "chocolate cake" (which was surprisingly good). But since when is it normal to take five shits a day? I mean, who even wants to take five shits a day? I don't.

"Alright," he said, and I heard him shuffling away from the bathroom door. "Just let me know if you need anything."

If I need anything? If I need anything? I sure do need something, I thought, as I rested my elbows on my thighs and my sweaty head in my hands. I need these bathroom moments to be the *least* of my concerns. I need you to live closer. I need Jeff to not be coming back. I need Bubbe Bobby Grace to tell me what to do. And I desperately need another roll of toilet paper, please. But mostly I need you to stop saving the Earth and to start saving me. Because I honestly don't see how this relationship is going to work if I'm on the can half the time. And I really, really want this to work, because you're special. You're one of the best people I've ever known. Even though we don't live in the same city, I think about you all the time. Bubbe Bobby Grace would have loved you, not your OCD, or the fact that you're not exactly a generous lover, or the vegan part of you — she would have forced you to eat her chopped liver whether you liked it or not — but your kindness and your wit and your curly hair and your glasses. And the fact that our children would go to summer camp. You are exactly who I know I should end up with. C'mon, Ruthie C. Make good choices for once.

MARCH 20

This morning a 12-year-old came into the Antler & Beaver and asked why we don't make any gluten-free baked goods. I told her it wouldn't be safe in our open kitchen, owing to cross-contamination. "We leave that to the experts," I said with a smile. (I have really been working on my customer service.)

"Do better," she sniffed, before heading out the door.

MARCH 21

After that last impromptu colon cleansing, things started to turn in my favour with Dean. I think he finally understood that as hard as I tried, his way of eating was never going to agree with my body, and he decided to choose me over mung bean dahl stew! We're going to try to MEAT in the middle (haha, nailed it).

MARCH 22

I'm not exactly pushing the beef and seafood on him, but now I'm able to take Dean to places like Pizza Nino and Café Tak when he visits. They don't exactly cater to vegans but there are enough options for him and enough fish and seafood dishes to satisfy me, so we can both be relatively happy at the same restaurants. Lilly recently informed me that this is what's called "a compromise."

"I know this is all new to you," she said, "but it's part of being in a healthy, committed relationship." (Committed! Relationship!) "Dean's giving of himself because he cares about you, but it doesn't mean you get to take advantage and have things your own way all the time."

"Well, I'm not so sure I like the sounds of that," I winked.

"It's worth it, I promise," said a glowing Lilly, who was truly back in love with Craig. (All was forgiven, but not yet forgotten.)

But there's a hitch. And darn it if there isn't always a hitch. Ever since we had come to a fair and reasonable compromise on the vegan front, I thought most of our core issues had been solved, but apparently not. Tonight, Dean's veggie pad Thai seemed to have been served with an extra spicy side of passive aggressiveness . . .

"What now?" I asked during a bit of a tiff regarding when my next trip to Chicago would be.

"It's nothing," said Dean. "I'm just getting tired of all the planning and flying black and forth on my sporadic days off when I really need to be sleeping. I'm exhausted. It's also getting expensive."

"I thought Toronto General and Sunnybrook were paying for the flights because of all the interviews!"

"For some, but not all. Forget I said anything. It's not really about the money . . . don't worry about it . . ."

"Wait a minute, hold up," I said. "Then what *is* it about?"

And then Dean backed down and said nothing at all, even though I still needed more information and was now raring for a spirited discussion. It's times like these I like to remind him of the Glicks.

"Don't forget about the Glicks," I warned him, since Dean knows the story of the Glicks by heart as it's one of my shortest and most effective cautionary tales.

The Glicks had two redheaded freckled children, Jessica and James, who were about my age and lived five doors down from us on the street I grew up on. All of us neighbourhood kids used to play together after school for hours every day like a pack of running, gum-chewing feral wolves. Until one sad summer afternoon when Jessica Glick informed the rest of us that her parents were getting divorced, and they were moving away to Ohio.

"I don't understand. What happened?" I asked Mom, so puzzled by the piece of bad news. "The Glicks never, ever fought."

"*Exactly*," said Mom with a sad shake of the head.

Ever since, I always try to get everything out in the open, but it doesn't really work if the person you're trying to argue with doesn't feel like fighting back.

"When you don't engage," I told Dean, "it makes me feel like you don't take me seriously."

"That's crazy, Ruthie, of course I take you seriously. I just don't like to fight." And then he explained how when he was growing up, unlike the Glicks, Dean's parents did nothing *but* fight, to the point that when they eventually divorced it came as a blessing. "Finally, there was peace and quiet in the house for the first time in my life," he said, popping some homemade tamari and maple roasted cashews in his mouth, and then signalling for me to "open wide" so that he could throw some into mine.

I felt bad for Dean. I suppose we all have our own cautionary tales, not to mention baggage, and I guess I understand his reasons for not wanting to fight. I'm tired, but I'm happy. Dean is wonderful, he really is. I'm lucky and I shouldn't rock the boat. Plus, he seems to think that everything with us is great, full steam ahead, stay the course.

I just hope he's right.

MARCH 23

Am I trying to convince myself that I've fallen in love with Dean, or have I actually fallen in love with him? When we met in Thailand we instantly connected, and it felt like magic. But things feel different now. I want to talk to the girls about it, but I'm afraid they'll judge me, and they probably should. They'll tell me I'm falling back into my bad habit of going for the unattainable, and I probably am. Because Dean is perfect. But what if I'm not falling back into old habits and am instead listening to my gut? Ugh, why can't anything just be easy? I hate that I've suddenly turned into such a fretter. I wish I could call Bubbe Bobby Grace. She'd say just the right thing.

MARCH 24

Last night, as I was lying in bed fretting about Dean, I remembered that Bubbe Bobby Grace already *has* said the right thing. After I had introduced her to my first real boyfriend at my Sweet Sixteen, for reasons unbeknownst to me she was clearly not taken with Darren Stern's polite demeanour and bookish charms. "Perfect on paper doesn't mean perfect for you, dollface," she said. "Don't sell yourself short: you're short enough as it is."

MARCH 25

We're doing some light renovations at the A&B ahead of our regular bistro service starting up soon. (Sad Phil seems to have everything under control in terms of plumbing and construction, but we'll have to call in an electrician to install the new range and hood.) Mom and Dad wanted to meet Chef Antoine to thank him for basically changing my life, so I invited them all to the restaurant for a tasting of some dishes we were working on for the bistro menu, and more importantly so they could gather en masse to praise moi. Also, some of the recipes were surprise odes to them.

"Pleased to meet you, Chef!" said Dad as he reached out his hand to greet Chef Antoine. "Have you heard the one about the Frenchman and the frog?"

"Dad, no!" I yelped, while Mom quickly covered his mouth with her palm. Sometimes it took teamwork to rein in Dad. They took their seats at a four-top, and Peter brought them water and poured glasses of an uncomplicated but lovely Chenin blanc as they warmly chatted.

I started the night off with a vol-au-vent made from Peter's puff pastry, filled with tender escargot in a creamy garlic and wine sauce, tossed with tons of springtime herbs. "Old-fashioned but also fresh," said Chef. "A nice dish, Ruthie."

"What he said," said Dad.

Next, Peter brought out the freshly broiled bowls of French onion soup, just how Chef Antoine taught us, only I hit mine with a touch of Calvados, plus Peter's baguettes make for incredible croutons.

"Why, it eez not even my anniversaire!" joked Chef.

French onion soup is Mom's favourite, too, and she was clearly loving it. "Excellent, Ruthie. Just excellent," she said.

From there we moved on to my foie gras terrine with a Sauternes jellée, which they liked, but in the end we all decided wasn't worth the cost or effort (or telling Dean I had foie gras on the menu).

The Bibb salad was simply adorned with my signature lemon-maple-Dijon dressing and was "Just what the doctor ordered," according to Dad.

For the main courses we served trout meunière; a half roast chicken; a vegan delicata squash dish with crispy chickpeas, ginger, and pear; and brisket boeuf Bourguignon. Plus, sides of potatoes dauphinoise and roasted baby turnips and French breakfast radishes.

At one point Mom worried aloud, "This is too much food, Ruthie!" only to have Dad shout her down, "Keep it coming, kiddo!" (Peter and I ate some of it, too.)

For dessert, there were slices of blueberry crumble pie, plus scoops of a vegan chocolate gelato I was working on, and a slice of my perfect lemon meringue pie, which I torched tableside. (Take that, Chef Bertrand! And Candy Feldman!).

Overall, a very successful night! Chef had some fair comments as they ate — he wanted a garnish here, more browning there — but I could tell he was pleased: "Very, very tasty, Chef Ruthie."

MARCH 26

Mom called to say that she didn't want to say anything in front of Chef Antoine, but she thought the escargot were too salty.

MARCH 27

Jeff's back. Fuck. Fuuuuck!

I didn't want to write it in here. That makes it real.

He texted me a few days ago — no doubt part of the reason why I've been non-stop fretting — to say he's back, feeling much better, and he wants to meet up.

"To apologize?" I texted back.

He texted back, "Yes," but added that there was also something he had to give me.

I thought the A&B was a good place to meet since it has sort of become my home away from home. My safe haven. Home advantage. Plus, Jeff said he was interested in seeing what I had been up to over the past few months, and I must admit I kind of felt like showing it off, especially since Peter and I had a discussion this week about me becoming part owner of the café.

"You've changed things around here in a big way," he said. "And I want you to feel more invested in it. Literally."

We had started doing more pop-up set menu dinners and the evenings were going really well — write-ups on *BlogTO* and in the *Star* certainly helped, and, "Sort of Secret: Café by day, bistro by night, what's on the menu at the Antler & Beavertail?" asked the bold headline font on *Toronto Life*'s website. I was also loving that Lilly and Craig and Trish had become regulars. (Craig loves our French onion soup burger.) Things are going way better than expected, to the point that it wasn't long before we started taking in twice as much through the pop-ups at night as we were during the day — the arugula salad with seared albacore tuna and preserved lemon vinaigrette, and the truffled roast chicken for two with a side of mac and cheese being two crowd favourites. We soon recognized that if we were going to keep up with the demands of a permanent evening dinner service, we'd have to hire a few extra staff. I scooped up Claire (turns out she wasn't loving the team at the Yorkville bakery), while Peter hired his brother-in-law Tom, a terrific front-of-the-house man and a talented rookie sommelier who takes pride in educating our youngish clientele by introducing them to burgeoning wine regions and interesting grape varietals, always with an entertaining story to go along with his reasonably priced picks. Meanwhile, Sad Phil also officially joined the roster as our star dishwasher and fix-it guy.

Acknowledging that the popularity of the new bistro-style pop-ups and the doubling of the café's revenue were mainly due to my evening menus (and let's face it, hard work from all of us), Peter made me a very generous offer: if I can come up with the $20,000 of seed money needed to make improvements to the kitchen, buy some necessary new appliances, and spruce up the bathrooms, he'd be honoured to make me a part owner of the Antler & Beavertail.

Isn't it funny how not so long ago I would have been able to hand over a cheque for the full amount to Peter, c/o Bubbe Bobby Grace's inheritance, with no problem?

No. Not so funny.

MARCH 28
3 p.m.
When I saw Jeff again for the very first time, all of those old feelings came bubbling up like a flute of Veuve Clicquot, and I honestly wasn't expecting that. FUCK. With Dean being back in the picture, I thought I'd be calm, cool, and collected. But at least our first face-to-face since the whole breakup-and-cocaine-driven-$30,000-theft thing was a planned meeting so there wasn't any threat of me bumping into him unexpectedly and having a heart attack and dropping dead in the middle of the street. Dead in a ditch, just like Mom's greatest fear.

Instead, I was throwing together a big bowl of mushrooms for that night's special of toasted brioche with gorgonzola and marinated mushrooms, with my heart in my throat and one eye on the door. I spotted him locking up his bike outside whereupon the butterflies in my stomach escalated to full-on monarch winter migration mode. I watched him straighten his shirt, then surreptitiously peek into the side mirror of a parked car and quickly fix his hair. He seemed to like what he saw, and rightly so. He looked hotter than ever. And, he had a club pack of Snickers bars with him, that bastard.

"Hi Ruthie," he said, nervously waving to me as he walked in the front door.

"Hi Jeff," I said, giving him a hug.

... More later, I'm late to meet the girls.

Midnight
"Okay, so I gave Jeff a big old hug and he gave me the biggest hug back, and since we were the only two people at the A&B until dinner service, he went and flipped the bolt lock on the front door and then ran back and swept me off of my feet — literally — and carried me over to the booth in the back corner, just like a princess chef."

"Oh my god, Ruthie, no!" said Trish, her green eyes now wider than salad plates. Lilly, meanwhile, had both hands covering her gaping mouth.

"And *then* what happened?" asked a breathless Lilly.

I slowly polished off my water.

"And then I said 'Stop.'"

The girls continued to look stunned.

"He apologized, put me down in the booth, and explained that it was just second nature, he was so happy to see me that he couldn't help it."

"So, what did you do?" asked Lilly through her cupped hands.

"It's kind of hard to explain," I said. "It was almost as if I were having an out-of-body experience. On the one hand, I was definitely there with

Jeff and loving both the hotness and familiarity of it all, but on the other hand, I was in Chicago with Dean."

"You mean you were with Jeff while pretending he was Dean?" asked Lilly.

"No, not really. I was sitting there smiling, knowing it was Jeff and happy to see him doing so well. And damn it, all of those feelings came flooding back like the Red Sea in *The Ten Commandments*. But I was also feeling guilty about Jeff not being Dean, because in a big way I wished Jeff *was* Dean."

"I'm lost," said Trish.

"I was, too. Okay, how can I better explain this . . . I was definitely happy to see him again, but after a little while all the recent memories of all the *extremely shitty* stuff he did kicked back in, and I stood up and I told him there was nothing going on with us and there would be nothing going on with us, because I'm with Dean. Because I *am* with Dean."

"Finally, some common sense," said Trish. "It's as if our friend group's new thing is making questionable romantic decisions."

"Hey!" said Lilly, raising her voice a little, because obviously she was included within that circle. "Ruthie, don't take me and Craig as an example. Things are good right now, but we have a long history together and a long way to go before I fully trust him again." Lilly said that just because she took Craig back doesn't mean I should take Jeff back: "There are some additional issues where Jeff is concerned."

"Yeah! Craig may have cheated but he didn't steal $30,000 from Lilly," said Trish by way of apology. "Don't throw away incredible Dean for Jeff."

"I just said I didn't! I chose Dean!" I said defensively. They both gave me this annoying *look*, as if they knew my insides were still swimming and confused.

"Could it be," Lilly waded in, calming the growing tension in the room, "that perhaps neither of them is right for you at this exact juncture in your life? You've got a lot going on right now. You just quit your job and changed your whole life. You're a new chef. A soon-to-be business owner . . ."

"I mean, maybe. But there's more," I said.

"Oh?" asked a slightly concerned Trish.

There is more. A lot more. I can't get that moment at the A&B out of my head...

"Do you love him?" asked Jeff, not willing to reference Dean by name, as I sat back down in the booth.

I nodded, even though I wasn't 100% sure anymore, and then Jeff said he was happy for me, but that it didn't mean he was going to give up on me.

"Ruthie, I've changed. I've changed in ways you can't even begin to imagine. Baby, you won't know what hit you. I will be good to you, and I will make you proud, and I swear I will never, ever hurt you again. I know we should be together, and I know you know that's true. And that's why I'm not giving up on us."

It was some John Hughes–level dialogue. And I'm pretty sure I believe him.

Inheritance Update:

Expenses: return flight to Chicago $551.47, vegan restaurant meals $134.55, normal restaurant meals $559.02, extra packs of triple-ply Charmin $62.

Balance remaining: $7,543.29.

April

APRIL 2

Bubbe Bobby Grace had a very straightforward method for making up her mind when it came to deliberating important life decisions. She would write a list of pros and cons and always insisted that I do the same. Even if it was something as basic as deciding between taking gymnastics or ballet lessons, no matter what advice my parents gave me and no matter what advice my friends gave me, and no matter what my horoscope said, Bubbe Bobby Grace always insisted that there was no better system for finding the exact right answer than by writing out a simple list of pros and cons.

"You've got all the information you need right up there in your keppe, dollface," she'd say as she tapped my head. "And except for maybe me, nobody knows you better than you." She said that's why a nice long list of things, both good and bad, "usually makes the answer as clear as the racks during a white sale at Nordstrom."

Along with my notebooks of Bubbe's life lessons, I also have a sock drawer crammed with my pros and cons lists dating back almost ten years, and I've got to say, about 72% of them have led me to the exact right decision.

So here we go. My future. Done in ink on paper. Black and white. Right. Now.

DEAN PROS	JEFF PROS
Responsible	Trying to become responsible
Stable	Trying to become stable
Loving	Hot

DEAN CONS	JEFF CONS

This is too hard. I'm putting my pen down in defeat.

It just feels inappropriate to make such a big decision based on a few random thoughts and a couple of hard facts. Maybe a list won't cut it this time. After all, how could Bubbe Bobby Grace have known that one day her granddaughter could be in love with two men at the exact same time?

Oddly, the girls weren't much help either. We went for a walk on College Street and popped into Coco's for a snack. There, I revealed my future, much like the exquisitely layered flavours of our slice of earl grey, plum and lavender buttercream cake.

"So, Dean's moving here?" asked Trish.

"Basically," I answered.

"What does that mean?" she asked.

Or perhaps not as exquisitely as I had thought.

"He's had job offers but I'm not sure which he's accepting. But he is accepting one. I think."

"You think or you know?" asked Trish.

"Look, he'll be accepting a position. I think he's having trouble deciding between Toronto General and Sunnybrook. We should know soon."

"This all seems a little vague, Ruthie," offered Lilly, who knows a thing or two about how these things work. "Are you sure he's telling you everything?"

Well, I had thought so, up until this exact second!

"You guys, I literally cannot deal with any more shocking boyfriend surprises," I whined.

"Sorry, you're right. Dean moving here is a giant, exciting step," said Lilly. "This is a good thing. We're happy for you."

APRIL 4

8 a.m.

Peter texted that there was an important letter waiting for me at the café. Peter is the least mysterious person I have ever met so this was beyond intriguing.

Sure enough, when I got to the A&B there was a crisp white envelope waiting on the counter beside the POS stand. The letter hadn't been mailed — it was hand-delivered. *For Ruthie*, it said in green Sharpie ink. I knew that green ink. And I knew that writing. I tore it open and smiled with relief. It was a cheque. *Part 1*, it said in the memo line to the left of Jeff's signature.

10 p.m.

When I informed the girls about the cheque, they were more inquisitive than they were happy for me, which stung a bit.

"But where did he get $10,000?" asked Lilly.

"I haven't got a clue."

"You'd better find out before you cash it," warned Trish.

Our discussion didn't end there. The great Jeff-versus-Dean debate continued on into the night, and even though they really didn't want to, at the end of it I made the girls choose sides. Surprisingly, they came back with a split decision. Lilly thinks I shouldn't give up on Jeff altogether because we truly have a shared passion for food, and she says our chemistry is undeniable. She said it reminds her of when she and Craig first met. "Sparks like that don't fly every day," she said. (Oddly reminiscent of my dad's Shazamo! take.) Obviously, she has serious misgivings about Jeff, but Lilly has always bravely followed her heart, and I admire her for it. She also floated the idea, yet again, that maybe now wasn't the right time to be dating either of them, but I don't like the sounds of that option.

Trish, on the other hand, was firmly on Team Dean, not only because she saw the best of him owing to our perfect time together in Thailand, but in general, she's not as trusting or forgiving as Lilly. "I don't know," said Trish, "I still have major misgivings about that guy. A smile that sexy is nobody's friend."

I've decided to wait until the next time I see Dean to tell him that Jeff has been back in touch. I'm not sure how he'll take it, and since I can read his face in person better than I can read it on FaceTime or his voice over the phone, I want to make sure he's truly cool with it, just in case he says he is but really isn't. He does that sometimes.

Obviously, I'm not going to tell him about Jeff trying to kiss me in the booth and I probably also won't mention the whole "not giving up on us" part, because I'm not an insane person. I'm just going to tell Dean that Jeff is back, that he texted me because he had something to give me, and that now I almost have the wherewithal to buy into the A&B and fulfill my dream of becoming a partial owner of the best café and bistro in the whole damn city! How could Dean not be happy about that? He'll be thrilled. Why wouldn't he be thrilled? I know he'll be thrilled. (I hope he's thrilled.)

But just in case he has further questions — and who wouldn't given the stickiness of the situation — I've prepared some casual answers for every eventuality.

Ruthie's Answers For Dean
1. Jeff seems fine.
2. No, I don't feel the same way about him as I feel about you.
3. He got the money from his parents, some sort of loan that they're dealing with privately as a family. He owes other people money, too.
4. We met twice in person. First, at the A&B, and then at my bank when he came with me to deposit the cheque to make sure it cleared. He also wanted to thank Trevor for being so kind.
5. This all happened this week.

I was practising my answers on Lilly and Trish, and Trish said that while they're all solid and concise, she still has major concerns seeing as I'm the world's worst actress.

"But I'm not acting," I told her.

"Then why are you rehearsing?"

APRIL 7

The A&B is busy as hell! Claire has started taking some of the morning shifts which is a huge relief, because obviously I hate early mornings, but also because it means I can focus more on dinner prep when I show up around 11 a.m. I can't believe this is all actually working! Chef Antoine even came by for lunch today to check on our progress, as if we were still at school. Adorable! He ordered a meatloaf baguette sandwich (our current bestseller, by the by) and an Americano with extra cream.

After he took the first savoury bites from his sandwich, and a sip of his coffee, he put down the ceramic mug and looked up at me. "I have taught you well," he said.

Holding back tears emoji.

APRIL 10

Three old friends, Helen, Lorraine and Nancy, come into the A&B for tea and treats at exactly 1:15 p.m. almost every Thursday and because of this, Peter and I have gotten to know them a bit. We've learned they met at summer camp in northern Ontario over 55 years ago and have been friends ever since. Helen swims laps most mornings, and Lorraine volunteers at the food bank on Fridays. I love the way they sit there gossiping and laughing and knee-slapping over lemon-poppyseed muffins (Nancy's favourite) and misshapen croissants.

"You know," said Peter while looking over at the ladies today, "they remind me of you, Trish and Lilly."

Two holding back tears emojis.

APRIL 12
3 p.m.
When Dean showed up at my door, I was so glad to see him that I almost burst into tears. I hate what a blubberpuss I've become lately! And then we went to my bedroom and had maybe our best sex ever: hot, meaningful, truly top-notch stuff. I honestly didn't know what had gotten into him. What had gotten into us. And then, afterwards, as he sat down at the kitchen table while I toasted up some sesame seed bagels, I noticed him taking off his glasses and looking all serious.

"What's wrong?" I asked.

"I've got something to tell you, Ruthie."

"What is it? What's wrong?" I had just about stopped breathing altogether.

"Nothing's wrong," he said. "I received some news before my flight yesterday. Some great news, actually, but I'm not exactly sure how you're going to take it."

"Try me."

"Well . . . I've been offered — and have accepted — a staff position at Northwestern Memorial Hospital."

The words "offered and have accepted" hit me like a sucker punch to the stomach.

Dean continued, "While I was doing my residency, it didn't look like there would be a position for me in Chicago anytime soon. But late last week Dr. Lee tendered his surprise resignation. From what I hear he's moving back to Hong Kong to help take care of his aging parents. I couldn't believe it, but they offered me his staff job," said Dean, now on his feet and circling my kitchen while giving me furtive glances to gage my reaction. "It's happening, Ruthie. This is the dream."

But whose dream? "Dean, that's amazing news. But . . . you know I'm about to buy into the Antler & Beavertail."

"Well . . . don't? This changes things. You can move in with me and open up an even better place in Chicago, one that's all your own, all new and exactly how you want it."

"But I love the Antler & Beavertail."

"More than you love me?"

"That's not fair. It's like me telling you to give up medicine. I've worked hard all year to make this happen," I said.

"Wow. One whole year."

Excuse me?

"Dean, what the fuck?"

"Have you ever heard of the word 'compromise'?"

"Yes, as a matter of fact I have. Lilly introduced me to the concept just last month."

Ladies and gentlemen, welcome to Dean and Ruthie's first big fight!

"Well then," continued Dean, "let's amp up the learning curve as I introduce you to another one, the concept of 'the ultimatum.'"

Holy shit. He seriously *does* suck at fighting.

"Ruthie, infectious disease staff positions rarely come up. In fact, almost never. I don't think you understand what a big deal this is. The bottom line is, I'm staying in Chicago, with or without you."

Whoa. "I understand why it's a big deal. I just don't understand why you're pretending like we never had a plan," I said, shaking, nauseous, but trying to remain calm. "Like we never discussed this — when we had fully discussed this and had planned on you moving here to work at Sunnybrook or Toronto General when you were done. I'm not imagining those interviews, am I? Or the offer you were mulling over? You didn't even tell me about this Chicago offer. You didn't even *try* to discuss it with me."

And then, get this: Dean just sat there at the kitchen table brooding, with his arms crossed and his face frowned.

"You know what this reminds me of," I started, trying to calm the situation. "*Say Anything*."

"What does that mean?"

"You know, the John Cusack movie, *Say Anything*."

"I've never seen it," he mumbled.

"What? That's unbelievable—"

"And I'm not a John Cusack fan."

Whoa.

"And I don't particularly like your chick flicks."

Whoa.

Whoa, whoa, whoa.

And from there, things went from bad to worse, the weekend slipping into a worrisome mix of tofu stir-fry, the cold shoulder treatment, and make-up sex. It was awful.

And then came this afternoon. "I've got to get to the airport. I'll call you when I land." And then he looked me in the eyes and hugged me one more time. Maybe his biggest hug ever. *Maybe for the last time ever?* And then Dean left.

I crashed out on the couch, trying to make sense of it all, watching the Food Network while forcing down some applesauce and microwaved frozen peas. I keep wondering if Dean and I had just had our first big fight, or if we actually just broke up . . .

1 a.m.

I can't sleep. Dean's "This is the dream" keeps reverberating in my head.

The thing is, with Jeff giving me the first installment of my stolen money back (the next $10,000 would come in a few months' time, he told me), he had given me the chance to live out *my* dream. (The irony of the situation isn't lost on me, since he obviously took it the first time.) And then there's this: when I popped by the A&B today, Peter handed me another mysterious package, saying it was from Jeff. I took the gift into the café's bathroom, locked the door, lowered the toilet seat lid, sat down, untied the ribbon, and pulled the tissue paper out of the gift bag. Inside was an old school photo album, the ring binder type with a puffy cover and sticky pages for scrapbooking. On the red cover was a black-and-white photo of me, beaming in my chef's cap during the Silver Platter competition in Vancouver. I flipped it open and greedily started turning the stiff pages. Honestly, I couldn't believe it. Jeff had put together a collection of recipes that tracked our relationship, from the early Apple Charlotte days at l'École de la Cuisine Française right down to our favourite "night in" pasta, and he even figured out a recipe for homemade Snickers squares. There are photos of us, of me, of inspirational dishes we ate out together, and of memorable kitchen disasters, too (stupid tarte au citron meringuée!). But here is the kicker. Sprinkled throughout are numbered lessons by Bubbe Bobby Grace. He either remembered them or, more likely, "borrowed" them from my sock drawer to glean tidbits such as "Never serve salsa to dinner guests."

It's so touching. It's beautiful. I'm getting worked up now just thinking about it again.

So, here's the question: do I choose a new love or a lost love? And which is which? I haven't been this confused since that time I got on the wrong train in Krakow.

APRIL 15

Bubbe Bobby Grace's biggest life lesson (#287) is about being true to oneself, but at the same time, letting others in. She said love is like a seesaw: "When you're equals in a relationship you level each other out, you support each other, sometimes with a few bumps." But, she said, "if one person makes a sudden or unexpected move, the other person ends up flat on their tuches."

In terms of unexpected love on the positive side, she would often recount the time she was having dinner with her friend Myrna Sobel at Charlie's Seafood Restaurant on 15th Street near her Miami complex. She had been single for years when a man wearing yellow slacks and a straw hat sat down beside them and asked her how the fish was.

"It's good, but it was better yesterday," answered Bubbe.

"Well, it'll be even better tomorrow when we dine here together," said Mort the jeweller, who would indeed take her back to Charlie's the very next day, where they'd split the house salad of iceberg lettuce tossed with canned mandarins, slivered almonds, and baby shrimp, doused in a poppyseed dressing, and the grilled salmon, done medium rare. Mort would become her second and final husband two weeks later, until his death, three years after that.

"Understand what I'm saying, Ruthie," said Bubbe Bobby Grace, newly in love at 72. "I was there for the fish, but I left with so much more." And she wasn't just talking about the bread rolls in her purse.

APRIL 16

As I've become a more confident baker (thanks to Peter and Claire), I've found that working with dough actually soothes my nerves as opposed to jangling them — quite the turnaround! Since we've had so many requests for classic cinnamon buns at the A&B, I decided to kill two birds with one stone and work on a recipe last night, starting with a butter and egg-enriched French brioche dough that I rolled out and spread with a homey cinnamon bun filling. After the second rise, I topped each swirl with a disk of craquelin before popping the buns in the oven. When I brought a batch in for Peter to try this morning, he took a bite and yelped, "Holy shit, Ruthie!" which was the first time I'd ever heard him swear *or* yelp. Then, when I dropped some off at Trish and Lilly's, they both moaned, "Holy shit, Ruthie."

I'll have to get Chef Antoine to try one too so I can hear him say "Holy sheet, Ruthie!"

It felt really good to nail this. I would be so much more braggy about it if I wasn't so torn up about everything else in my life. But at least I know I make a mean cinnamon bun.

APRIL 17

Dean tried to FaceTime me twice yesterday and three times today. I didn't pick up. Still marinating in my hurt feelings.

APRIL 18

The girls and I met up for drinks tonight to discuss Dean and what I should do. Or if I should do anything at all.

"I mean, you have to answer him eventually . . ." Lilly said, squeezing a lime into her first gin and tonic of the season. "I know it sucks, but communication is key, even if that communication is just . . . breaking up."

"I know," I said, sheepishly. "I just . . . I don't know what to say to him yet."

"I mean, do you want to move to Chicago?" Trish asked, never one to mince words.

"Well, no. But we could be so great?" I sighed. Could we? I don't know anymore.

"Well, what *would* be great would be another drink," Trish said, raising her hand for the server. "This isn't a one-drink problem, my friend."

No, this is a problem only Bubbe could have solved.

APRIL 21

I texted the girls in our "Ride or Dies" group chat to rant more about Dean but they were oddly silent. I know I'm probably being too needy, but they can't give up on me yet. They have to help me decide my future first!

4 a.m.
Prepare to be stunned, Diary.

It was still dark outside, but something woke me. I rubbed my eyes and hit the snooze button, but the music played on. It wasn't my alarm. Trying to gather my bearings, I sat up in bed, saw that it was 1:37 a.m., and finally realized the music isn't coming from my vintage clock radio at all.

I followed the familiar song down my hall, into the living room, and as it got louder and louder, I realized that it was coming from outside. I grasped the sticky overpainted corners of the window casing and, using all of my might, shoved it wide open. It was cold out. I looked out towards the street and realized that the music was coming from right below my big open window, but I still couldn't quite see the source.

That's just like Jeff to go in for the kill, I thought, as I pulled on my jean jacket and slid on my clogs. I knew that amazing photo album wasn't the end of it. Only the beginning. So, here we go, the fantasy becoming reality . . .

I figured he'd be dressed in his chef's whites — fresh from work — Chef Antoine got him an interview at EchoEcho, and Jeff totally dug what Chef Nick Zane was doing and, of course, Chef Zane totally dug Jeff (who doesn't?). And now Jeff had come to me, and was very likely standing under my window, probably holding a giant rib roast over his head (with gelatinized mint oil pearls?), while Peter Gabriel's "In Your Eyes" played from a Sonos speaker sitting on the grass beside him. I could see from my bay window that it wasn't raining, like in my favourite scene from *Say Anything*, but I knew that whether he was trying to duplicate it or not, Jeff would totally nail Lloyd Dobler's defiant, hurt puppy dog facial expression and valiant body language as the music played on.

Wait a minute ... it could be Dean!

Sure, we just had a big fight and he lives in another country, but he's an incredible person with a great big heart and he did try to FaceTime me a lot this week. Maybe he had second thoughts about how shitty he'd acted. Maybe he remembered the mangoes of Thailand and the kale chips of Toronto, our instant connection and our growing bond. Could this perhaps be *his* grand gesture, showing up from Chicago to win me back after being such a thoughtless asshole? He probably also has on the perfect Lloyd Dobler face, but of course Dean would be holding a Tofurkey over his head, and he'd be here to apologize *as* John Cusack for slandering John Cusack. He's sharp enough to pull it off.

My heart was beating twice as fast as the rhythm of the song as I ran down two flights of stairs, two steps at a time, and out the front door. I was getting the chase scene! Every woman's dream!

I turned the corner of the building and ...

It wasn't Jeff.

And it wasn't Dean.

(And for what it's worth, it wasn't John Cusack.)

And get this.

I felt — *relief?*

"Don't be mad, Ruthie," said Lilly, offering me a dish of the potatoes dauphinoise that I had taught Trish how to make. (She could have gone further with the browning, but they smelled delicious.)

"What sort of insane prank is this?" I said, confused. "It's almost two in the morning!"

"Ruthie," said Lilly, "we were afraid Jeff would follow up that incredible scrapbook with something even bigger and bolder ..."

"Or Dean would sway you with memories of Thailand," added Trish. "So, we thought we'd beat them to the punch. After all, we love you, too."

Oh my god, right?

"Ruthie, right now, it should be about beginnings," said Trish. "You've been going from one crisis to another, and now things are finally going your way. Why rush back into the chaos?"

"If one of them is the real deal, it'll happen," said Lilly, "but it doesn't have to be tonight. If it's meant to be it can be tomorrow, or a month from now..."

"Or never," coughed Trish.

And that's when it finally — properly — sunk in.

The third option.

When dispensing her especially useful dating advice, Bubbe Bobby Grace always said, "In this life you'll meet some knights, and you'll meet some scoundrels, and they'll often be the same guy. But you know who you can count on, who you can always trust? Besides your parents and me?" She gently pinched my cheek and said, "It's you, dollface. It'll always be you."

Bubbe was right. My girls are right. Holy shit. This has been such a wild, crazy mess of a year, but the best parts of it have been... *me*. Cooking. Figuring out what I want. Spending time with my girls. I don't want to change anything. I don't want to tweak my life, my *recipes*, for anyone right now. I choose *me*.

I punched the girls on the shoulder then gave them each a big hug, tears brimming.

"You guuuyyysssss," I cried, happily.

And then we plunked down on the cozy blanket they had laid out before us, and we dug into those soul-satisfying potatoes as if there's no tomorrow and it wasn't 2 a.m. and mildly freezing.

Inheritance Update:

Expenses: $7,543.29 plus $10,000 reimbursement from Jeff, minus $17,543.29 downpayment on partnership in the Antler & Beavertail.

Balance remaining: $0.

Acknowledgements

Particular thanks to Mika Bareket, who put the manuscript in my magical editor, Kenna Barnes's hands. Thanks, too, to the whole ECW crew, including David Caron, Jack David, Sammy Chin, Jess Albert, Jen Knoch, Laura Pastore, Claire Pokorchak, and Emily Ferko. I'd like to also thank my family and friends who may have inspired a few scenes, though I cannot stress enough that this novel is a total work of fiction.

Recipes

HEARTBREAK COOKIES FOR LILLY

(Makes 3 dozen cookies)

1 cup unsalted butter, softened
½ cup brown sugar, packed
1 tsp pure vanilla extract
good pinch of salt
2 ½ cup all-purpose flour
2 regular-sized Toblerone bars, chopped into large chunks

Preheat oven to 325 degrees Fahrenheit.

In a medium bowl, cream together butter and sugar until it gets light and fluffy. Stir in vanilla extract, a pinch of salt, and little by little, the flour. You should be able gather it into a ball (if it's too sticky, add a bit more flour).

Lightly flour a work surface, roll out the dough to desired thickness, and cut it into 1 ½ inch squares. Arrange on a cookie sheet then, using your thumb, make a light imprint in the centre of each cookie and place a nice chunk or two of Toblerone in the dent. Bake for 10 to 15 minutes, or until cookies are lightly browned around the edges.

TOMATOES PROVENÇAL FOR CHEF ANTOINE

(Serves 2)

2 garlic cloves, chopped
2 tbsp breadcrumbs
1 tbsp chopped parsley
2 tsp olive oil
Salt and pepper to taste
1 large, ripe, juicy tomato

Preheat oven to 400 degrees Fahrenheit.

Place chopped garlic on a cutting board and the breadcrumbs and parsley on top. Chop everything together until very fine. Put in a little bowl and stir in oil, and salt and pepper to taste.

Cut tomato in half horizontally, then cut a thin slice off the bottom of each half so that they can stand upright. Place in a little baking dish, season tomato with salt and pepper, and then top with breadcrumb mixture. Bake in preheated oven for 5 minutes or until hot and soft (but not mushy).

APPLE PECAN BREAD PUDDING FOR THE SILVER PLATTER COMPETITION

(Serves 8 to 10)

For bread pudding:
one 5–7 oz loaf stale French bread, or enough crumbled to make 3–4 cups
2 cups milk
1 cup sugar
1/4 cup butter, melted
1 egg plus 1 egg yolk
1 tsp pure vanilla extract
1 Golden Delicious apple, finely chopped
1/2 cup toasted pecans, chopped

For Calvados butter sauce:
¾ cup butter
1 ½ cups sugar
¾ cup heavy cream
2 tbsp Calvados
Pinch of salt

In a large bowl, combine all the ingredients for bread pudding in order listed. Mixture should be quite thick and moist, the consistency of oatmeal.

Pour into a buttered 9" x 9" baking dish, then place in a non-preheated oven. Turn oven on and bake at 350 degrees Fahrenheit for about an hour, or until browned and smelling like heaven.

Combine sauce ingredients in a medium saucepan and bring to a boil, then lower to a simmer for about a half hour, whisking now and then and until sauce is thickened and smooth. Set aside.

Once bread pudding is out of the oven, let cool slightly then drench in Calvados butter sauce. Slice into diamonds or squares and serve topped with extra sauce. (Any remaining sauce can be refrigerated for up to 2 weeks.)

POTATOES DAUPHINOISE FOR TRISH

(Serves 6)

1 garlic clove, peeled and smashed
1 ½ lbs potatoes, peeled and thinly sliced with a mandoline or food processor
1 cup heavy cream
1 tsp sea salt
A grating of nutmeg
50 grams Gruyère (about ½ cup), grated

Preheat oven to 375 degrees Fahrenheit.

Rub a large gratin dish with a smashed garlic clove, then take the same clove and rub a big bowl with it. Toss prepared potatoes in the garlic-rubbed bowl. Pour heavy cream over potatoes and add sea salt and a gentle grating of nutmeg. Mix together, add Gruyère, and toss some more.

Separate the potato slices and layer them in the gratin dish, making sure the top layer is especially pretty and evenly fanned. Pour remaining cream and cheese over top and bake in the preheated oven for one hour or until gorgeously browned and burbling.

RUTHIE'S EASY LEMON MERINGUE PIE

(Serves 8)

15–20 Social Tea biscuits, crushed or blitzed into crumbs
½ cup unsalted butter, melted
1 can sweetened condensed milk
3 eggs, separated into yolks and whites
¾ cup freshly squeezed lemon juice
5 tbsp sugar

Preheat oven to 350 degrees Fahrenheit.

Mix biscuit crumbs with melted butter. Pat down firmly into an 8" greased pie dish.

To a medium bowl add condensed milk, egg yolks, and lemon juice. Beat for several minutes with a whisk until well combined. It will be smooth but runny. Pour filling into the pie crust and bake for 30 minutes in the preheated oven. Remove and let cool for a half hour.

With a whisk, whip the egg whites until foamy and then gradually add sugar. Beat until firm peaks form in meringue, and then pour the meringue on top of baked, cooled pie, artistically smoothing and mounding it. Turn the oven on to broil. Put the pie under broiler for about 30 seconds, or until meringue browns slightly. Take that, Chef Bertrand!

NEWFOUNDLAND SUMMER FOOL

(Serves 6)

½ lb rhubarb, roughly chopped
½ cup white sugar
1 tbsp water
½ lb fresh strawberries, stems removed
1 cup 35% cream
½ tsp vanilla
2 tsp brown sugar

Put rhubarb, sugar, and water in a saucepan, bring to a boil, then simmer until soft — about 15 minutes, stirring every once in a while. Once softened, remove from heat and let cool to room temperature.

In a separate bowl, crush the strawberries with your hands or a spoon, then add to rhubarb mixture and chill in the refrigerator for an hour.

Whip the cream to soft peaks, adding the vanilla and brown sugar in the last couple of minutes, then gently fold cream together with chilled rhubarb and strawberry mixture and spoon into pretty little dessert bowls or mason jars.

LYONNAISE PINK PRALINE TART

(Makes one 9" tart)

For pink pralines:
1 cup whole almonds, skin on
1 cup sugar
1 cup water
A few drops of pink food colouring

Line a baking tray with parchment paper and spray with cooking oil.
    In a saucepan over high heat, bring almonds, sugar, and water to a boil. Add food colouring. Continue cooking and stir consistently until sugar begins to caramelize and crystallize around the almonds.
    Spread onto parchment and let cool completely before using.

For the pastry:
1 ¾ cups flour
⅓ cup sugar
Pinch of salt
¾ cup cold butter, cut into small pieces
1 egg

Whisk the flour with sugar and salt. Add in butter. Mix together with your fingertips until well-blended and no big lumps remain. Add egg.
    Mix until the dough comes together then gather into a ball and wrap in plastic wrap.
    Refrigerate 30 minutes.

Preheat the oven to 350 degrees Fahrenheit.

For the praline filling:
1 cup crushed pink pralines (if you don't want to make them and can only find regular candied almonds, use a touch of red dye in the cream)
1 ¼ cups heavy cream (35%)

Heat the cream with the crushed pink pralines in a saucepan on medium-low heat. Stir slowly until the cream mixture thickens and large bubbles form, about 10 minutes.

    Remove from heat and let cool.

    Roll chilled pastry out on a lightly floured surface until it's large enough to fill your tart tin at 1/8th of an inch thickness. Line the tin with pastry, cut off any excess, then add pie weights or dried beans onto parchment lining the pastry. Blind bake for 20 minutes, then remove the parchment and pie weights and continue baking for an additional 10 minutes or until the pastry is lightly browned. Set aside to cool.

    Add the praline cream to the tart shell and chill for at least an hour to set. Top with additional chopped pralines.

VEGAN SZECHUAN CARROT SOUP FOR DEAN

(Serves 4 to 6)

2 tsp vegetable oil
1 medium onion, chopped
2 garlic cloves, minced
6 large carrots, peeled and chopped
1 inch fresh ginger, peeled and minced
1 tsp red pepper flakes
4 cups vegetable stock
2 tbsp creamy peanut butter
4 tsp soy sauce
1 tsp sugar
A few drops of sesame oil

Heat vegetable oil in a large pot over medium heat.

Add onion and sauté for a few minutes, or until softened, then add garlic and cook for a minute more.

Add carrots, ginger, red pepper flakes, and stock.

Bring to a boil, reduce to a simmer, cover, and cook for 30 minutes.

Remove from heat and add peanut butter, soy sauce, sugar, and sesame oil. Using a hand blender, purée the soup in the pot.

Reheat over low heat until it's hot enough to eat, without letting it boil.

Dish out in bowls to your favourite vegans and enjoy!

JEFF'S SHAZAMO! FRIED CHICKEN

(Serves 4)

1 cup kosher salt
4 cups hot water
12 cups cold water
1 whole 3 to 3 ½ lb. frying chicken cut into parts (breast, thighs, legs, etc.)
1 cup flour
½ cups matzo meal
2 tsp seasoned salt (such as Lawry's)
1 tsp fresh cracked pepper
2 cups buttermilk
1 ½ cups vegetable shortening (like Crisco) or lard
Extra salt to taste
Maple syrup or honey, for drizzling

Mix salt and hot water in a big bowl. Once the salt is dissolved, stir in the cold water. Add the chicken to the brine and put in the refrigerator. Brine chicken for a minimum of one hour but up to four hours, then rinse chicken very well and pat dry with paper towels and set on a wire rack to dry some more.

Make a mixture of the flour, matzo meal, seasoned salt, and pepper. Pour buttermilk in a shallow bowl. Dip chicken pieces in buttermilk, shaking off the excess, before dredging in seasoned flour until well coated.

Over medium heat (in a cast iron skillet if you have one), melt shortening and heat to about 350 degrees Fahrenheit. Brown the chicken on all sides, a few pieces at a time, and cook through; this should take approximately 15–20 minutes, or until the internal temp is at least 160 degrees Fahrenheit. (Alternatively, you could brown it in the pan and finish it off on a baking sheet in a preheated 350-degree oven.) Drain on paper towel.

Shake a bit of salt over the hot chicken, and then tell people to drizzle with maple syrup at the table.

DAD'S FAVOURITE BLUEBERRY CRUMBLE PIE

(Makes one 9" pie)

For crust:
2 cups flour
1 tsp salt
2 tbsp sugar
¾ cup canola oil
2 tsp vanilla
2 tbsp milk

Preheat oven to 350 degrees Fahrenheit.

Put flour, salt, and sugar into a pie plate. In a small bowl, whisk oil together with vanilla and milk. Pour oil mixture into dry ingredients, right into the pie plate. Stir with a fork, and then with your hands work it into a ball of dough. Remove a small handful of dough and set aside for the crumble topping.

Press crust dough evenly into pie plate, making sure it isn't too thick on the bottom. Prick the crust with a fork and bake in the preheated oven until golden, approximately 10 minutes. When baked, set aside to cool.

For filling:
2 ½ pints (about 4 cups) fresh blueberries
Freshly squeezed lemon juice from half a lemon
¼ cup brown sugar
1 tbsp flour
1 tbsp cornstarch

Combine filling ingredients and add filling to prepared and cooled pie crust.

For crumble topping:
½ cup flour
¼ cup white sugar
¼ cup brown sugar
½ tsp salt
2 tbsp unsalted butter, softened
2 tsp vanilla
Reserved handful of pie dough

Raise oven temperature to 425 degrees Fahrenheit.

Put flour, sugars, and salt into a bowl. With a pastry blender, blend in butter until mixture is crumbly. Toss with vanilla. Add the handful of pie crust dough to the crumble, blending it in with your fingers. Crumble the mixture on top of pie and bake at 425 for 15 minutes. Lower heat to 375 for another 25–30 minutes, or until pie is golden. Let cool for several hours before eating. Shazamo!

FRENCH ONION SOUP FOR MOM
(AND CHEF ANTOINE AND HIS WIFE)

(Serves 4 to 6)

3 tbsp unsalted butter
6 large yellow onions, thinly sliced
¼ cup brandy
6 cups good quality beef broth
Pinch of sugar
Salt and pepper to taste
½ stale baguette, sliced
2 cups shredded Gruyère cheese

In a large soup pot over medium heat, melt butter, add onions, and cook, stirring frequently, for about 30 to 40 minutes, or until onions are tender and very browned. Add brandy, simmer until liquid is gone, then stir in beef broth, making sure to scrape the browned bits from the bottom of the pan, and simmer for 20 minutes more. Taste for seasoning, add salt and pepper and a pinch of sugar if onions aren't already sweet enough.
    Preheat broiler. Put a slice of baguette on the bottom of each oven-proof onion soup bowl, ladle stock overtop, and top with a good handful of shredded Gruyère. Place bowls on a baking sheet to avoid spillage, and pop under the broiler until cheese bubbles and browns and looks like a bowl full of everlasting love.

THE ANTLER & BEAVERTAIL'S MEATLOAF BAGUETTE SANDWICH

(Makes enough meatloaf and spread for 8 to 10 sandwiches)

For meatloaf:
1 lb ground sirloin
1 lb ground chicken
2 eggs
½ cup toasted breadcrumbs
1 tbsp Dijon
1 medium tomato, chopped
2 shallots, minced
2 garlic cloves, minced
1 tbsp fresh thyme
Sea salt and fresh ground black pepper

For artichoke spread:
two 169 ml jars marinated artichokes, drained
1 tsp Dijon
1 tsp mayonnaise
1 garlic clove
2 tbsp extra virgin olive oil
Sea salt and pepper to taste

For sandwich:
Fresh baguette
Arugula
Olive oil
Fresh lemon juice

Preheat oven to 375 degrees Fahrenheit.

Combine all meatloaf ingredients then bake in a greased loaf pan in a preheated oven for about an hour or until firm to the touch.

In a food processor, puree artichoke spread ingredients, making sure not to overprocess. Lightly dress the arugula with extra virgin olive oil and lemon.

Assemble the sandwich: cut baguette in half then slather with artichoke spread on both sides of the bread. Add a nice slice of warm meatloaf on the bottom and dressed arugula on the top. Place top back on top. Enjoy.

HOMEMADE BAGELS FOR BUBBE BOBBY GRACE

(Makes 12)

3 ½ cups flour
two 8 g packets instant active dry yeast
1 ½ tsp sea salt
1 ¼ cups warm water
½ cup honey, divided
2 tsp vegetable oil, for coating bowl
1 egg yolk beaten with 1 tbsp water
¼ cup sesame or poppy seeds

In a stand mixer fitted with the dough hook, combine the flour, yeast, and salt. Slowly add the water and ¼ cup of the honey. Knead on a low setting for 5 minutes, until the dough comes away from the sides and a soft, smooth ball forms.

Lightly oil a medium-sized bowl, and place the dough ball inside, turning it over to make sure it's fully coated in oil. Cover with a moist tea towel and set aside in a warm place for 30 minutes.

Lightly flour a work surface and roll the dough into a long snake, then cut into 12 equal pieces. Roll each piece into a rope about 8" to 9" long. Pinch the ends together, then roll with the palm of your hand to seal the ends and form a bracelet. A bagel bracelet. Cover the bagels with a tea towel and let them rest on the floured surface for 15 minutes.

Place an oven rack on the lowest level. Preheat the oven to 450 degrees Fahrenheit. Line two baking sheets with parchment paper.

Bring a large pot of water (at least 10 cups) to a boil and add the remaining ¼ cup of honey. Lower the heat to a simmer, then add 4 bagels at a time, simmering for 1 minute, flipping each one over, and simmering for 1 minute more. Remove the bagels and place on the prepared baking sheets. Repeat with 2 more batches of 4 bagels at a time. Divide the bagels equally between the prepared sheets. Brush with egg wash and sprinkle or gently press each bagel into some sesame or poppy seeds on a plate, one at a time.

Bake one sheet at a time, for 18 to 20 minutes, or until cooked through and deeply golden brown. Let cool, then slice and schmear like there's no tomorrow!

Entertainment. Writing. Culture. ─────────────

ECW is a proudly independent, Canadian-owned book publisher. We know great writing can improve people's lives, and we're passionate about sharing original, exciting, and insightful writing across genres.

───────────────────────── **Thanks for reading along!**

We want our books not just to sustain our imaginations, but to help construct a healthier, more just world, and so we've become a certified B Corporation, meaning we meet a high standard of social and environmental responsibility — and we're going to keep aiming higher. We believe books can drive change, but the way we make them can too.

Being a B Corp means that the act of publishing this book should be a force for good — for the planet, for our communities, and for the people that worked to make this book. For example, everyone who worked on this book was paid at least a living wage. You can learn more at the Ontario Living Wage Network.

This book is also available as a Global Certified Accessible™ (GCA) ebook. ECW Press's ebooks are screen reader friendly and are built to meet the needs of those who are unable to read standard print due to blindness, low vision, dyslexia, or a physical disability.

This book is printed on FSC®-certified paper. It contains recycled materials, and other controlled sources, is processed chlorine free, and is manufactured using biogas energy.

ECW's office is situated on land that was the traditional territory of many nations, including the Wendat, the Anishinaabeg, Haudenosaunee, Chippewa, Métis, and current treaty holders the Mississaugas of the Credit. In the 1880s, the land was developed as part of a growing community around St. Matthew's Anglican and other churches. Starting in the 1950s, our neighbourhood was transformed by immigrants fleeing the Vietnam War and Chinese Canadians dispossessed by the building of Nathan Phillips Square and the subsequent rise in real estate value in other Chinatowns. We are grateful to those who cared for the land before us and are proud to be working amidst this mix of cultures.

ecwpress.com